DEATH VALLEY

EDEN FRANCIS COMPTON
WITH DIANE TAYLOR

Level 4 Press, Inc.

Published by:
Level 4 Press, Inc.
14702 Haven Way
Jamul, CA 91935
www.level4press.com

Library of Congress Control Number: 2019944584

ISBN: 978-1-64630-052-5

Printed in the United States of America

Other books by
EDEN FRANCIS COMPTON

Emily

PROLOGUE

Mac Brown didn't know how long he had been lying unconscious with his face pressed into the scorched earth of Death
Valley. Was it minutes? Hours? Days? However much time
had elapsed, he hoped against all logic it was enough to have altered
his situation.

He resisted the urge to open his eyes, instead listening intently. He
strained to detect even the slightest hint of an approaching car, the
sound of tires speeding across gravel and dirt, an engine revving in the
distance but getting closer by the second. He reasoned Slim must be
out there somewhere, looking for him. They were supposed to have
met at the silver mine that afternoon. Mac was supposed to have handed Slim the money. Slim needed that money. Surely, he would come
looking for him.

Despite his best efforts, the only sound Mac heard was his own
rasping breath. With the sun beating on his back, his thoughts drifted
to the day Slim had first brought him to this godforsaken wasteland.
The scene played out in his fevered mind as if it were happening then
and there. He and Slim, standing opposite one another in the meager
shade of a weathered wooden shack, surrounded by the desolation of
an abandoned silver mine on the outskirts of Las Vegas.

"It's insane," Mac said.

"It is," Slim agreed. "But it'll work. I guarantee it. We just need the money, Mac. We get the money, we get the deal, we're made men."

"It's a gamble."

"It's a sure bet."

Mac had heard such assurances from Slim before, since they were kids, it seemed. He knew from experience Slim's guarantees were, at best, a fifty-fifty proposition, as likely to fail as they were to succeed. Mac averted his eyes from his best friend's face to avoid telling him straight out that he didn't want in on this deal. Tension built up in the silence that stretched between them.

"You owe me," Slim finally said in a hushed voice. Mac tensed as Slim stepped forward, all six-foot-four of him looming. Mac defiantly brought his eyes up to meet Slim's.

"We made a deal, remember?" Slim continued. "And I upheld my end of the bargain. *I* went in. *I* did the time. And we can both be glad that I did because I learned some important shit in Southern State. I came out with a plan, Mac, and I'm asking you, as your friend, the one who saved your sorry ass, to help me with it."

Mac held his ground and relented at the same time. "I didn't say I wouldn't do it. I just said it was a gamble."

As those last words played out in his mind, Mac's eyes suddenly shot open. The gamble had panned out, hadn't it? He had the money, didn't he?

Mac lifted his head from the desert floor and scanned his surroundings. He spotted what he was looking for—a charred, battered Samsonite suitcase, its sides burst open, one-hundred-dollar bills fluttering out of it with every tug of the arid desert air.

The sight of the suitcase, not more than three feet away but just out of reach, reinvigorated Mac. He summoned the strength to try to lift himself up on his elbows and inch toward it. But he couldn't raise his right arm. A heavy weight held him back.

Marcus! In his delirium, Mac had forgotten about Marcus, who had handcuffed his wrist to Mac's as they had battled in the desert.

Mac pulled on his brother's arm, trying to wake him and drag them closer to the suitcase.

"Come on, Marcus! We're so close!" Mac struggled to get the words out of his parched throat. "We're almost there! Help me!"

But he got no response. Mac used the last of his strength to drag Marcus's limp body up to rest at his side. The sight of his brother's face, frozen in a deathly grin, broke his will to continue.

Mac rolled onto his back and opened his eyes against the glare of the sun and the endless expanse of blue sky. His eyes roamed across the jagged, rust-colored ridges that hemmed him in on all sides, still hoping against all hope for some sign of Slim on the horizon. What he found, instead, was the flicking, forked tongue and cold, darting eyes of a lizard.

Mac stared at it. He studied its every detail—its pale-yellow legs, the alternating bands of pastel gray and yellow splashed with white polka dots across the creature's back, the curved rows of black and white rectangles that adorned its head, the band of royal ermine around its neck.

In reality the small reptile had crawled to within inches of Mac's face. But in Mac's dehydrated, deranged state, his mind blew the lizard up to gigantic proportions. The creature grew and grew until it dominated the horizon, and Mac imagined he lay prostrate beneath the contemptuous, regal gaze of the Lizard King of Death Valley.

1

Marcus Brown didn't have to be a forensic expert to piece together what had happened to his parents. When he and his older brother, Mac, had stepped inside the trailer the day before, the evidence told a story that was easy even for them to read.

Empty Canadian Club whisky bottles had littered virtually every level surface in the open area of the combined kitchen and living room. The bottles overflowed the single trash can and cluttered the floors, some standing up straight like good soldiers, others lolling around like an army of town drunks.

To their immediate left, in the kitchen area, a straight-backed metal chair lay flat on its back on a yellowed linoleum floor, topped off by a three-foot-wide circle of blood that had dried from red to black. Marcus had walked around the chair, reluctant to touch it, but eventually picked it up and set it back on its feet. He picked up a set of silver handcuffs and shuffled them nervously from one hand to the other.

"Christ!" he said, more to himself than to Mac. "He handcuffed her to the chair."

"Yeah, he did," Mac agreed. "And then he blew her fucking head off."

In unison, Marcus and his brother had turned their eyes to the right, to the evidence in the living room that revealed what must have happened next. A green and white plaid couch was pushed up against a white wall. Above the middle cushion, on the wall behind, they confronted a large splatter of dried blood with one perfect small hole in the middle of it.

Mac leaned over the couch and stuck his right index finger into the hole. He whistled appreciatively. "It went right through the back of his head. Perfect shot!"

"His aim was true. Both times," Marcus said.

"The Colt 35 is a good pistol."

"They gave it back to us, right?" Marcus couldn't remember much about their stop at the Inglis Police Department, he'd been too shocked to retain anything beyond the basic facts.

"Yeah, they did." Mac lifted his shirt to reveal the firearm tucked into the waistband of his jeans.

"Here! Take these, too. You keep 'em." Marcus passed the handcuffs to his brother.

Mac slipped them into the other side of his waistband. "Family heirlooms."

For the past twenty-four hours, Marcus had tried to digest what had happened, make sense of it all. He stood in the kitchen surveying the grisly scene with his hands on his hips until he caught himself, and quickly adjusted his stance. Mac regarded the pose as ridiculous, feminine-looking, and he always let Marcus know.

"Christ, Marcus, it's bad enough you're scrawny," Mac said. And, it was true. Marcus was slim, and short, clocking in at just five-foot-six. "Why do you have to make it worse by wearing your hair long and acting like a damned girl?"

Marcus didn't reply. He put his attention back on the chaos that had been their parents' home. "What a mess." He sighed. "I feel like we ought to do something. Pick up all these bottles. Take the couch out to the dumpster. Clean the place up. I just don't know what to do first."

Mac straightened up. "We're not doing shit. Joe Next-Door paid up this morning. All of this is his problem now. He bought it all."

"We don't even have to clean anything? He's taking it all?"

"Everything. The whole shebang. The trailer, the Thunderbird, the

John Deere, the fishing boat, everything inside here and everything in the shed."

Marcus looked around wondering why anyone would want all this shit when the woman they knew as Betty Down-By-The-Dumpster poked her white-haired head inside the open door. She'd been by the day before, too.

"Once again, I am just so sorry for your loss," she twanged.

Marcus rolled his eyes. For the last day, everyone in the Driftwood Mobile Home Resort had been sorry for their loss . . .

"I've got a sister in Louisiana I've been trying for years to get a place she could move into here. I sure would love to see her more often. She's bad off these days. I was wondering—"

"Already sold it to Joe," Mac said, cutting Betty off and jerking his head toward the trailer next door.

"Oh dear!" Betty's age-spotted hands flew to her chest, as if she were reacting to a sudden pain. "I was trying to give you a little time to sort things out. I guess I'm too late."

Betty's eyes darted around the interior of the mobile home. Her thin shoulders sagged in toward her chest as she took in the grisly details of the demise of Fred and Myrna Brown. But in her next breath, Betty straightened right back up. "What about the dinette set?" she asked.

Marcus stared in disbelief. The old lady wanted the chair their mother, her neighbor, had been shot to death in? Marcus started to say something, but Mac jumped in.

"Sold to the man next door. Everything. We sold it all to Joe."

"Oh, I see." Betty cast her eyes askance and sniffed disapprovingly. She pulled herself up a little taller. "You should put a sign on the door then. You should let people know. It's not fair that Joe—"

Mac shut the door in Betty's face. Marcus watched the frail, tiny old lady stumble down the dirt road to her own trailer a stone's throw away from the dumpster.

"Vultures!" Mac said.

Marcus was sure the fact that the residents of the Driftwood Mobile

Home Resort wanted his parents' trailer and their possessions was a definite sign of the general degradation of the place.

Marcus could hardly fathom where their parents had taken such a wrong turn. He had always known his mother to be a fastidious housekeeper and their father to be a capable repairman. He imagined his parents' place had stood out like a gem among the dozen or so mobile homes with collapsed roofs, rusted exteriors, rotted floors, leaky plumbing, and busted windows patched over with cardboard. One trailer was a blackened, burned-out shell, the remnants of a former meth lab that had met its end in a spectacular explosion.

Residents still relished the details of that explosion, and the brothers were told every possible version of the story as they had fielded inquiries from seemingly every occupant of the Florida mobile home park their parents had called home for the last few years. When the first tentative knock on the door had come, Marcus had jumped to answer it. He had expected to find someone handing him a hot casserole or a bottle of Jack Daniel's. That's what he would have done, because that's what he had seen his mother do countless times. Someone dies, you bake a damned casserole. Or if you're a man, you buy a bottle of booze. Bastard that he was, even Dad had done that, Marcus thought. Not the cheap stuff, either. Good hard liquor—something that shows a little respect for the dead and sympathy for the living. That's what his father always said.

By contrast, every one of their parents' neighbors had shown up at the door with their hands out, looking for favors, unabashedly surveying the wreckage, eager to snatch something up on the cheap.

"You selling Fred's weed whacker?"

"They didn't die in the bed, did they? How much for the bed?"

"I sure could use those plastic totes. You gonna empty those out?"

"Now, I know Myrna had a ton of Mason jars. She was always making those pickles! Don't throw those jars away. I can use them!"

"What about those binoculars Fred had? How much you want for them? You ain't gonna use them, are ya?"

"Heathens!" Joe Next-Door had pronounced, although he also had stood at the door eager to make a deal. Difference was, Joe had offered ten thousand in cash for the whole kit and caboodle—as is, no questions asked—they'd have the money in their hands the next day. Marcus watched his brother shake on it, then he and Mac made a trip to the Minit Mart for beer, Apple Jacks, milk, instant coffee, and Marlboros. Marcus made sure to include some Hot Pockets since the neighbors were not going to feed them.

Mac retrieved a can of cold Budweiser from the refrigerator, popped the lid, handed it to Marcus, then grabbed one for himself. They drank in silence for a long moment, leaning side by side against the kitchen counter, each of them staring at their feet.

Marcus knew they must have come across as an unlikely pair of brothers to all the neighbors in their parents' trailer park. They both had their mother's dark brown, almost black, hair, but that was where the similarities ended. It wasn't just that Marcus was small, he was almost delicate. At least that's what he always heard Mac and others say about him growing up. And Mac wasn't just big—to Marcus, he was like a rock. He was five inches taller and outweighed him by a hundred pounds, and never let Marcus forget it. He wore his hair in a Marine-style crew cut. His biceps bulged out of the short sleeves of his T-shirts. Though he loved to talk, especially when he and Marcus were at the bar, Mac rarely smiled, and when he did, he was usually putting someone or something down.

For those who knew Marcus and his brother well, however, there was a more telling detail that set the brothers apart. It was the color of their eyes. Marcus had the pale blue eyes of both their mother and their father. Mac's eyes were a chocolate brown. It was a detail Marcus had never given any thought to until the night a drunk Billy Stanley called Mac the "brown-eyed bastard," and Mac left Billy a bloody pulp on the sidewalk outside the Riverside Pub.

The incident left Marcus trembling and speechless as he and Mac resumed their seats at the bar. It took two more beers before Marcus found his voice again.

"So . . ." Marcus drew the word out, long and slow.

"So yeah," Mac said. "Dad married Mom after he came back from the Army. He found her knocked up with some other man's kid. Married her anyway. You never figured that out?"

Marcus shook his head and sipped his beer.

"Well, now you know." Mac took a gulp of beer. "Explains a lot, doesn't it?"

Marcus supposed it did. He had spent years of his childhood watching his brother and their father square off against one another, most notably at the dinner table, their father at the head of the table, Mac directly opposite him at the other end, Marcus and their mother stuck in the middle. On a good night, food was passed and portioned and eaten in a state of repressed silence. If the boys were good—that is, if they kept their thoughts to themselves and ate everything on their plates—they could ask to be excused and expect to be set free within a few minutes after they finished eating.

Always timid, Marcus had adapted by scooping tiny portions of food onto his plate, eating quickly, and hoping for the best. But on a bad night, of which there were many, Mac would court a confrontation with their father. It was always something stupid, and always deliberate. Mac would lock eyes with their father and simply refuse to eat something on his plate, even if it was something he liked, and the battle of wills would begin. Their father commanded Mac to eat, Mac clamped his lips tight, their mother stared out the window, Marcus prayed to himself, *Please Mac, just eat the mashed potatoes, just eat the mashed potatoes . . .*

Marcus couldn't remember how any of those dinnertime contests had ended. *Who won?* he wondered. He could only recall the fury in their father's face, the defiance in Mac's eyes, and the fear rumbling in his own gut. That fear had stirred in him again as the full weight of Billy Stanley's revelation had sunk in. Only now, Marcus was a man sitting at a bar, not a child, and within seconds the old childhood fear turned into anger.

"Dad was the bastard," Marcus had pronounced. "We're brothers, dammit!"

Mac had stared straight ahead and pretended not to notice Marcus was crying. "Life's a bitch."

That was a year ago, but Marcus found himself once again with Mac, holding onto his beer, too self-conscious to look at his brother, too upset to speak.

Finally, Marcus said. "I had no idea things had gotten this bad. I called them once in a while. Not regular. But I did call. I checked in with them now and then. I swear, they never told me a damned thing."

Mac looked up from the floor and snorted. "You're a better man than me then. I never even did that. I couldn't make myself do it."

"I understand," Marcus said. And he really did. When he looked back at the last few years of his parents' lives, he couldn't explain to himself, much less to someone else, why he had stayed in touch.

As a child, Marcus himself had many times been on the receiving end of the handcuffs that had bound his mother to her death bed, so to speak. When their father drank, there was no telling what form his rage might take. But it had often wound up with Marcus handcuffed to radiators, bedposts, and table legs. Who knew why? When the liquor flowed, Marcus kept his head down and his mouth shut, hoping to avoid his father's wrath. Sometimes he remained invisible, sometimes he didn't. Those times when Marcus's father spotted him, or sought him out, he always shouted the same thing.

"You little shit! I'll learn you a thing or two!"

Many times, it was Mac who saved Marcus. The old man was built like Marcus, small and wiry. Mac, on the other hand, even in his teen years, had grown bigger and stronger than their father. Mac could have taken him on years before he did. But the night their father handcuffed Marcus, just thirteen, to the boiler in the basement, Mac finally flexed his muscles. He'd grabbed hold of their father's shirt collar, hoisted him three feet off the floor, and hurled him against the cement wall of the basement. The blow to his head had left him unconscious. Mac fished the key to the handcuffs out of their father's pants pocket, set Marcus free, and tossed the key back into their father's lap.

"Fucker!" Mac had said. "Come on, baby brother. Let's go get a beer."

Marcus got drunk for the first time in his life that night. He'd stayed in his brother's truck and watched in awe as Mac strode into a convenience store as if he were a full-grown man and came back out with two six packs of Budweiser, one for himself, one for Marcus. Mac took Marcus to the old cemetery out on the wooded section of Mascoma Street. They'd leaned their backs against lichen-covered headstones and drank in silence until Marcus was halfway through his second beer and he started sobbing uncontrollably.

"I love you, Mac," he'd wept. "I don't know what I'd do without you. That house! It's just . . ."

"It's hell." Mac finished the sentence for him. "But it's temporary. Serve your time. You'll get out eventually. We both will."

"You graduate this year." Marcus was still sniffling.

"That's right. And I'm moving out as soon as I do. He can't make me stay."

The prospect of being alone with his parents for the next five years of his life was all the incentive Marcus had needed to keep drinking that night. He finished the six pack, puked, and passed out. Mac must have carried him into the house. He'd woken up the next morning in his own bed.

That had been more than ten years ago. Now Marcus stood next to his brother, his shoulder still only reaching Mac's bicep, confronted with the grim truth that their mother, just like Marcus all those years ago, had been handcuffed and helpless, and neither brother had been there to help her.

"Hell," Marcus sighed. "It wouldn't have made any difference if both of us had called every day. Every call was the same."

Marcus shifted into a parody of their father's gruff New England accent. "'Yup, I'm good. Mother's right here. You want to talk to her?' Then he'd hand the phone to Mom, and she'd say, 'Hi, Marcus. I'm fine. Okay. Bye-bye.' Every call was the same. They never told me a thing. And what if they had? What if Mom had actually told me what was going on? It's not like we could have done anything about it."

"I could've done something. If I'd known how far things had gone, I would've done *something*."

"Like what?" Marcus demanded.

The words escaped his lips an instant before he remembered what had happened the last time he'd challenged Mac's idea of himself as the conquering hero. It had only been a few weeks since the two of them had been leaning against the bar at Than Wheeler's in downtown White River Junction, their hometown. The sight of their old friend Barb showing up with the usual bruises on her arms and taking her usual seat next to Jon, who regularly gave her those bruises, had set Mac off. Back in the day, Barb had been Mac's girl. Marcus knew he still had a thing for her.

Mac had tossed back a shot of Canadian Club and leaned in close to Marcus.

"If that were my woman I'd treat her like a queen. She'd never work a day in her life. She'd have everything she ever wanted. And no one, I mean, no one, would dare raise a hand against her. I'd make sure of that."

Marcus had snorted into his beer and found himself sprawled out on the floor two seconds later.

"You got something to say, baby brother? Spit it out!" Mac demanded.

Every eye in the place turned to the Brown brothers, the little one cowering on the floor, the big one towering over him, fists clenched for battle. It was nothing they hadn't seen before.

"You're sleeping in your truck in the Walmart parking lot." Marcus's words were slurred but still audible to everyone in the joint.

"What's that to you?" Mac's foot landed a blow to Marcus's ribs. "Huh? What's that to you?"

Marcus rolled over, clutching his side. His long dark hair fell over his face. Spit dribbled from his mouth. He was too drunk to care, too far gone to know when to shut his trap. "You can't even hardly take care of yourself. How are you going to take care of someone else?"

"I'll take care of you, that's for damned sure! I'll learn you a thing or two!"

The next thing Marcus knew, Mac was shaking him awake. He was lying in the bed of his brother's pickup under a streetlight of the Walmart parking lot. Mac had to lower the tailgate for Marcus to crawl into the Walmart men's room to clean himself up. A man had walked in, taken one look at Marcus's battered face while he stood before the mirror, and laughed out loud.

"And I thought I had a rough night," he'd chuckled.

And now, standing next to Mac in their parents' disgusting train wreck of a home, Marcus braced himself for whatever abuse Mac might dish out. To his relief, nothing came.

"I could have at least beat the shit out of him," Mac answered dejectedly. "Not that it would have made any difference. She never would have left him. If I'd dragged her out of here, she would have crawled right back. I can't believe she stayed. Look at this place!"

Marcus stared at the trailer in glum silence. He had assumed he and Mac would be staying in their parents' mobile home, but once they arrived, Marcus was relieved they could retreat to Mac's truck to sleep. You could say what you wanted about their mother, Myrna Brown, that she had married poorly and stuck with a drunken brute for no good reason, for example. But by God, the woman had kept a decent house. If Dad was chaos, Mom was order. She had vacuumed and dusted, mopped and waxed, folded and tucked, washed and dried, sometimes until her hands were chapped. Marcus remembered her as a woman constantly in motion, forever tidying up, always putting everything in its place. When her work was done each night, she settled into her comfy chair in front of the TV and smoked a single cigarette. Dad had been parked in his recliner for hours, drinking.

Marcus's knees weakened at the thought of their mother living in filth. "She was dead long before he killed her."

"You got that right," Mac agreed. "At least he finally put her out of her misery. May be the one decent thing he ever did."

Tears welled in Marcus's eyes and he kicked a whiskey bottle away from his feet.

"Come on," Mac said. "Let's go sit by the lake. Tomorrow, we get the hell out of here."

2

Marcus grabbed two rusted lawn chairs from the carport that sheltered the old Thunderbird, Mac brought the cooler with some ice and what was left of their case of Buds, and the two brothers walked down to the rotting wooden boat dock that marked the pinnacle of the amenities available at their parents' trailer park.

"Welcome to the good life at the Driftwood Mobile Home Resort." Marcus sank down into his chair.

"More like the Mobile Home of Last Resort," Mac scoffed. "They had a nice place back home. Friends. Family. Good jobs. Why the hell did they move down here?"

"Money?" Marcus guessed. "Dad always said taxes were too high in Vermont. Said he wanted to fish. He did do a lot of fishing on the lake. Joe Next-Door said he was kind of famous for his fish fries."

"Fuck Joe! Fuck the old man's fish fries!" Mac exclaimed. "If I never see this dump again it'll be too soon."

Mac popped open a new Bud and handed it to Marcus, something he always did when it was just the two of them, and something that always secretly pleased Marcus. "Baby brother" first, big brother second, whether it was handing over takeout from McDonald's or shaking out a cigarette from a pack of Marlboros. But, in a group setting, Mac was more inclined to make Marcus beg. Marcus would hear himself quietly ask, "Can I have one?" and wait to see if Mac would grudgingly decide he could.

Marcus accepted the cold Bud and gazed wistfully across the still water of Lake Rousseau. Spanish moss hung from live oak and willow trees, framing the man-made body of water like a natural curtain. With the sun setting, Marcus felt as if he were seated before a stage, as if he were in a place of possibilities, the lights being turned down low to reveal a scene that produced happy endings.

"I wonder if it was nice here once," Marcus mused.

"This part of Florida has always been a shithole. Always will be." Mac took a long drag on his Marlboro and looked out into the gathering darkness.

"Did you know that the citrus industry, when it first started in Florida, like back in the 1920s, they locked up Black people who refused to work in the orange groves? No shit! That's a fact. Treated those people like slaves. Threw them in jail until they agreed to go back to work. Burned down their houses. Whole neighborhoods. You ever hear of Rosewood?"

Marcus shook his head.

"A community of Black people. Right nearby here somewhere. Sometime in the twenties, I think, white bastards burned Rosewood to the ground. These woods here"—Mac waved his lit cigarette in a wide arc—"these woods are overrun with the ghosts of Black men and women. You couldn't pay me to live here. Haunted as hell."

Marcus scanned the horizon. All seemed peaceful to him. He shook the idea clear from his head. It was just like Mac to plant some unwanted seed in Marcus's mind.

Mac was one of those guys who always had a story to tell, and Marcus had been falling for Mac's stories since he was a kid. Like the time Mac convinced him there was a whole tribe of Abenaki Indians living in the woods behind their house back in Vermont. He'd had proof—arrowheads and feathers, moccasins and beads—and Marcus had believed him, right up until the moment he was talking up the

Indian tribe to a group of kids on the school playground and their laughter had sent him home in tears.

The thing with Mac was there was always just enough truth in his stories to make the lies almost plausible. Once upon a time, Vermont *had* belonged to the Abenaki and the Mahican. The rivers *were* their highways. They *did* once build their villages in the woods behind the Browns' house. They just weren't doing it in the twenty-first century.

"How do you know that about the citrus industry?" Marcus asked.

"Google, I guess. I don't know. I read shit." Mac leaned forward in his chair and jabbed his beer in Marcus's face. "Do you know what they call Nevada?"

Marcus shrugged.

"The 'Silver State.' These days, everyone thinks Nevada is nothing but slot machines and whores. But back in the day, it was silver that put Nevada on the map. It still does, too. No shit! You ever heard of the Comstock Lode?"

Marcus had never heard of the Comstock Lode.

"Biggest silver rush in Nevada history. Everyone knows about the California gold rush. But no one remembers the Nevada silver rush. It was huge! I'm telling ya, back in the 1860s, men made fortunes mining silver in Nevada."

"Huh," Marcus said.

Mac crushed their empty beer cans in his hands and tossed them into the lake. Marcus winced.

Mac handed him another cold Bud, then lit each of them a fresh cigarette.

"There's still silver to be mined in Nevada, too, baby brother," Mac continued. "Every county in Nevada has mining operations. Well, every county but one. There's no mining in Douglas County. But that's beside the point. The point is there's money to be made mining silver in Nevada even today. You just gotta get your head out of your ass and come up with a plan to make some money on it, is all."

Marcus shifted uneasily in his seat. He didn't know exactly where this conversation was headed, but he had a feeling it wasn't going in a direction he liked. He suddenly had a sick feeling in his gut.

"Listen!" Mac lowered his voice and inched closer to Marcus. "It's do or die time, you know? We got ten thousand dollars in our pockets, and nothing holding us back. Nothing holding us back! So, what're we gonna do with it? What're we going to do?"

Marcus swallowed hard. "We split the money and go home, right?"

"Fuck no! There's nothing for us in Vermont. Nothing! We gotta think big! We gotta strike out on our own, take control of our lives for a change."

Marcus didn't entirely agree there was nothing waiting for them, or for him, at least, back in Vermont. He had an apartment and a job, a good one, entry level at a high-tech plasma cutting plant famous for its profit-sharing plans. Every year around Christmas, the local newspaper ran a happy front-page story about the thousands of extra bucks even the grunt workers at Plasmatherm got from the annual profit share. This was going to be Marcus's first year to cash in. That didn't seem like nothing to him.

"I was going to open a savings account," Marcus said.

"Fuck that! Less than one percent interest? We can do better than that, baby brother. Listen! I'm going to Vegas. You gotta come with me. Me and Slim have a plan to make us some real money. I mean *real* money!"

"Slim? Jim Daniels?" Marcus asked in disbelief.

Marcus pictured Slim Daniels. Tall, gangly, and pockmarked, Slim wore his white-blond hair long, pulled it straight back from his face, braided it, and let it dangle between his shoulder blades. Among the men Marcus knew, such a hairstyle should have branded Slim a pussy. Somehow Slim got away with it. Probably because everyone knew Slim Daniels was badass through and through, and the long, braided hair made him seem even more so.

Slim was also Mac's best friend. Marcus had grown up seeing the two of them together: Mac and Slim, Slim and Mac. He rarely saw one without the other. He supposed the friendship was, in some ways, a precious thing. But to Marcus, the fierce loyalty that existed between them was inexplicable. He privately wished his brother had ditched Slim years ago because wherever Slim went, trouble followed. And justly or not, Marcus blamed Slim for a good portion of the trouble Mac had gotten himself into over the years.

"What's Slim got to do with anything?" Marcus asked, trying to keep his tone neutral.

"He's out of jail."

"Yeah, I knew that, but—"

"Slim's in Vegas. Been there for a few months now. He knows the lay of the land. He can help us settle in."

Marcus sank down lower into his lawn chair.

"Yeah, yeah, yeah," Mac snapped. "You don't like Slim."

"He killed a man!" Marcus shot back.

"Christ! He was a kid when that happened! He was *sixteen years old.* He pled guilty. He served his time. Are you gonna hold that over his head forever? Are you never gonna let him forget it?"

"He beat a man to death with his fists. It's kind of hard to forget."

"You don't know the whole story. Nobody does. Slim had reasons for what he did. He's not as bad as you think. He says what he means, and he does what he says he's going to do. You don't appreciate that about him, how trustworthy he is. I trust Slim with my life. He's always had my back. Always!"

Mac had delivered versions of this impassioned defense of Slim for years. Each time he heard it, Marcus wanted to ask: "So, what *is* the whole story?" Marcus had been a kid, not quite a teenager, when he eavesdropped on enough conversations and picked up on enough rumors to know that Slim was going to jail for murder. He knew the police had questioned Mac, and that had scared Marcus—the possibility Mac might get locked up, too. But then Slim had pled guilty and been sent away, and the story had died down. Marcus had pressed his mother once for details. She'd told him to "let sleeping dogs lie." Marcus hadn't exactly understood what that meant, but he had followed the lead of those around him and tried to put the incident out of his mind.

He had let the sleeping dogs lie and hoped he'd never have to see Slim Daniels again. But now Slim was back, reviving in Marcus the same dread he had felt as a child whenever he was around his brother's best friend. He still couldn't help but wonder what the whole story was, but neither could he summon the courage to demand point blank that Mac tell him.

"So, what's Slim doing in Las Vegas, anyhow?" Marcus finally asked.

"Silver mining, dumb shit! Haven't you been paying attention?"

"Slim Daniels owns a silver mine?"

"No, not yet! Jesus!" Mac paced the dock. "Look! It's complicated. You wouldn't understand. But Slim has a plan. He's got it all worked out. He's smart! He hooked up with a guy in the joint and they worked the whole thing out together. Slim got out first and he's been waiting for this guy to get out. That time has come, brother! We can either take a chance and be a part of it—right now—and make something of ourselves, or we can go home and be the same chump losers we've always been. A lousy five grand apiece. We'll blow it all at Than Wheeler's in a year. We'll be back to square one, with our tails between our legs like whipped dogs."

Marcus would have given his left arm to be sitting at the bar at Than Wheeler's rather than having this conversation with his brother in some backwater town in rural Florida. The sun had set, leaving the two of them engulfed in darkness, sitting at the edge of three thousand acres of black water, with a park full of poor people in rusted tin shacks at their backs. Marcus stared at the lit ends of their cigarettes as if those hot red specks of light were his only glimmer of hope.

"What about Dotty?" Marcus asked, though he knew he was grasping at air.

"My ex? What about her?"

"She's the mother of your child. What about Amanda? She's five years old. Are you gonna just leave her behind?"

"Of course not!" Mac grabbed hold of Marcus's arm and squeezed hard. "Don't you get it? I'm no good to anybody right now. Christ! I'm still sleeping in my truck."

"I told you, you could bunk with me," Marcus interjected, more forcefully than he had intended.

"That's not the point!" Mac shouted, beer splashing out of the can, sparks flying from the end of his cigarette.

"Not a damned thing has ever gone my way." Mac lowered his voice, which Marcus found more ominous than the yelling. "Nothing has ever gone my way. Not from the start! And you know what I mean." Mac jabbed his cigarette toward Marcus's face.

Marcus did know what he meant. The brown eyes.

"Dad treated me like shit. You know he did. Wasn't nothing I could do that was ever going to be good enough for him. I never stood a chance."

Marcus could have easily countered that Fred Brown had treated both his sons, and his wife, like shit. But he held his tongue.

"But that's okay. That's in the past," Mac said. He tossed his beer can and cigarette stub into the lake. Marcus pressed himself even deeper into his lawn chair as Mac strode across the rotting dock and loomed over him in the darkness.

"Look! This isn't about Slim. It isn't about Dotty or Amanda or anybody else. This is about you and me! They're dead!" Mac jerked a finger toward their parents' mobile home. "They're both dead. And the only thing we're getting from them, the only thing we're ever going to get from them, is ten thousand dollars. This moment will never come again. We've got a chance right now to take that ten grand and do something big with it."

"I just want to go home," Marcus confessed, not wanting to look at his brother.

"And you will!" Mac got down on his knees in front of Marcus and held him by his forearms, gripping so hard Marcus felt the blood stop flowing into his fingers. "You'll go home a made man, Marcus. You, me, and Slim, we're going to be local heroes when we get back home. We've just got this one thing to do first, then we'll go home. I promise!"

Marcus's fingertips tingled, then went numb. "Can't you do it without me?"

"I can. And I will if I have to. But I don't want to," Mac said in an intimate whisper. "I know I wasn't always the best brother. I was always afraid of what the old man would do to you, or to Mom. But the old man's gone. He killed himself and took Mom with him. It's like a clean slate! We can be brothers now without all that bullshit."

Marcus lifted his gaze and looked into his brother's eyes for the first time that night.

"We're free. We can have an adventure, make a shitload of money, and then go home. Wouldn't that be nice?"

Marcus grinned weakly. "Yeah, that would be nice." He wasn't sure that was true, but he knew he couldn't say that to Mac.

"All right then!" A rare smile lit up Mac's face. "Let's do it, bro!"

3

The brothers left the Driftwood Mobile Home Resort late the next morning, carrying with them all the possessions they would ever claim from their parents' "estate." Mac took the handcuffs that had bound their mother to the chair where she was shot to death by their father, slipping the key inside his wallet. He laid claim to the Colt revolver, silver with a black handle, which he stashed under the front seat of his truck. Mac also had possession of the ten grand from Joe.

"One hundred one-hundred-dollar bills," he told Marcus, patting the plain white envelope Marcus had watched him tuck into the inside breast pocket of his jacket.

Marcus had never actually laid eyes on the money Mac said he'd received from Joe Next-Door—he'd only seen the envelope. But he was certain that if he asked to see it, whatever way the words came out of his mouth, Mac would take the question as a challenge and some sort of ugliness would ensue. So he left well enough alone.

Marcus took it upon himself to care for the two polished mahogany boxes that housed their parent's cremated remains. Treating the boxes as if they were fellow passengers, he placed them in the back seats of Mac's Ford F-150. But when Mac discovered them there, he ordered Marcus to put them in the truck bed along with their two suitcases, a large, padlocked metal chest, and an assortment of loose copper wire.

"It's not right," Marcus muttered under his breath.

Mac ignored the comment and covered their meager possessions with a blue tarp he secured to the truck with bungee cords. Marcus glared at him beneath his shaggy bangs. Mac grabbed Marcus by one arm and led him over to the cab of the truck.

"Get in!" he said. "And stop pouting like a girl."

Marcus climbed into the front passenger seat, still scowling, while Mac revved the engine. He slammed the gas pedal to the floor, and they roared out of the park, kicking up a cloud of gravel behind them.

"Smile, goddammit!" Mac ordered.

It was the exact command that used to issue forth from their father when the family was gathered around the dinner table and their mother did not appear sufficiently happy. Fred Brown's fist would hit the table, and Marcus's heart would jump in his chest as their father fixed angry eyes on their mother.

"Smile, goddammit!"

His mother would smile feebly, and Marcus would spend the remainder of the meal trying not to gag on his food, watching Mac do the same. It all had to go down, or they would never be excused from the table.

"Smile!" Mac said again, but in a gentler tone. "We're free, brother. We're on our way!"

Marcus stared gloomily out the window. Travel brochures always presented Florida as a paradise of swaying palm trees. But in the rural pocket of the state where Fred and Myrna Brown had lived their last days, all Marcus saw out his window was acre after acre of scraggly pine trees. They seemed like sad genetic mutations of the lush conifers he was used to in Vermont and New Hampshire. The landscape that whizzed by in a blur was so bleak, he imagined it being used as the backdrop for a movie set in some sci-fi ravaged-Earth dystopian future. It had neither the charm of a New England countryside nor the stark beauty of a desert.

"Look. I'm sorry," Mac said. "I don't want shit on the back seats—easier for when we fold 'em down to sleep."

Marcus glanced around the cab of his brother's domain. A fire-engine red F-150 with black interior, the truck was Mac's prized possession. Marcus knew he took care of it with the kind of loving attention a cowboy might show his horse, and he seemed to actually take a certain amount of pride in the fact he really had been living in it for most of the last year. When the girl he'd been shacking up with had called the cops on Mac after he got drunk one night and kicked in the front door of her apartment, he spent the night in jail, and then retreated to his truck. He never went back to the girl's place, shrugged away Marcus's offer of his couch, and never bothered to find a place of his own. He'd said he could've scraped together the money for a deposit and first month's rent, but he'd never bothered to make the effort.

Marcus preferred not to think in too much detail about how Mac made living in his truck work. But now that they were striking out on an adventure together, he found the topic suddenly worth further investigation.

"I don't see how you can stand it," Marcus said. "Living in your truck, I mean."

Mac raised his eyebrows. "It's been good enough for you this week.

"Well, yeah, but—"

"It's pretty easy, actually. If you get your head out of your ass, you find out pretty quick you don't actually need a house. You think it's awful to spend the night at Walmart? It's not. RVers boondock at Walmart all the time. They're open twenty-four hours. You wake up in the middle of the night and need to take a shit, you go inside and use the restroom. No one cares."

"But what about showers and stuff like that?" Marcus asked.

"Truck stops. Truck stops have everything," Mac said. "Showers. Laundry rooms. TV rooms. Restaurants. Barber shops. Christ! The big ones even have chapels. Not that I ever went to one. But they're there!"

Mac drove in silence for a moment. Marcus assumed he was lost in his memories.

"Sometimes in the summer," he started up again, "I'd drive all the way up to that truck stop on 91. You know the one I mean?"

"The P and H. The one with the homemade pies," Marcus said. "After you got your license, you'd wake me up in the middle of the night sometimes and we'd drive up there at like two in the morning for pie."

"That's right! We did, didn't we? It's a haul to get up there. But I'd take a shower, and have some dinner and a couple beers, then head back down to Goose Pond and find someplace around the water to park my truck for the night. You know, follow the little dirt roads all around the lakes and ponds back home, you find great places. Real quiet, you know? Nobody there to bother you. Hell, I'd blow up an air mattress and sleep under the stars in the bed of my truck. It was beautiful. I really liked it. Wake up the next morning and go to the Four Aces Diner for breakfast. What could be better than that?"

Marcus looked at his older brother and smiled at the thought of him living the bohemian lifestyle of a modern-day gypsy. He hadn't ever pegged him for the part. To Marcus, Mac was just the big guy always sitting next to him at a bar. Mac was the guy with the hair trigger temper who could toss back more whiskey shots than anyone else in the joint and still manage to drive off in his truck and never once get arrested for a DUI. Marcus imagined Mac passed out every night, but he never once imagined him staring up at the Milky Way and the Big Dipper.

Mac suddenly slapped the steering wheel with the open palm of his hand. "I tell you what, baby brother! The best fucks of my life have taken place right here in this truck!" he bragged with glee. "Stick with me, kid! I'll learn you a thing or two. You've lived a sheltered life."

They barreled north on I-75, then jogged west on I-10 when they reached the outskirts of Jacksonville. Marcus knew they were headed for Vegas, but he hadn't given much thought to the exact route that would lead to their destination. He left that to Mac, who stayed awake at the wheel while Marcus dozed in and out of sleep for several hours, always pulled out of his slumber with sudden thoughts of something left undone for their parents.

"We still need to write obituaries," he said after a bump jostled him awake. "Or get someone to write them for us. I don't know what to say. Do you think Dotty or Barb would do that for us? We need to get something printed in the paper so people back home will know what's happened."

"Believe me. They already know," Mac said.

"How?"

"Beats me," Mac shrugged. "The *Valley News* must have picked the story up from a wire service or something. Barb called and told me she saw it in the paper. 'Former Plainfield Road Agent and Wife Die in Murder-Suicide.' Some headline like that. Everyone knows, baby brother. We're the talk of the town now."

"Oh." Marcus contemplated the shame of it all, then went back to sleep. He woke up an hour later in a recurring ethical quandary about utility bills.

"I still think it's weird we couldn't cancel the gas or electric on the trailer. The phone and the cable, too. I kind of feel like we should have sorted that stuff out."

"They all wanted death certificates," Mac shrugged. "I wasn't going to stick around and deal with all that shit. We could've been ordering death certificates and mailing them to people for weeks."

"I guess Joe will have to deal with it," Marcus said.

"That's right. He owns the place. It's his problem now."

"I guess you're right." Marcus stared out the window, trying and failing to suppress a suspicion that had nagged at him for days. "It was legal, right? The deal we made with Joe?"

"Legal enough," Mac responded.

Marcus glanced sideways at Mac, in the general area of where the hundred one-hundred-dollar bills nestled up against Mac's chest.

"Joe made out like a bandit. He'll sell that shit for twice what he paid us," Mac said.

"So maybe we should've stuck around longer and taken care of things ourselves," Marcus offered.

"No, sir." Mac patted the envelope through the faded brown leather of his jacket. "This ten thousand is our get-out-of-jail-free card, brother. If Joe wants to wallow around in that swamp, that's his business. We. Are. Free."

Marcus smiled wanly and closed his eyes. He slipped into a vivid dream of their mother, ensconced in her living room chair, smoking a cigarette at the conclusion of all her housework. He dozed in peace for a brief spell, until a thought shot up like a rocket from his conscious mind and his eyes flew wide open.

"They planned it, didn't they?" Marcus said, half to himself, half to Mac. "Before they moved to Florida, they prepaid for their plots at the Lyme Cemetery and had their headstones carved with everything except the death date, remember? They prepaid and arranged for the cremations. All we had to do was make a call, and everything was taken care of. They already had the urns. They had the boxes. Everything was in place."

"Looks that way, doesn't it?" Mac said, not taking his eyes off the road. "Mom dotted all the *i*s and crossed all the *t*s, then Dad drank himself half to death before he did the both of them in."

"I guess we'll have to plan some kind of a service for them, won't we?" Marcus dreaded the thought. "They want their ashes buried in the cemetery. Don't most people have their ashes scattered somewhere? Are we supposed to bury the boxes or just the urns?"

"Damned if I know. But look. It's February. The ground is frozen solid back home right now. We can't do a burial until spring, at the earliest. Stop worrying, okay? We'll take care of all that once we're back home."

"Okay. Hey! Pull over here!" Marcus spotted a liquor store off the interstate. "I want to get something."

Marcus left Mac by the truck, lighting up a Marlboro, and went into the liquor store. He emerged moments later waving a brown paper sack. "Jack Daniel's. Since no one at the damned Driftwood bought us any."

"Good man!" Mac said. "Now drink that and leave me alone for a while, will ya?"

Marcus did as he was told. He took liberal gulps from the bottle, then reclined his seat all the way back and fell completely asleep. He didn't wake up again until Mac was shaking his shoulder. He opened his eyes to a wall of purple light that seemed to extend from the ground to the heavens.

"Where are we?" Marcus asked.

"Biloxi, Mississippi. Hard Rock Hotel and Casino."

The brothers stepped out of the truck, stretched, and gazed up at a ten-story hotel and an equally tall guitar, both bathed in purple. They took deep breaths of warm air blowing in from the Gulf of Mexico— Marcus could see the water from the parking lot. The breeze played with his hair, pushing the long strands back from his face.

"You know, I've never been inside a casino," Marcus said.

"Tonight's the night." Mac slung an arm across his shoulders and handed him two crisp one-hundred-dollar bills. Marcus accepted the money as if Mac were playing a trick on him.

"Seriously? We're going in? We can afford this?"

"Yeah. Why not? We deserve a break, don't you think?"

Marcus smiled as they strode toward the darkened glass doors of the casino, Mac's arm still draped across his shoulders. It was the best he could recall feeling for a long time. When the glass doors parted, they stepped into the flashing lights and cacophony of bells and whistles, the laughter and shouts of the casino. Marcus let loose with a joyous "Yes!"

Mac slapped Marcus's hand with a high five. "Baby brother, you're free! You don't have to call Mom and Dad ever again! We don't have to worry about them anymore. Now let's have some fun!"

The brothers shared a couple of drinks at a bar, then Mac found a Mississippi Stud poker game, while Marcus wandered around the casino floor trying his luck on slot machines, roulette wheels, and blackjack, which was the only card game he understood. He overindulged in the free drinks the cocktail waitresses handed out like candy. The more Marcus drank, the more he tipped, which one petite waitress with coal black hair and neon pink lipstick quickly caught on to. She brought Marcus more shots of Cuervo than he could count.

When Marcus's two one-hundred-dollar bills dwindled to a handful of ones, he staggered out to the truck and opened the door on a brown-haired beauty riding Mac in the back seat of the cab. Marcus shut the door, leaned against the truck, slid down the side of it, and passed out with his back resting against the truck.

At some point, Mac must have lifted Marcus into the cab and put him to sleep on the reclined seat. When Marcus woke up with the sun in his eyes, he found Mac glaring at him from the driver's seat.

"Enjoying your inheritance, baby brother?" Mac asked.

Marcus opened his door, hung his head out, and vomited. Once the sickness passed, he wiped his mouth with the back of his hand and collapsed into his seat.

"Damn straight I'm enjoying it," he said, because he thought he should.

"Christ! You never could hold your liquor."

"And you never could keep your pecker in your pants."

Mac slapped the steering wheel with the palm of his hand, then threw a fake punch at his brother's head—twice. Marcus flinched both times and braced himself for the real punch he expected to follow. That was a favorite ploy of Mac's, had been since they were boys. A play fight turned into a real fight in the blink of an eye, leaving Marcus stunned and bawling for justice from whichever parent was present.

Typically, his mother would look Marcus over for any signs of blood, then pretend to believe Mac's protestations that he was "just playing." "You're all right. You're not bleeding," she'd say to Marcus, unless he was, in which case she'd grab a kitchen towel and have him hold it over the bloody wound while she searched for Band-Aids in the bathroom.

"I don't have time for this nonsense" was the closest thing to a reprimand against his older brother that Marcus had ever heard their mother issue. At some point in his childhood, it dawned on him, almost as an unconscious thought, that his mother was afraid of Mac just as much as he was.

His father didn't seem to believe Mac was just playing, but he also never punished him, nor did he ever express any sympathy for Marcus. Quite the opposite.

"Hit him back! For Christ's sake, don't just stand there and take it," he'd say, lips curled in disgust while he watched Marcus blubber.

In those instances, it was Mac who finally took pity on Marcus. He'd get the kitchen towel, he'd staunch the wound, he'd find and apply the Band-Aids. "You're gonna live," he'd say, then slap his younger brother, somewhat affectionately, on his ass.

This time, Mac retracted his fist, put the truck in gear, and sped out of the Hard Rock Casino parking lot.

"Where are we going now?" Marcus asked.

"What difference does it make? I'll get you there. Don't bug me about it."

For the next several days, Marcus tried not to bug his brother as Mac charted a haphazard course across the country that landed them in casinos in several different states. From Biloxi, they jogged over to a riverboat casino in New Orleans, then headed north to the Osage Casino in Tulsa. Marcus won more than two hundred dollars at a blackjack table that night. He gave half to his waitress and tucked the rest into an envelope marked SAVINGS he stored in his suitcase. He told Mac he was going to open a savings account once they got to Vegas.

They drove on to Colorado and the Black Hawk casino outside Denver. Marcus's enthusiasm for slots and booze and Mac's habit of turning their truck into a whorehouse every night had dimmed. He was ready for the party to end, and it was a relief to be in a state where he could smoke his weed in peace like he had back in Vermont. To sit in the truck and smoke a joint and drink a beer at the same time was the equivalent of a day at the spa. The weed smoothed the rough edges of his nerves, which were beginning to fray every time he wondered, as he did with increasing frequency, just how much of their inheritance was left.

He asked Mac about it, the morning after the night at the Black Hawk. He waited until they were on the road, heading toward Utah. His thinking was if Mac was driving with at least one hand on the wheel, he'd be less likely to pummel him.

"So, how much is this celebration costing us anyhow?" Marcus asked as casually as he could.

"Fuck if I know," Mac said.

He offered no further information. An awkward silence hung between the brothers for several minutes. Marcus knew in his bones he should just endure it, sit there with his mouth shut until the tension dissipated like a foul odor. But, instead, he took another stab at it.

"I was just wondering, you know, if like you win money at the poker games? You know, like I won at blackjack the other night? I mean, like maybe we're coming out ahead. Like maybe we're *investing* the money rather than just throwing it away."

Mac swerved the truck to the right and off the interstate. He slammed on the brakes, sending Marcus flying out of his seat and slamming his head against the windshield. Red with rage, Mac turned on Marcus, who was backed up against the car door, feeling blood drip down from a cut over his eye.

"So, that's what you think? You think I'd blow the whole ten grand on whores and bad bets? Huh? Is that what you think, baby brother?"

Marcus wiped blood away from his eyes. His lips trembled. "I don't know what I think. Honest, Mac, I don't. I've never even *seen* the money. What do I know?"

"You want to see some money?" Mac yanked his wallet out of his back pocket and started hurling bills at Marcus's face. Small bills—ones and fives, a lone twenty—fluttered against Marcus's cheeks like bedraggled greenish butterflies caught in a storm. Enraged, Mac jammed his fist into the pile of loose change he collected in the console of his truck and let fly a barrage of coins into his brother's face. Marcus sat stunned as pennies, dimes, nickels, and quarters hit his cheeks, his forehead, his chin.

"Is that enough? You want to count it? You need more?"

"I don't know!" Marcus was crying now. Tears mixed with the blood already rolling down his cheeks.

"Well, it's all you're going to get! So, take it and get the fuck out!" Mac reached across the cab and swung open Marcus's door. "Get out! Get the fuck out of my truck! Right now!!"

Marcus grabbed at the bills that had landed in his lap, gathering them up as quickly as he could, then stumbled out of the truck. Alone on the side of the highway, blood and snot smeared across his face, Marcus stared at Mac in helpless misery.

"You're on your own now, baby brother. Let's see how long you last without me!" Mac yanked the passenger door shut and gunned his truck back onto the highway, pelting Marcus with a wave of gravel and sand as he sped off heading west on Interstate 70.

Marcus remained glued to his spot for several minutes, watching the endless flow of vehicles speed by. He stood mesmerized until he regained enough of his senses to move. He slid down the embankment and found shelter under the shade of a spindly aspen tree.

He wiped his face with his T-shirt, which came up smudged with snot, blood, and tears, then sat cross-legged on the ground, smoothing and counting the bills. They didn't add up to much, just fifty-seven dollars, if Marcus counted correctly, which he figured he didn't. He remained dazed from the confrontation, uncertain what to do next.

However much he did or didn't have, it wasn't enough to get him back to Vermont.

Marcus stood, fished his own wallet out of his back pocket and stuffed the small stack of bills inside of it.

"Fuck it!" Marcus said aloud, brushing dirt off his backside. "I'll walk home if I fucking have to. I'm going home."

He walked back up to the highway and set out, trudging east against traffic at the edge of the interstate. What else could he do?

He made it less than a mile when it occurred to him he should cross over to the other side of the interstate. On that side of the road, at least, he stood a chance of hitching a ride with someone who could carry him in the right direction toward home. He was watching and waiting for a break in the flow of traffic when a fire engine red pickup truck slowed and stopped beside him.

"No way," Marcus muttered aloud. He resumed his trek, his eyes angrily glued to the ground.

Mac stepped out onto the gravel shoulder, but Marcus didn't halt until Mac caught up to him and grabbed his arm. But even then, Marcus shook his stronger, older brother off. He took two steps back and faced Mac with a defiance he rarely had the wherewithal to muster. He felt it in his clenched jaw.

"What? What now?" Marcus spat the words at his brother's face.

"Look. I'm sorry," Mac said. "I'm sorry. Okay? What more do you want from me?"

"Nothing! I don't want shit from you!" Marcus's voice, high pitched like that of a terrified girl, quavered with rage. "Why can't you just leave me alone?"

Mac's shoulders slumped. He glanced up, as if searching for an answer in the scattered clouds. He blew out a long breath and pointed an accusing finger at his own chest. "I'm an asshole. You think I don't know I'm an asshole? I do. I go off on people. I go off on *you*. I don't know why. I just do. I always have. I probably always will. But look . . . !"

Mac took one step toward Marcus. "But look. You're my brother. Christ! You're my *only* brother! I'm *your* only brother. It's just you and me now. This is it. This is all we've got left." He paused, took another step toward Marcus, narrowing the distance between them. Marcus was aware Mac could reach out and put a hand on his shoulder or punch him in the face.

"You have to forgive me." Mac's voice verged on brotherly compassion. "You have to. I'm your brother."

"I always have to forgive you. It's not fair."

"I know. But that's the way it is. That's what we're stuck with." Mac extended a hand toward Marcus. "So come on. Let's get over it and move on. There's water and food in the truck. I'll take you straight to Vegas now. The party's over. I promise. It's time to go to work. There's shit I have to do."

Marcus didn't move. The boiling hate he felt had simmered down to a lukewarm dread. He struggled to understand where he was, what he was doing. He cast his glance beyond his brother, to the seemingly endless line of cars speeding down the highway, to the empty horizon spread out before him. He smiled a little. "I always kind of wanted to go west. See the horizon, the wide-open sky."

Mac nodded. "Damned trees and mountains back home make it impossible to see beyond your own nose. Everyone in New England wants to go west. Everyone wants to see the horizon. At least once."

"When I close my eyes," Marcus said, "I always see Mount Ascutney. Know what I mean? Like when you're driving south on 91, and you see Mount Ascutney in front of you for miles and miles? That's what I see when I close my eyes. Fucking Mount Ascutney right up in my face. It's always there, closing in on me, like I'll never get away from it."

Mac held his hand out for Marcus again. "Come on. I'll get you away from Mount Ascutney. I promise."

4

Mac tore through Utah with just a couple of pit stops. He told Marcus there weren't any casinos in the state and he couldn't imagine any kind of fun with a Mormon whore. He'd promised Marcus the party was over and, for the moment, at least, it seemed to Marcus that Mac was honoring that promise.

Marcus fell into a deep sleep for most of the ride, but as they crossed out of Utah and into Nevada, he found himself suddenly wide awake and in a mood to cut loose. He smoked a joint and swigged what was left of the Jack Daniel's, and as the desert scenery passed by, he felt a novel sense of freedom expanding in his veins.

His parents were dead, reduced to ashes, a coarse blend of gray grit and dust poured into a plastic bag and sealed with a twist tie. He and Mac had stuffed the bags into their fancy metal urns and tucked them into the fancy mahogany boxes, which were now bouncing around with their suitcases and some scrap metal in the back of Mac's truck. Never one to disrespect the dead, Marcus now struggled to suppress his merriment. His father would never berate, belittle, or beat him again. His mother would never again turn away from him and cast her pale blue eyes toward some nonexistent distant horizon while the abusive man she called a husband demanded she smile for him.

By the time they reached Vegas, Marcus felt like a free man.

As Mac crawled the Strip and gunned his engine, Marcus couldn't keep the massive grin off his face. At first, he gawked at the lights and the throngs of people like any other tourist, but soon he rolled down his window and stuck his upper body out of the truck.

"Whoo-hoo! Yeah, baby!" he yelled. "We're here, Vegas! We're here!"

Mac honked his horn as if to announce their arrival as well. They passed the Bellagio as the fountain show started, and Marcus whoo-hooed again. Then Mac pulled him by his shirttail back into the cab of the truck.

"Enough already," Mac snapped, as if he were scolding a child. "Have at least a little self-respect."

As Marcus was trying to think of a comeback, they passed a tall platinum blonde in black stiletto heels and silver hot pants on the sidewalk outside Planet Hollywood. Mac grabbed his crotch and rubbed himself.

"Hey baby! he yelled to her. "Make my dreams come true!"

The woman on the street rubbed her fingers together in the universal sign for money, and Mac slammed on the brakes, ripped a fifty out of his pants pocket, and threw it toward her. "That's for having the best view in town!"

She tossed her head back and laughed, stooped to pick up the money, and blew Mac a kiss as they continued up the Strip.

Marcus fell back into his seat and grasped his chest, feigning a heart attack. "My inheritance!" he wailed in mock distress. "You're wasting my fucking inheritance! What would Dad say!?! What would Mom think!?!"

"Fuck them!" Mac cried.

They both laughed with unbridled glee.

Mac drove them up and down the Strip half a dozen times, and Marcus called out excitedly every time he spotted yet another fabled Vegas institution.

"There's the Mirage!"

"That's Caesars Palace!"

"The Flamingo! Man, that place is a classic! We gotta go there. And Harrah's! That's old school, too, right?"

"Hey, there's the Eiffel Tower! I don't think the real Eiffel Tower is gold, though, do you?"

"The Venetian! That's like from Venice, Italy. I think you can ride gondolas in there, like in the real Venice, only it's fake."

As they neared the north end of the Strip, Marcus announced he had to take a piss. Mac pulled into the parking lot of the Circus Circus Casino. Marcus hopped out of the truck, leaned against it, and promptly pissed. Sounded to him like Mac was doing the same on the other side. They could've walked a few hundred yards to find a restroom inside the casino, but in that moment, at three in the morning at the bleaker end of the Strip, taking a piss in a parking lot seemed the more appropriate thing to do.

Stoned and drunk, tired but exalted, Marcus zipped up his jeans, leaned his back against Mac's truck, and lit up a Marlboro. He closed his eyes and tried to savor the moment, tried to make sense of what they'd done. Him and Mac. Together. Through thick and thin. For better or for worse. They had survived their parents. They had survived one another. They had crawled out of the dank swamps of Florida and transported themselves to the bright lights of Las Vegas. Their asses weren't glued to bar stools at Than Wheeler's anymore. He felt as if he'd accomplished something.

"No one can take this away from us," Marcus slurred. "Whatever else happens, we had this."

"Had what?" Mac asked.

"Nothing." Marcus shook his head. "I'm wasted."

He crawled back into the cab of the truck and reclined his seat to go to sleep. Marcus assumed they'd spend the night right there in the parking lot of Circus Circus and set about finding a permanent place in the morning. Wasted as he was, however, one eye popped open when he heard Mac on his cell phone in the seat next to him.

"Yeah, we're here. Got in about an hour ago. Just taking in the sights. Where you at?"

Marcus stopped breathing. Every muscle in his body tensed as he listened to Mac's side of the conversation.

"South end of the Strip. Couple of blocks west of the Boulevard. Corner of Russell and what? Sandbar Suites. Yeah, I'll find ya. Be there in a few."

As Mac turned the key in the ignition, Marcus rolled to his left side and faced his brother.

"Where're we going?" he asked weakly.

"Huh? I thought you were passed out." Mac tousled Marcus's hair. "We're going to the Sandbar Suites."

"What's at the Sandbar Suites?" Marcus said.

"A place to crash. A place to call home, actually. Slim set it up for us."

Marcus pushed himself up into a sitting position, alert to the mention of Slim. He'd known all along Slim was as much a part of their destination as Las Vegas itself. But for days he'd put the specter of Slim out of his mind.

Not thinking—it was a habit Marcus had developed at an early age. If he didn't think about it—his father drunk and belligerent, his mother looking the other way, Mac bullying him—it didn't exist. He blocked out the bad and lived relatively worry-free during the interval between the last awful thing that had happened and the next awful thing that hadn't happened yet. Marcus lived inside the parameters of a blank, neutral space where the past was suppressed and the future might turn out okay—if he just didn't think about it. Marcus didn't think unless he had to. And now he had to think about Slim.

"You look like you're about to puke," Mac said. "Don't you dare puke in my truck, brother!"

Marcus didn't puke in his brother's truck. He fell to his knees and puked in the parking lot of the Sandbar Suites. Slim was there waiting for them, leaning against his banged-up purple Chevy Cavalier, a lit cigarette dangling from his lips.

"Christ! Some things never change, do they?" Slim laughed. He waved an oddly shaped milky-white bottle in one hand and three paper cups in the other. He handed the bottle to Mac, slapped his old friend across the back. "Baby brother's still a lightweight, I see."

Marcus wiped his lips, his queasiness still lingering as he witnessed the easy bond between the two old friends.

"Ain't that the truth?" Mac shook his head in disgust, then suspiciously eyed the bottle Slim had handed him. "What is this shit?"

"That shit, my friend, is Azul Reposado tequila," Slim pronounced the Spanish words with some pride. "It's the smoothest damn tequila you'll ever taste. Try it!"

Mac brought the bottle to his lips and tipped his head back for a sip. "Damn! That is good. You must've paid a pretty penny for that!"

"I didn't pay nothin'," Slim bragged. "I picked it up half full about a week ago, right on the sidewalk outside the Bellagio. Been savin' it for my buddies. You won't believe the shit you can find for free around here, Mac. Fucking tourists, man! I can't wait to show you the ropes!"

Marcus stumbled to his feet, wiping his mouth on the back of his hand. "Can I try it?" He tentatively held his hand out for the bottle.

"Fuck no!" Slim slapped Marcus's hand. Marcus dropped both hands to his sides and focused his attention on the pavement.

"I'm just teasin'!" Marcus looked up to see Slim wink at Mac, and then he punched Marcus playfully in the shoulder. "Come on. Follow me. I'll get ya seated someplace safe and then I'll pour you a drink. I don't want your pukey lips all over my pretty bottle."

Marcus followed Mac and Slim across the parking lot and through the squeaky metal gate of a battered chain-link fence that surrounded a small oblong swimming pool. They took seats under the faded red umbrella of a concrete patio table set up with three curved, concrete seats bolted into the deck of the pool area. Slim set the paper cups on the table and poured each of them a shot. Marcus felt Mac and Slim watch him take his first sip.

"Mmmm, that is good," Marcus said.

The two older men snorted contemptuously.

"What?" Marcus asked, feeling sheepish.

"Nothin'," Slim said. "You're just such a pussy, is all. Always have been, always will be."

Marcus shrugged and downed the rest of the tequila in his cup. "Cheers! Pour me another!"

Slim poured them all another shot. Out of the corner of his eye, Marcus spotted something moving in the pool. "Are those ducks?" he asked.

"Ducks? Are you out of your fucking mind? You think there are ducks in my pool? Boy, you're seeing things!" Slim glared at Marcus, then winked at Mac.

"Just teasin'," Slim said. "There are, in fact, ducks in my pool. They showed up about two weeks ago. Now kids and chicks are always down here tossing breadcrumbs to the damn ducks. They're never gonna leave."

"Where'd they come from?" Marcus asked.

"Fuck if I know." Slim shrugged. "Golf course would be my guess. There's golf courses with duck ponds all over the place out here. Poor fuckers got confused and wound up here."

Marcus felt an immediate kinship with the ducks in the pool. He made a mental note to get some bread for them first thing tomorrow.

Marcus lit a cigarette and surveyed his surroundings. In the glare of the streetlights, he could see an L-shaped, three-story brick structure painted a garish yellow, with white wrought-iron fencing around the second- and third-floor balconies. Here and there, men and women, dressed in jeans or shorts and tank tops or sweatshirts, leaned their bellies against the white railings, smoking cigarettes and listlessly scanning the city streets below or night sky.

"What is this place?" he asked. "It looks like a motel."

"It was a motel. Now it's apartments. You find places like this all over Vegas. Every bum fuck who wanders into the city winds up in a place like this at first, including me," Slim said. "Cheap housing."

"How cheap?" Mac asked.

"Six hundred a month, plus three hundred upfront. I got you guys set up on the third floor two doors down from me. You owe me nine hundred and twenty-five dollars. That includes an application fee."

"Does it have a kitchen?" Marcus asked.

"Kitchen, bathroom, TV, duck pond. This place has everything a man needs. Come on. I'll show ya."

Slim snuffed out his cigarette in a black plastic ashtray overflowing with stubs. Marcus trailed behind as he led the brothers out of the pool and up the three flights of exterior stairs.

"That's me, in 308," Slim said, "And this is you, in 310."

Slim unlocked the door and swung it open. He ushered Marcus and Mac into the room as if he were a real estate agent showing prospective buyers a choice piece of property rather than a couple hundred square feet of utilitarian renovations. They entered a tiny kitchen set up with a small table and two chairs on one side of the room. On the other side of a half-wall partition was a full-size bed, dresser, TV, and recliner. An A/C unit sat in the window next to the bed, ready for the warmer months ahead. Faded orange drapes were closed on the picture window to their left.

Marcus stood with his hands on his hips and shrugged. "I guess this'll work."

"You guess?" Slim sneered. "You find someplace better, you let me know. I'm telling ya, this place is a palace compared to some of the rattraps I've seen in this town."

"It's perfect," Mac said. "Ain't that right, baby brother?"

"Yeah, it's great. I like it." Marcus fell in line as he was expected to do.

Somewhere on the third floor, a door slammed opened. "Go ahead, you fucking whore! See what I care!" a man yelled.

Slim and Mac rushed out the door and Marcus followed eagerly. He stepped out onto the walkway in time to catch sight of a pudgy brown-haired woman in a mini skirt and halter top clamber down the exterior stairs in a pair of clackety platform heels. As she opened the driver's side door of a silver Oldsmobile parked almost directly beneath them, the boys, in unison, took a step back as a man in faded boxer shorts rushed in front of them and hurled a rusted hibachi grill over the railing.

"Take that, you bitch!" the man screamed.

The grill landed with a thud on the hood of the woman's car. It sat there in the cosy indentation it had created, as if it were a bird settled into a nest.

"You think I give a fuck?" the woman screamed back. She tossed her handbag into the car, climbed in, revved the engine, backed up, and roared out of the parking lot. The hibachi grill rolled off the hood and came to rest upside down in the empty parking space.

"Fucking whore," the man muttered to himself. Paying no mind to the three men standing on the balcony watching him, he plodded back to his apartment and slammed the door shut.

"Oh, man, this place!" Slim shook his head and nearly giggled. "Welcome to Vegas! You guys are gonna love it here!"

5

Marcus woke up late the next morning, fully clothed, his face pressed against his brother's bare back. He had only scattered recollections of the previous night, and no memory at all of getting into bed with his brother. It was something he'd never done before. When they were kids, Mac had alternately tortured and protected his younger brother. If there was an internal logic to Mac's moods, Marcus failed to discern it. He got used to the fact Mac was as likely to grip him in a headlock and force him to his knees as he was to dare the neighborhood boys to even look sideways at his kid brother.

Marcus grew up never knowing which way the wind might blow. When he had cowered alone in his bed, on high alert as his father staggered about the house in a drunken rage, Marcus had often longed to tiptoe over to Mac's room across the hallway. He had imagined slipping in beside Mac under the covers, the two of them weathering the storm of their father's temper together.

That had never happened. Marcus had remained paralyzed in his bed, terrified by the prospect of his drunk father crashing into his room and utterly uncertain as to the reception he might receive from his brother. Eyes wide open, the covers pulled up to his chin, Marcus had willed himself to be invisible. Sometimes, it worked. Most times, it didn't.

Marcus tried to climb out of bed without disturbing Mac. He succeeded to the extent that Mac rolled over, opened his eyes long enough to recognize his brother, then turned his back to him again.

Marcus opened the door of the little refrigerator in the kitchenette. It was empty, as he had expected. He grabbed his cigarettes and stepped out to the third-floor walkway. Slim was there, leaning his elbows on the railing, sipping black coffee from a white Styrofoam cup. "You want some, Sleeping Beauty?" Slim asked.

"Sure. Thanks."

Slim handed him the cup, half empty, then went into his apartment and came back out a moment later with a new, full cup for himself.

"Where can I get some food?" Marcus asked.

"There's a 7-Eleven just around the corner. You can see it from here." Slim pointed with a lit cigarette. "They got hot dogs and pizza, all the usual shit. Play some slots while you're there if you want."

"They have slot machines at the 7-Eleven?" Marcus asked.

"They got slot machines everywhere. *Everywhere*," Slim said. "You know, like in grocery stores back home where they store the shopping carts right inside the entrance? Here they got slot machines."

"Really? Do people play 'em?"

"Play 'em? Fuck man, slots are like heroin. One shot, you're hooked. You can't turn sideways in this town without bumping into some damn fool humping a slot machine. They're everywhere. Gas stations. Convenience stores. Grocery stores. Shit man, I half-expect they're in the fucking schools."

"Strange place." Marcus imagined slot machines sprouting like dandelions all over Las Vegas.

Slim shrugged. "Shit, I've seen stranger places than this."

"Like where?" The question slipped out of Marcus's mouth before he considered what he was saying.

"What? You think this shithole town is the strangest place I've ever seen?" Slim's eyes narrowed to steely slits.

"I don't know." Marcus shrugged and looked away.

"That's right. You don't know because you're an ignorant son of a bitch." Slim moved a step toward Marcus. "You don't know shit about where I've been and what I've done. You got that, my friend?"

"Yeah, I got it." Marcus tried to inch away from Slim's fury. "I was just asking, like where, you know? It didn't mean anything."

"The hell it didn't." Slim spat over the railing. "You need to watch yourself, my friend. I've seen things and done things you don't even *want* to know about. You don't want to forget that." He moved in even closer to Marcus. "You know who never forgets that?"

Slim pointed his lit cigarette at the closed door to Room 310, where Mac presumably was still sleeping, unaware of the conversation outside on the walkway.

"Your brother never forgets who I am and what I've done. He knows where I've been. He knows what I *did* for him. He minds his fucking manners around me. And you damn well need to do the same." Slim tossed his cigarette over the walkway railing.

Marcus wished he had the courage to stand up to him. In his mind, he shouted, *"What? What did you do? Exactly what does my brother owe you?"* But Marcus didn't dare, and he was spared from having to decide what to do or say next when Mac shuffled out of Room 310. He shoved a hundred-dollar bill and the keys to his truck into Marcus's hands.

"We need beer and bread," he said. "And cigarettes."

"And toilet paper," Slim added, looking directly at Marcus. "So this pussy can wipe his ass. I think he just shit his pants."

Marcus made his way to the 7-Eleven. Sure enough, just as Slim had said, to his right as he walked into the store, Marcus spotted three slot machines. They were set up in a row, conveniently located next to an ATM. A padded stool with a backrest was at each machine, and each stool was occupied. The sight of a young woman in a pretty sundress, an old white man in a shabby Dallas Cowboys T-shirt two sizes too big for him, and a grandmotherly Black woman with a small child wrapped around each of her legs brought a nervous smile to his face. The intensity with which each of them focused on the colorful images flashing before their eyes, to the near total exclusion of everything else around them, struck him as bizarre. He hadn't found it peculiar at the casinos he and Mac had visited. But at a convenience store, it just seemed weird.

Marcus stood in line to check out, a grocery cart loaded with beer, bread, potato chips, Little Debbie coffee cakes, and a stack of frozen Red Baron pizzas, when one of the slot machines went wild with flashing lights and an explosion of bells and whistles. All eyes turned to the bedraggled man in the oversized Cowboy's T-shirt. He waved his hands over his head and danced in place in front of his machine. "I won! I won!" he cried, clearly astonished by his own good luck.

Everyone in the 7-Eleven applauded, except the middle-aged cashier behind the counter. "All right," he said, waving the man toward him. "Let's settle you up."

Everyone in line stood back to let the winner go ahead of them. Some patted him on the back. Others offered congratulations. Even the cashier's face cracked into something like a fleeting smile as he handed the man his winnings.

"You be careful out there," he warned the old man solemnly. "Take care of yourself."

When it was Marcus's turn to pay, he tried to initiate a conversation with the cashier.

"So, how much did the old man win?" he asked.

"Ain't none of your business." The cashier fixed Marcus with a stern glare.

"Just curious," Marcus said, taken aback by the firmness of the cashier's response. "I'm new here. Got in last night. Just wondering, like, how much do people win at those things?"

"Just enough to be dangerous," the cashier answered cryptically. "You watch your back, newbie. You hear me?"

"Sure, sure." Marcus was still confused by what he'd done or said to elicit such a response.

As he rolled his cart out to Mac's truck, Marcus noticed a young guy in a pink sport coat had assumed the old man's seat at the slot machine. He shook his head. How much time and money would it take, he wondered, before that machine blessed another gambler with a winning spin?

It wasn't until he pulled out of the parking lot, glancing to his right to check for oncoming traffic, that Marcus noticed a commotion taking place around the corner from the 7-Eleven. Two teenaged boys, slim and dressed alike in low-slung jeans, oversized white T-shirts, and black baseball caps, stood on opposite sides of a prone figure on the sidewalk, taking turns kicking at them. It was a fleeting glimpse of a Dallas Cowboys logo that clued Marcus in to what was happening. The old man who'd been congratulated and applauded not more than five minutes ago for winning at the slots was being robbed. Only now the old man might as well have been invisible. Pedestrians and drivers alike, including Marcus, saw what was happening, and did nothing. Marcus stared for a second, his mouth hanging open, appalled at what he was witnessing. The old man curled up in a ball, trying to protect himself from the repeated blows to his body. Blood streamed from a gash on his face.

Marcus hesitated at the intersection. Should he intercede on the old man's behalf or mind his own fucking business? The decision was made for him when a woman in the convertible behind him laid on her horn and yelled, "What the fuck!?"

Marcus turned away from the plight of the old man and focused his attention on the flow of vehicles coming and going along the busy street.

Shaken, he traveled the short distance back to the Sandbar Suites in a state of shock. Mac and Slim were still on the third-floor walkway, smoking cigarettes and drinking coffee, when Marcus approached. Breathless from carrying grocery bags in both arms up three flights of stairs, and still aghast at what he'd just witnessed, Marcus deposited the groceries at Mac's feet.

"You won't believe what just happened," he gasped.

"I bet I will," Slim retorted.

"Some old man won at the slot machines at the 7-Eleven," Marcus continued, "and two guys jumped him and robbed him, beat the shit out of him, right there on the sidewalk, in broad daylight."

"Slot muggings," Slim pronounced, nodding his head sagely. "If you stand here and watch the 7-Eleven, you'll see shit like that every day."

"Seriously? People win at the slots that often?"

"Nah, not really." Slim directed his words more to Mac, although it was Marcus who asked the questions. "Just meth heads and whores picking off the low-hanging fruit. They know what to look for— tourists with money in their wallets, the occasional slot winner. It's all the same shit."

Marcus turned his eyes back to the 7-Eleven. His view from the third floor was unobstructed. The old man was alone on the sidewalk now, wiping blood and tears off his face with the hem of his Cowboys T-shirt.

"Poor bastard," Marcus said. "I feel sorry for the guy."

"I don't," Mac spoke up. "Fucking idiot, if you ask me."

"Damn straight," Slim agreed. "People get what they deserve. Slot monkeys? They're practically asking for it. Feel sorry for some asshole who humps a slot machine at the 7-Eleven? I don't think so."

Marcus watched the old man struggle to his feet and walk away on unsteady legs. He wondered how much he had won, and how much he had lost.

Neither Slim nor Mac had made any motions to assist Marcus with the groceries, so he carried the bags into the apartment, put the food away, and rejoined the two men on the walkway.

"There's more stuff in the truck," Marcus said. Mac and Slim stared at him indifferently. He sighed, bit his tongue, and hiked down to the parking lot. He retrieved the mahogany box that bore his mother's name, carrying it in his arms back up the three flights of stairs, past Mac and Slim and into Room 310. He set the box on the dresser, then returned downstairs for his father's ashes.

"Is that your parents?" Slim asked Mac as Marcus passed by them the second time.

"What's left of them," Mac said.

When Marcus trudged past a third time, Slim guffawed. "There's more?" He grinned at Mac. "How many bodies are you boys traveling with?"

"I'm getting my suitcase," Marcus muttered.

"Get mine while you're at it!" Mac called out to him.

Marcus walked wearily down the stairs, the sound of his brother's and Slim's laughter fading behind him. His suitcase was in the back seat of the truck. But for some reason, he opened the driver's side door and sat, unmoving, for several minutes. Exhausted, his heart racing, the keys to the truck in his pants pocket, he gripped the steering wheel until his knuckles turned white.

A voice in his head screamed at him. *Leave! Don't go back up those stairs again! Fuck Slim! Fuck Mac! Fuck your dead parents! Go home to Vermont! Go back to your job, your apartment, your clothes, your PlayStation, your DVD player, your friends! Get out now, before it's too late!*

Too late for what, Marcus couldn't say. But a sense of impending doom threatened to swallow him whole if he walked back up those stairs even one more time. He pulled the truck keys out of his pocket. He inserted them into the ignition. He pictured himself on the open highway of the wild west, alone in the truck, the windows open, the wind blowing through his hair. What was to stop him?

"Mac would fucking kill me," Marcus said aloud. "And Slim would help him do it."

He sat for another minute, catching his breath, unwinding his fingers from the steering wheel, removing the keys from the ignition, returning to reality. He grabbed his suitcase out of the back seat and trekked one more time up the stairs. His face burned with humiliation as he passed by the grinning faces of Slim and Mac. He set his suitcase down inside the door of their room and fetched the bag of Wonder Bread he'd bought at the 7-Eleven.

Mac and Slim howled with laughter as he passed by them on his way to feed the ducks.

6

All the way from Florida to Nevada, Marcus had pushed back against his misgivings and propped up his enthusiasm for the move with the idea that finding work in Las Vegas would be easy. All those casinos. All those hotels. All those restaurants and bars. Surely, a reasonably intelligent and hardworking young man such as himself would find gainful employment within days upon his arrival in the city.

Mac had encouraged his optimism.

"You can be a dealer!" Mac had declared between swigs of Jack Daniel's.

"I don't know how to deal cards. Do you?"

"They'll train you," Mac had said with confidence.

"Will they?"

"Shit, yeah. No one knows how to deal cards. They must provide training."

Marcus had a hard time picturing himself at the head of a gaming table. He was too shy, too easily intimidated. Mac on the other hand—tall, stone-faced, unreadable, in command of everyone around him—he would be good at it.

"I think I'd rather be a bartender," Marcus had said, taking the whiskey bottle from his brother's hands. "Pretty girls. Tips. Do you think they train guys to be bartenders?"

"Probably. Or you train yourself," Mac had offered. "Learn some basic drinks. Go online. Take a state test or something. Get a certificate, I think."

The prospect of going online and taking a test seemed daunting to Marcus. But there were plenty of other, more likely jobs to occupy his imagination. Dishwasher. Bell boy. Grocery bagger. Gas station attendant. Something would come along. He'd wrapped his lips around the Jack Daniel's bottle and pretended to be confident about his future.

Two days after they'd settled in at the Sandbar, Marcus journeyed on foot alone out to the Strip to look around. He walked up one side of Las Vegas Boulevard and down the other, wandering in and out of every casino he passed, utterly overwhelmed by the alien quality of everything he saw. It was one thing, he soon discovered, to wade into a casino high on booze or chilled out on weed and lose himself in the lights and the press of bodies, the endless rows of slots, the eager tourists gathered around a roulette wheel, waitresses dodging and weaving through the crowds with drinks spilling over onto their trays. It was quite another thing to walk into a casino stone cold sober in the harsh light of day and try to figure out how to apply for a job.

Marcus didn't have a clue where or how to start. He roamed the Strip for hours, accomplishing nothing. He hadn't submitted a single job application when he made his way to the far north end and sat down alone at a bar at Circus Circus. It was the one place that seemed even slightly familiar to him, and not just because he had pissed in the parking lot his first night in town. The Circus was a better fit for Marcus. It wasn't as glitzy or glamorous as other places. It showed a little wear and tear around its edges. Its carpets were worn, its fixtures less polished, the hookers less alluring than at casinos like the Bellagio and the Mirage. In his faded white polo shirt and clean khakis two inches too long, Marcus could take a seat at a Circus Circus bar and start to feel like he had finally found a home.

He ordered a beer, then another, and since he was the only person at the bar on a late Tuesday afternoon, he struck up a conversation with the bartender. Maybe thirty, dark skinned with black hair slicked straight back from his forehead, a little paunch hanging over his belt buckle, the bartender polished highball glasses with a towel. Marcus sized him up as an okay guy and caught his attention for a third beer.

"So, how does a guy get a job around here?" Marcus asked as the bartender set a beer down on a cardboard coaster in front of him.

"At the Circus or in general?" the bartender asked.

"In general, I guess. I just got into town. I'm staying at the Sandbar Suites. I need a job."

"Your best bet is to go online. All the casinos list their jobs online. There are all different types of jobs. Scroll through. Find something you like. Upload your résumé. See what happens next."

"Right. My résumé." Marcus nodded as if he actually had a résumé.

Back home, finding a job had been a casual affair. He'd get a tip from a friend, or a friend of a friend, or a heads up from Mac, show up at a job site on Monday morning or Friday afternoon and get hired on the spot. "You Fred Brown's kid?" or "You Mac's brother?" That's all employers had wanted to know.

Marcus had never typed up a résumé or submitted a job application online, even when he'd landed the plum job at Plasmatherm. On a Saturday night, someone at Than Wheeler's had said they were hiring. Monday morning, Marcus had shown up in his white shirt and his khaki pants. The nice lady in the HR office had taken one look at him and said: "Are you Myrna Brown's youngest? Me and her were in the same class at Handley High." She'd sat Marcus down in front of a computer terminal and walked him through the entire application process.

"I'll put in a good word for you," she'd whispered conspiratorially.

Marcus wondered if people at work missed him yet. He'd only been there a few months. He was still working under the guidance of a more experienced man in the plasma cutting room. All the same, when he announced the unexpected death of both of his parents, his coworkers had murmured sympathetic words and his supervisor had told him to take as much time as he needed. People were good to him there. He felt guilty for not having called to let anyone know he wasn't coming back anytime soon. He kept telling himself he would call them soon.

"You're gonna want to get a headshot, too," the bartender interrupted Marcus's musings.

"Get a what?" Marcus brought himself back to the bar and the conversation.

"A headshot." The bartender placed his fingers around his face to simulate a frame. "Any job on the Strip, any job anywhere *near* the Strip, you're gonna have to submit a headshot. A professional one. Not some amateur thing. You need an actual headshot, like you're auditioning for a movie role or something."

"Are you shitting me?" Marcus asked.

"I wish." The bartender laughed. "You can't get a damned job at a Denny's anywhere near the Strip without a fucking headshot."

"Even if it's kitchen work, like washing dishes or something?"

"Even if it's kitchen work. I shit you not."

The two men shook their heads in unison. Marcus drank his beer. The bartender polished his highball glasses.

"It's bullshit," the bartender said. "But you just gotta do it."

"Well, that's good to know, I guess." Marcus drained his glass, stood up unsteadily, and fished a fifty from his pants pocket and placed it on the bar.

"I'll get your change."

"No. You keep it. For the free advice."

"Thanks, man." The bartender extended his hand across the bar. "I'm Jake, by the way."

"Marcus."

"My man, Marcus. You keep looking. You'll find something."

"Yeah. Just gotta touch up my résumé," Marcus laughed. "And get a headshot."

The sun had already set, the moon high in the desert sky, when Marcus exited Circus Circus. To get back to the Sandbar Suites, home as it were, he steered himself away from Las Vegas Boulevard and forged a path along streets that were named after Vegas luminaries, like Frank Sinatra and Sammy Davis, Jr. But the class and sophistication associated with those names had not rubbed off on these avenues. There was nothing suave about the raggedy old man Marcus passed, pushing a pilfered grocery cart piled high with aluminum cans. There was nothing hip about the harried grocery clerk who rushed by him with her name tag still attached to her store vest, a cell phone pressed to her ear, a cigarette clenched between her lips, tears spilling from her eyes.

In the gathering darkness, Marcus plodded on with a growing impression he was walking through an area of Vegas that might properly be called Nobody Gives a Rat's Ass About You Here. His pace slowed to a crawl, and then to a standstill, as the reality of his situation took hold of him. He was nobody here. Not Fred Brown's son. Not Myrna Brown's baby. Not even Mac's kid brother.

Another man might've found the revelation liberating. Marcus himself had rejoiced in a sense of newfound freedom as he and Mac had cruised the Strip for the first time. But that was then, when he was high as a kite and the lights were bright and the girls looked pretty. This was now. The lights were dim, and the girls were not only plain, they were sobbing on their way from work.

"What the fuck am I doing here?"

Marcus uttered the words out loud as he glanced in despair up and down Frank Sinatra Boulevard. He scanned his surroundings as if he were searching for something, anything, that might quell the sudden, paralyzing fear that gripped him. In that moment, his eyes landed on the figure of a girl. She was on the other side of the street, leaning up against a brick wall, smoking a cigarette. And at first, his eyes skidded across her as if she were an object that offered no interest.

Then the girl unloosed a rubber band from her hair, setting free a cascade of auburn curls so wild and so extravagant, Marcus zeroed in on them as if they were the one thing he'd been searching for all his life. He'd never seen anything so unruly and also so spellbindingly beautiful.

The girl's hair didn't fall around her shoulders so much as it exploded like fireworks, scattering light around her head and all the way down to the small of her back.

Marcus stared transfixed as the girl sucked on her cigarette and scrolled aimlessly through her cellphone. She was oblivious to his presence, for which Marcus was grateful. If she'd looked up and found Marcus fixated on her every detail, he knew her very justifiable alarm would've broken the spell. As it was, her complete disregard allowed Marcus the time and the liberty to take in everything about her that he could, to try to fathom what weird power pulled him toward this girl with a seemingly irresistible force. Because she was not, by conventional standards, exceptionally attractive. She was an odd mismatch of features—high, small breasts, and wide, pear-shaped hips. And even from a distance, Marcus could discern she wasn't a real beauty. She had a small, pale face with a weak chin and a little upturned nose, and thin, rosebud lips. She was, at best, cute.

And yet, Marcus could not take his eyes off her. More specifically, he couldn't turn his gaze, or his imagination, away from her hair. He beheld her in reverence, like a worshipper before the altar of a goddess. His fervent prayer was he be allowed to bury his face and hands in that intoxicating mass of curls at least once in his life. Just once! And he would die a happy man.

Marcus was jolted back to reality when the girl stubbed her cigarette out under her heel and pulled her magnificent auburn hair back into a hair tie. Only then, with cars speeding by him and the full darkness of night settled around his shoulders, did Marcus realize the girl was on a work break. She was resting against the brick wall of a Waffle House. She was even dressed in a Waffle House uniform—short sleeved blue shirt, black apron, hair pulled up under a black baseball cap with the letters "WH" printed on it.

His spell broken, Marcus laughed aloud as he watched the girl re-enter the Waffle House, no doubt returning to her shift. He shoved his hands into his pants pockets, grinning and blushing as he continued his walk home to the Sandbar Suites. He wouldn't have used the word *miracle* to describe what he'd experienced. He just knew he was suddenly stoked, revived, uplifted, giddy with excitement. With his own eyes, he'd seen the Goddess of the Waffle House! There was hope for him in Vegas after all.

7

Weeks passed, and Marcus was no closer to employment than he was that first night Mac had driven him up and down the Strip, and he'd hooted and hollered in joyful celebration of his dead parents and the promise of a brighter future. He told Mac he was looking, that he had put in a lot of applications, but nothing had panned out yet. He knew Mac knew he was lying, and he assumed Slim also knew he was lying. But neither of them bothered to call his bluff. Mac didn't have a job. Slim didn't have a job. Marcus didn't have a job. They still had beer in the fridge and cigarettes in their shirt pockets, so no one had any cause to worry.

Except Marcus. He kept his mouth shut and minded his manners as Slim had warned him to do. But he worried plenty, because he had no idea how much of the ten-thousand-dollar inheritance was left, or where it was, or how he might get his hands on it. So far, whenever Marcus asked Mac for money, Mac doled it out according to his whim and whatever he happened to have in his wallet. A fifty-dollar bill one day, a twenty the next, occasionally a hundred, sometimes a handful of fives, tens, and ones. Marcus didn't complain. He had enough money to afford one meal, once a day, sometime between the hours of midnight and 7:00 a.m., at The Waffle House on Frank Sinatra Boulevard. And that was really all he cared about—sitting alone at the counter and being waited on, once a day, usually around three or four, by the Goddess.

Marcus established something of a routine. He slept through most of the day, his back pressed against his brother's in their shared bed. He woke when Mac did, but stayed in the bed, pretending to sleep until Mac finished in the bathroom and left. Then Marcus got up, took a shower, grabbed a couple pieces of Wonder bread, and joined his brother and Slim down by the pool. February wasn't exactly pool weather in Vegas. The nights were cool, and no one was swimming in the chilly water. Still, the pool was always where Marcus found them, bundled up in sweatshirts or jackets, seated around the concrete patio table, smoking and talking and drinking beer as if they were gathered around a campfire on a fall evening back in Vermont.

They ignored Marcus when he arrived. He rolled up his pant legs, took a seat at the edge of the pool, and dangled his feet into the cold water. Something about his calves turning numb until they almost felt warm appealed to him as he tore off bread for the ducks.

"You keep spoiling them ducks, they ain't never gonna leave," Slim said.

Marcus hesitated a moment. "Why would we want them to leave?"

"Because they're shitting all over the pool and the deck, you fucking idiot."

Marcus glanced up from the ducks and surveyed the deck area. Slim wasn't wrong. The deck was slowly but surely becoming carpeted with a layer of brownish duck turds.

"Maintenance should hose this area," Marcus suggested. "That's gotta be a health hazard."

"Maintenance should shoot them fucking ducks and eat 'em for dinner," Slim said. "Hell, we should shoot 'em, shouldn't we Mac?"

Mac shrugged noncommittally.

"Good sport, right Marcus?" Slim pointed his fingers like a gun at Marcus's little trio of paddling companions. "Kaboom! Kaboom! Kaboom! Do us all a fucking favor, right Marcus? Health hazard gone, right Marcus?"

"Yeah, right." Marcus had been saying that to Slim since he was a child. And like a child, he wished Slim would magically disappear, go back to prison where he belonged.

Marcus tossed in the last of his breadcrumbs. As he lit up a cigarette, the ducks paddled off to the opposite side of the pool, and Marcus eavesdropped as Slim and Mac resumed their conversation. For the last couple of weeks, they'd fixated on the same subject—copper and silver mining.

"I found an untapped copper mine over on the west side," Slim said to Mac.

"Oh, yeah?"

"Yeah. Brand new development. Bunch of houses just been framed and plumbing put in. Easy in and out."

"Excellent." Mac took a drag on his Marlboro. "We should inspect that industrial site tonight, too. I think it's doable if we deal with the dogs."

Marcus turned to look at Mac and Slim. "What're you guys talking about?"

"Copper mining," Mac said. "You know."

"No, I don't know," Marcus said.

Mac's expression registered genuine surprise. "You've seen the back of my truck. The copper wire I collect."

"Yeah. So what?"

"So, that's copper mining," Mac said, a hint of annoyance in his voice.

Marcus stared blankly at his brother.

"Oh, for fuck's sake," Slim interjected. "You find scrap copper wires and pipes and sell it to the scrap yards. Copper mining, you dumb shit."

"Oh. Like collecting aluminum cans," Marcus said.

"Aluminum cans? What the fuck kind of an idiot do you take me for?" Slim challenged. "There ain't no money in aluminum cans."

"Yeah, I know that." Marcus tried to defend himself. "But copper isn't lying around like cans are either. How do you find it?"

"Construction sites," Mac explained. "New housing is the best. Like the place Slim found last night."

"Damn straight," Slim said. "It ain't like dumpster diving for a fucking soda can. Any fool can do that. Hell, you could do that, Marcus! Copper mining is a business. You have to know where—"

"And when," Mac added.

"Where and when. That's right. Timing is everything. You have to monitor the situation. When the plumbing's going in. When the wiring's going in. How long you have before the fucking sheetrock goes up and you can't access it anymore. You plan things right, you can hit the same place at least two, maybe three times."

"How?" Marcus asked.

Slim scowled at Marcus and turned to Mac. "Did you get *all* the brains in this family?"

"Think about it, baby brother. Someone rips out your copper wiring, what're you going to do? Stop construction? Abandon the project? Fuck no! You put it back in."

"And we take it back out." Slim cackled. "It's like taking money out of an ATM. It's that easy."

The two friends clicked their beer cans together and swigged in unison.

"But what if you get caught?" Marcus asked.

"I knew it! I knew the little pussy would ask that question!" Slim exclaimed.

"Cost of doing business," Mac answered, as if a robbery conviction and a prison sentence were reasonable parts of doing business.

Marcus mulled the idea. "Did you guys steal copper back home?"

"Shit, yeah," Mac replied. "We started, what—when we were fourteen, fifteen?" he asked Slim. "We couldn't even drive yet. Ben Murphy took us out in his old truck. He's the one got us started on that gig."

"Yeah, he did! We were ambitious little shits, weren't we?"

The two friends smiled at the memory of their adolescent selves.

They weren't kids anymore. They were men now, edging up close to thirty, but to Marcus they both seemed older than that. He couldn't exactly say why. It was just a sense that, given their relative youth, they seemed unduly old to him. Slim in particular. He'd gone into prison a gangly teenager with long blond hair done in a rebel braid and come out a decade later his hair shaved closed to his head and missing two of his front bottom teeth. There was nothing young about Slim anymore.

"Whole different ballgame back home, though." Mac spoke directly to Marcus. "There weren't any apartment complexes getting built there. Or office buildings, either. You had to head into the hills. Follow those back roads where wealthy fuckers from Boston and New York build their second homes. It took a lot of time to find those places and scope 'em out, to figure out the right time to strike."

"Your old man was a gold mine of information," Slim recalled. "Road agent. Selectboard member. Volunteer firefighter. He knew every road, every house. Shit! He was even a deputy sheriff for a while. Remember? Your old man knew *everything* that happened in that town."

Marcus yanked his legs out of the swimming pool and joined his brother and Slim at the table.

"Dad was in on it?"

"Not 'in' on it so much. But I picked his brain pretty regular at the dinner table. I had money but no job all through high school. He might've put two and two together, and just looked the other way."

Marcus sat in dumbfounded silence for a long moment. As bad as Fred Brown had treated his family, the idea their father might have condoned criminal behavior, even passively, struck him like a lightning bolt. The idea of adolescent Slim and Mac prowling the country roads back home was less shocking but startling in its own way. He knew those roads, how completely dark they could be at night, how ominous they could feel, with dense forests crawling right up to the edge of your car on a winding, narrow dirt road. He could have never done what Slim and Mac had done. The spook factor alone would've made him turn back.

"He looks like he's about to shit his pants," Slim pointed his beer can at Marcus and laughed.

"You all right, brother?" Mac asked, one part tender, two parts derisive.

"Yeah, I'm good." Marcus grinned at his own bewilderment. He brushed his long hair out of his eyes and looked at Slim and Mac anew. "And you never got caught?"

They both shrugged and looked away from him.

"Well, how profitable is it? Copper mining, I mean. How much money are you making here in Vegas?"

"The fuck you care?" Slim snapped. "More than you make, sitting your ass around the pool every night, that's for damn sure."

"Enough. We make enough," Mac said, less confrontationally. "Don't worry about it, okay?"

"I'm not worried," Marcus lied. "Just asking."

"Well, don't," Slim ordered. "Mind your own fucking business. You're as spoiled as these fucking ducks, Mac handing out bread to you like the fucking pussy you are."

Slim snuffed out his cigarette in the overflowing plastic ash tray and stood. "I'm going to work." He turned to Mac. "You coming?"

"Yeah, right behind ya." Mac kept his eyes on Marcus while Slim exited the pool area and strode to Mac's truck.

"What? What did I do?" Marcus demanded, his temper starting to get the better of him.

"Nothing." Mac started to leave, then hesitated and turned back around. "Just keep your questions to yourself. That's all. Can you do that?"

"Yeah, I can do that," Marcus said. Only he couldn't. Mac had just closed the pool gate behind him when Marcus's heart skipped a beat.

"Mac!" he called out. "If that's copper mining, what's silver mining?"

Mac turned back to his brother. "You'll find out soon enough."

Then Marcus was left alone with his ducks.

8

By the third week, Marcus was an official Waffle House regular. He showed up around three o'clock every morning, perched on a stool at the counter, and ordered coffee and breakfast. He tried not to stare, but it hadn't taken long before everyone from the line cooks to the dishwashers and the Waffle House Girl herself—Catrina, it read on her name tag—knew he had a crush on the waitress with the curly auburn hair. He knew she knew it. He recognized the slight expression of disdain that crossed her face each time he showed up. He saw how her shoulders sagged a bit when she came toward him with a menu and forced a smile on her face. She said, "Hi, how are you tonight?" but her body language screamed, "You again! What a little creep!"

But he kept coming. Always quiet. Always polite. Never pushy. Never trying to impress her with big tips like he saw other guys do. Those were the real creeps. Men staggered in drunk and leered at her. They made crude comments about her ass. They slapped down twenty-dollar bills for tips and acted like she owed them something in return.

Marcus made a dent in her armor the night one of those assholes called her a bitch after she pocketed his tip and turned her back on him without another word. She was refilling Marcus's coffee when he managed to catch her eye.

"You deserve better," he said.

She paused in her pouring and, for a change, looked at him without suspicion or professional courtesy.

"You get used to it. Just part of the job. You need anything else?"

"No, thank you, Catrina," he said.

"It's Trina, actually. Short for Catrina." She looked down at the Waffle House name tag pinned to her uniform over her left breast. "I don't know why they put Catrina on this. I sure as shit didn't tell them to do that."

"Catrina's nice." Marcus slipped two dollars under his coffee cup and stood to leave. "It's got an exotic flair to it. Like you're a Russian princess or something. Like Katarina."

"I'm about the farthest thing from a Russian princess you'll ever meet." But there was a small, bemused smile on Trina's lips that sent an electric shock through Marcus's body. He suddenly stuck his hand out as if he were a salesman greeting a new client.

"I'm Marcus, by the way."

Trina glanced skeptically at his outstretched hand, then met his gaze, and finally put her hand in his.

"Nice to meet you, Marcus. Now go home. I have work to do."

Marcus walked back to the Sandbar Suites feeling ten feet off the ground. He'd done it! He'd broken through Trina's defenses! Not that he had anything to offer her. He was unemployed. He lived in a flea-bag apartment. His brother was a thief. His brother's best friend was probably a psychopath. But for the moment, none of that mattered. The only thing that truly mattered was Trina. In the hour before Mac straggled in from a night of copper mining and slipped into bed beside his brother, Marcus smoked a joint and daydreamed about Trina.

She was an all-consuming mystery to him, this not-so-pretty girl with a little pointed chin, carrying too much weight in her hips and not nearly enough in her breasts. Her imperfections endeared her to him a hundred times more than conventional beauty ever would have. The way Marcus saw it, if God had shortchanged Trina in some areas, he had fully compensated for those slights by topping her off with that magnificent cascade of wild red hair. That's where Trina's beauty lay. Any fool could see that, Marcus thought.

But that was just the surface. Marcus sensed that underneath the tough act, Trina felt vulnerable. He fell asleep well after sunrise and arose in the afternoon with a newfound sense of purpose. He was determined to change, to become a new man, someone capable of not just supporting himself but of taking care of Trina, too. He was going to rescue her from the Waffle House.

He showered and shaved and combed his hair out of his eyes. He put on his best pair of khaki pants and a clean polo shirt. He walked out of the Sandbar Suites and made his way on foot to an Albertson's and a Von's grocery store, where he submitted actual job applications. That night, he avoided the usual routine of joining Mac and Slim at the pool. He stayed inside and watched television. He smoked a joint and took a long nap. Around 2:00 a.m., he woke up hungry, and headed over to the Waffle House.

To his delight, both Trina and Becky, the other nighttime waitress, greeted him with candid, open gazes such as they had never offered him before. In the space of twenty-four hours, his relationship with Trina had changed. Everything was casual and friendly between them now. When she refilled his coffee cup, she looked him in the eye. She even smiled.

"So, how's Marcus tonight?" she asked.

"Marcus is fine. How's Trina?"

"Trina's tired, and she needs a smoke. Care to join me?"

"Sure. I'll keep you company." Marcus tried not to sound as eager to accept the invitation as he felt. But he was already off his stool and ready to go.

"You okay if I step outside for a minute?" Trina asked Becky, who was brewing a new pot of coffee and had no customers to wait on.

"Go for it," Becky said. "I can handle this."

Trina turned to Marcus with another smile, and he followed her out the door like a puppy on a leash. She leaned against the corner of the building, the very spot where Marcus had first seen her, and put a cigarette between her lips. Marcus managed to steady his hand enough to light it for her and get his own smoke going without dropping the lighter, which he was sure he'd do. Trina inhaled a lungful of smoke, then exhaled and unloosed her hair all in one movement. The absolute grace and beauty of the moment nearly brought Marcus to his knees.

"There!" Trina sighed. "Now if I could just take off my bra and my shoes, I'd be all set!"

Marcus glowed with affection. So pretty. So smart. So funny. Trina had it all.

"Long night?" he asked.

"Honestly? All the nights here are long. I mean, it's okay. Tips aren't half-bad. I like most of my customers." Trina nudged Marcus's elbow with hers. "But I'd like to find something better. I'd like to be out there on the Strip. I could buy a new car with the kind of tips that cocktail waitresses make at the high-end casinos. But I can't seem to get my foot in the door."

"Did you get a headshot made?" Marcus asked the question as if he might have some real helpful job-hunting advice for her.

"Yeah. I had to, even to work here at the Waffle Hovel. When I first got into town, I tried to get a job as a cashier at a 7-Eleven. They told me to come back when I had a headshot and a résumé. What's with that?"

"Was it the 7-Eleven over by the Sandbar Suites? That's where I'm staying. For the time being," Marcus added quickly.

"Yeah, that's the place." Trina laughed and pulled another cloud of smoke into her lungs. "My boyfriend and me stayed at the Sandbar when we first got into town, too. We were stuck there for two months. Felt like forever. Neither one of us could find a job to save our lives. Then Ben met a guy who got him a sweet deal at a weed farm."

"Your boyfriend's growing weed?" Marcus was astonished. That sounded like something he would love to get into.

"Ben's a weed farmer! Go figure!" Trina looked pretty astonished herself. "It's very scientific, though, very regimented, professional. Nothing like it was before it went legal. Big business, weed. It pays good. We're renting a house over on the west side now. Living the dream." Trina smiled a half-rueful smile.

Marcus's heart was breaking. He'd suspected from the beginning Trina couldn't be single. Still, he'd clung to a sliver of hope. It wasn't inconceivable. Girls *do* break up with their boyfriends. Even the prettiest of them have brief periods where they're in between the old and the new. If Marcus had stumbled upon Trina in a moment like that . . .

Marcus breathed in the scent of coconut from Trina's hair and commanded his hands not to touch it. He felt so much tenderness for this girl. He wanted desperately for her to love him, but even more, he wanted her to be happy.

"If Ben's making good money, maybe you don't have to work at the Waffle House at all." Marcus spoke tentatively, the same way he'd have touched Trina's hair, had he been allowed to do so.

Trina crushed her cigarette under her heel and shook her head.

"Not gonna happen. I'll make my own money, thank you. You can't depend on a man for support. I learned that lesson the hard way. More than once." She laughed bitterly. "You gotta stand on your own two feet."

Trina pulled her hair back into a ponytail and walked back into the Waffle House. Marcus trailed behind her and resumed his place at the counter while Trina went back to work on the other side. She cleared away his dirty plate, picked up his coffee cup, wiped the counter clean, and set the cup back down in front of him. Then she said "hello" to the man who'd walked in behind them and taken a seat two stools down from Marcus. He looked like the Marlboro Man—cowboy boots, cowboy hat, a huge silver belt buckle, and the rugged good looks to carry it off without looking like some faggot, as Mac would have said.

The Marlboro Man looked Trina up and down, and Marcus decided to leave before he witnessed yet another round of customer flirtation. He caught Trina's eye as he was heading out the door.

"Tomorrow night?" he asked as casually as he could.

"I'll be right here," Trina said with professional cheer.

"Living the dream," Marcus said. Both Trina and Becky laughed out loud.

Marcus stepped out into the cool desert night feeling as if he really were living a dream. It was four in the morning. He had nowhere to be and nothing to do, and the Strip was still throbbing with its usual mixture of lights, cars, and people. It was legal to open carry alcohol on the Strip, so Marcus stopped at a convenience store, bought himself a six-pack of Bud, and entered the stream of life that was always flowing through the veins of the city. He popped one can open, and carried the rest tucked under an arm like a football.

He felt more relaxed than he had in weeks. He'd known from the get-go that Trina would never be his girl. She was way up high, in a league of her own, way too special for the likes of him. Still, she'd invited him into her world. She'd accepted him as a friend. She talked to him, and he talked to her as if it were the most natural thing in the world.

Marcus cradled his six-pack in one arm and pondered the miracle of his newfound friendship with Trina. What he felt for her was like a small, precious, vulnerable thing, and he carried it up and down Las Vegas Boulevard, happily lost in a state of wondrous gratitude for the blessing that had been bestowed upon him that night.

He made his way to the Bellagio, hoping to catch the fountain show, not knowing that the waters would not dance again until 3:00 p.m. that afternoon. He drank the rest of his six-pack while he waited, enjoying the murmur of voices that passed by him like water in a stream. He smiled and waved at inebriated partiers hollering and dancing out of the sunroof of a black limousine. He benignly tolerated a mime who took to entertaining the passersby by imitating Marcus drinking beer. He could see the humor in it, and it was only a matter of seconds anyhow before the mime grew bored with Marcus and moved on up the Strip to someone more worthy of imitation. No harm done.

It was past six in the morning when Marcus drained the last Bud and turned his feet toward the Sandbar Suites. Once there, he stretched out on a lounge chair next to the pool and smoked a joint. He felt at peace with the world, except for one thing—Trina's boyfriend, Ben.

When Trina had stood close to him outside the Waffle House, he'd noticed a fading bruise on her left arm. Marcus had seen bruises like that before, on the arms of women like Mac's Barbara, women whose men manhandled them to get what they wanted or to make themselves feel like men. It was discouraging to Marcus the number of abused women he'd known throughout his lifetime, starting with his own mother and now leading straight to Trina. He hated it, but he'd never done anything about it. He'd never protected his mother, never stood up for a girl, even when he felt he should have. Like the time he'd watched Mac knock the teeth loose on a drunk girl who dared ridicule the size of his dick.

Marcus and Mac had grown up in the same house, they'd been molded by the same parental influences. But where Mac had taken after their father, becoming belligerent and brash, Marcus had adopted the coping skills of their mother. He cowered in fear, he placated angry men, he kept himself small and quiet, hoping to save his own skin. He never stood up for himself, let alone someone else.

He'd stood in the shadows protecting himself rather than protecting others. Ben was a bastard. He was sure of it. And Trina needed protecting. He was sure of that, too. And he was going to protect her if it was the last thing he ever did. Those were the thoughts swimming through Marcus's mind when he crawled into bed next to his snoring brother and went to sleep with the sun coming up over the horizon.

9

Mac spent so much of his time with Slim, Marcus started to see them as a single entity again, just as he had when he was a boy. He'd come to Vegas on the promise he and Mac would be brothers striking out together to make their mark on the world. In the wake of their parents' deaths, with money in hand and the West beckoning a new beginning, Marcus had dared to hope. He should've known better. He kicked himself for being a fool. He told himself he should've kept heading east after Mac forced him out of the truck in Colorado. He told himself to buy a bus ticket for home and be done with the Mac/Slim show.

Marcus told himself he could leave, but in truth he couldn't do it. He'd told himself similar things when he was a kid. When things got bad at home, a voice in his head told him to leave, get out, run away. But fear had glued him in place. He was afraid to stay, but he was even more afraid to leave. There are consequences, after all, any time a prisoner makes an escape. In Marcus's case, he'd vividly imagined his father tracking him down, hauling him back home, and making his life even more hellish than it already was. A similar fear now paralyzed him in his relationship with Mac. The mere thought of running, of turning his back on his older brother, put a big knot in his stomach. Mac, too, he feared, would track him down and make his life even more hellish than it already was.

Another thing Marcus couldn't do was directly question Mac/Slim about what their plans in Vegas were. Back in Florida, at the edge of Lake Rousseau, Mac had floated the idea of a silver mining operation, but he'd never elaborated on the scheme, and he'd deflected the few inquiries Marcus had dared make with brusque responses. "We're working on it" or "It's complicated" or "Give it time" or "It's too hard to explain. You'll see soon enough."

Night after night, Marcus lay awake right next to his brother in their shared bed, longing to press Mac for details. But he couldn't bring himself to do it. It was easier to turn away from Mac, roll over onto his own side of the bed, and just live with the uncertainty.

Marcus had managed to fall asleep on one such night when he was suddenly awoken by the sounds of an altercation taking place outside. Nothing new there. Husbands and wives, friends and roommates, neighbors and strangers frequently aired their grievances in loud, public, curse-laden confrontations everyone pretended not to see or hear. Most settled their differences relatively quickly. Emotions boiled over and died down. And then, peace, by Sandbar standards, prevailed.

But the skirmish heating up outside that night was different. It involved two men, and they were "fuck you"-ing one another with an intensity Marcus hadn't experienced before. Even Mac, who typically slept through such encounters, was suddenly awake and alert.

"Can you tell who it is?" Marcus whispered to his brother.

"Black Bob and White Will."

Marcus knew the couple, as did most Sandbar residents. Bob and Will were hard to overlook. One Black, one white; one big, one small; one reserved, one flamboyant—that was Bob and Will, respectively. The two men had been looking for work without much success, and it was rumored that Will had started turning tricks on the Strip to earn money. Which probably explained why Bob was accusing Will of being a whore.

"You fucking bitch! You fucking little white-assed cunt!"

Bob's baritone voice was followed by a shrill squealing from Will.

"Let go of me! You're hurting me!"

"Suck my dick, you little bitch!"

"For fuck's sake! Can't you faggots take this shit to your own fucking room?"

Marcus recognized Slim's voice as he inserted himself into the fray. It sounded like it was all happening just the other side of Slim's room. That was Rhonda's place. Rhonda was quiet. She kept to herself, and Marcus imagined her cowering under her covers the same as he was, her anxiety, like his, even higher now that Slim was on the scene. Mac, on the other hand, was energized. He was out of bed and into his pants, grinning, yanking the covers off Marcus.

"You don't want to miss this, brother. Come on!"

Marcus pulled on a pair of sweatpants and followed Mac out to the walkway. Will was on his knees with Bob towering over him, one hand ensnared in his boyfriend's long blond hair.

"Mind your own fucking business!" Bob yelled at Slim.

Slim spotted Mac on the walkway and, without a word passing between them, they seemed to settle on a plan of action as each man strode purposefully up to Bob and Will.

"I'll mind my own fucking business!" Slim said.

He punched Bob hard and square on the nose, not once but twice, spattering blood onto Rhonda's plate glass window. Bob's hands flew to his face. Will crawled out of Bob's reach, crouching up against the balcony railing as Mac stepped between him and Bob.

"You broke my nose, you bastard!" Bob wailed.

"I'm gonna break more than that. Grab his arms," Slim told Mac. "I'll get his feet."

From the safe distance of his own doorway, Marcus stood by in his bare feet as Slim and Mac hoisted Bob off the walkway and swung him through the air as if they were playing with a child. Three times they swung him out toward the railing and back toward Rhonda's window. On the third swing, they let him go. Glass shattered in every direction. Rhonda and Will both screamed.

"Oh my god, Bob! Are you okay?"

Will crawled toward Rhonda's window, heedless of the glass shards embedding themselves into his knees and hands.

Marcus stopped long enough to slip into his sneakers, then he too approached the window. By then, a light had come on in Rhonda's apartment, and he could see her two roommates, Jess and Sylvia. They huddled together, gaping in astonishment at the sight of Rhonda and Bob suddenly thrown together in Rhonda's small bed, right there under the window. Her bed, her hair, and her nightshirt were spattered with glass and blood.

Rhonda opened the door. "What the fuck is wrong with you guys?" she cried, turning terrified eyes to Slim and Mac standing on the walkway outside.

"Ain't nothing wrong with us, sister," Slim replied. "Can't say the same for these two faggots, though."

Slim cocked his head toward Mac, and the two friends went into Slim's apartment, closing the door behind them.

Someone had called the cops, but by the time they arrived, Will had already bundled Bob off to a nearby ER. That left Marcus and the three girls to explain to the police what had happened. They did the best they could, but they knew better than to name names. No one mentioned Bob or Will, and none of them were crazy enough to mention Slim and Mac. Their reticence incensed the two cops.

"Why are you protecting these scumbags?" the younger of the two officers asked the three women. Jess and Sylvia shrugged. Rhonda burst into tears.

"I just want to be left alone. I can't take this shit anymore."

"You don't want to press charges?" the older officer asked.

"No! I want to go home. Today!" Rhonda spoke through her tears even as she pulled a green Army duffel bag out from underneath her sullied bed. She stumbled about the dismal apartment, grabbing clothes and cosmetics, blindly shoving them into the bag.

The young cop shook his head in disgust and forced a business card into Rhonda's hand.

"In case you change your mind and want to press charges," he said gruffly.

Rhonda crammed the business card and a handful of panties into her bag. "I'm leaving," she sobbed. "You'll never see me again."

The cops left with a trail of slurs—"animals, punks, white trash"—lingering in the air as they descended the three flights of stairs to their cruiser down below.

"Fuck them! What do they know?" Marcus balled his hands into fists. He wanted to punch both of those cops in their faces, just like Slim had done to Bob. He settled, instead, for slipping a protective arm around Rhonda's shoulders. "Are you really leaving right now? You don't want to wait until morning?"

"Yeah, think about it. Maybe calm down a little," Sylvia added. "You don't have to leave right this minute. Everything will be okay."

Rhonda's hands were shaking but she managed to zip the duffel bag closed with Marcus's help. She looked at him, trying to give him a smile, and cast her gaze at her two roommates sitting in their nightgowns and robes on the edge of their shared bed. They were all younger than Marcus, the three women. One night, sitting with their feet in the pool as Marcus fed the ducks, Rhonda had told him how each of the girls had journeyed into Las Vegas from different directions. She was from Kentucky, Jess from Colorado, Sylvia from California. They'd met, three strangers, standing in line at a food bank.

"You girls are the only good thing that's happened to me in this shithole of a city," Rhonda said. "I'm sorry. But I'm done. I'm going home. Whatever that means."

Sylvia and Jess nodded their heads sympathetically.

"It's okay," Sylvia said. "We understand."

"Hell, I may follow you to Kentucky!" Jess added. "Why the fuck not? I've tried everything else!"

The three friends laughed wearily.

Marcus stood awkwardly at Rhonda's side, not sure where he fit in with the scene unfolding around him. He held back, trying to give the women a little privacy, half expecting they might go for a group hug before they parted ways. But no one made a move. For a long moment, the three friends merely gazed upon one another with silent, mutual understanding.

"Go on then," Sylvia finally said. "Before you change your mind."

Rhonda hauled the duffel bag across her shoulder and nearly swung it into Marcus.

"I'll get that," Marcus offered, taking it off her shoulder.

He followed her down the stairs. The sun was rising when Rhonda settled in behind the steering wheel of her run-down Ford Fiesta. Marcus leaned in through the open window to light her cigarette.

"So, Kentucky," he said. "That sounds nice."

"There's nothing nice about it, or I wouldn't never have left in the first place."

Marcus waved weakly as he watched Rhonda pull out of the parking lot of the Sandbar Suites. He trudged up the stairs to his own apartment, intent on crashing and getting a few hours of sleep. But he ran into Mac, already dressed and shaved, smoking a cigarette on the walkway outside their room.

"Clean yourself up," he ordered Marcus. "I've got something to show you."

10

Marcus didn't protest. He stood in the shower with steaming water pouring over his back and fantasized about the acid he'd like to throw in his brother's face. *Fuck you! I'm going to bed! Who died and made you king? Who the fuck do you think you are? Suck my dick! I'll come when I'm fucking ready!* It would feel so good, he mused, to stand up to Mac, to see the astonished look on his face, to watch him back down.

But by the time Marcus toweled himself dry and combed his hair in the mirror, the adrenaline rush of fury had subsided. The imagined satisfaction of pushing back against his brother was replaced with more probable scenarios of what was likely to follow if he so much as dared to even look cross-eyed at Mac, much less if he told him to fuck off. The impact of Mac's fist hitting his nose was something Marcus could nearly feel. And after what he'd witnessed a few hours ago, the possibility of Mac/Slim hurling him off the third-floor walkway seemed far more plausible than that of Mac taking a step back in amazed silence.

Marcus slipped into some clean clothes, walked down the stairs, and slouched into the passenger seat of his brother's truck without uttering a word.

Mac treated Marcus to coffee and a breakfast burrito at a Taco Bell drive-through, then steered them on a course heading northwest out of Vegas. With food in his belly and caffeine coursing through his veins,

Marcus started to wake up and take note of his surroundings. He was amazed at how quickly the entire city of Las Vegas disappeared in the rearview mirror. One minute it was there—all the lights and bells and whistles, all the people, all the places—and the next it was gone. Vegas was like a desert mirage, a figment of desperate men's imaginations. Marcus had now lived in Vegas for more than two months, but in that moment, he doubted whether the city even existed at all.

"Where are we going?"

"Into the shadow of death."

Marcus stared dumbly at his brother.

"Death Valley," Mac said. "We're going to Death Valley. Me and Slim have been doing some work out there. I want to show you what we've done."

"What kind of work?" Marcus asked.

"It'll be easier to explain if you just let me show you. You'll see. We're almost there."

Marcus said nothing and the brothers traveled in silence as Mac pulled off the freeway and, several miles later, took a left down an unmarked dirt road. Marcus saw nothing but scrub brush, rock, and sand. There were no houses, no convenience stores, no gas stations, no nothing. It was the kind of desolate place, Marcus thought, where Vegas gangsters carried out executions. He'd watched *Casino* more times than he could remember. He knew how such things were done, some poor fuck sobbing, kneeling in the dirt with his hands cuffed behind his back, his brains blown out with a single shot to the back of his head.

Marcus looked askance at his brother. *Surely not*, he reassured himself. *Mac wouldn't go that far.* But the farther Mac drove them into an increasingly remote area of the Mojave Desert, the more Marcus's breakfast burrito soured in his stomach. He scanned his surroundings for any sign of Slim's car, the purple Chevy Cavalier. Slim called it the Shit Mobile. There were limits on what Mac could, or would, do on his own. But Slim/Mac . . . that was another story.

Marcus's anxiety lessened when he spotted a collection of gray, rickety buildings in the distance and realized that's where Mac was taking him. The ramshackle buildings were old and weathered, and they seemed misplaced in the desert wilderness. But Marcus saw no sign of Slim or his car anywhere on the premises, so he relaxed, just a little.

Marcus slid out of the truck and shut the door behind him almost in a daze. "What is this place?"

"An abandoned silver mine," Mac said.

"Wow." Marcus gaped in wonder.

They trudged past a big hand-painted sign with black letters on a white background that said: KEEP OUT!

"Should we be here?" Marcus glanced at the warning sign behind him as they advanced toward the array of deteriorating buildings.

"Probably not. But me and Slim have been coming out here for weeks. No one's ever bothered us."

"What are you coming out here for?"

Mac pointed at the tumble-down gray structures in front of them. "Mining the silver that's still in those mines."

"Seriously? This place looks like it's been abandoned since like forever."

"It has been abandoned since like forever, but look around. Take a close look. Tell me what you see."

Marcus scanned the area. He turned a full circle and swept his eyes across an empty expanse of desert. He looked at the ground. He looked at the spotless blue sky. He didn't see anything of interest.

"What exactly am I looking for?" he asked apprehensively.

Mac squatted and scooped up two handfuls of dirt. Then he stood back up and stuck the handfuls of dirt under his brother's nose. "Use your eyes. Tell me what you see."

Marcus peered into Mac's hands. What he saw was rust colored dirt and maybe, just maybe, a hint here and there of something of a silvery metallic composition. He squinted and stared harder. He nudged the dirt with his finger.

"Is that silver?" he dared ask.

"Bingo!"

Mac tossed the dirt behind him and wiped his hands on his jeans. "Welcome to the Brown Brothers and Slim Jim Silver Mine!"

Marcus's mouth hung open as he turned another full circle and surveyed the abandoned mine again. "Are you kidding? You can't be serious!"

"I've never been more serious. Come on. Let's get out of the sun."

Mac led Marcus to a sagging overhang still clinging to the front porch of one of the old buildings. They each lit a cigarette. Marcus sucked on his to calm his rattled nerves. Mac took in deep full breaths of smoke as if he were reviving himself with fresh air.

"This is it. This is where I stake my claim," Mac announced, pointing his cigarette toward the abandoned land. "Slim learned about this place from a buddy of his in the joint. But he cut me in on the deal. He came out here ahead of me, got things moving. I was getting ready to follow him. You weren't even in the picture. Then Mom and Dad died. They were gone! History! It was just you and me together. So, I brought you out here with me. I'm cutting you in on the deal, too."

It was, perhaps, the longest speech Marcus had ever heard his brother deliver. That was unnerving on its own. It was even more unsettling to have Mac, after weeks of estrangement, now looking Marcus directly in his eyes.

"It started out just me and Slim. But this is big, brother. There's real money to be made here. So, I'm bringing you in. I *fought* to bring you in. I'm not leaving you out of this deal."

Marcus swallowed hard. "What deal?"

"Our deal! It's brilliant! It really is. Me and Slim have been copper mining. You know, to make money, pay expenses, and shit like that. But we've also been coming out here, seeding this area with silver. Slim owns the land. That's his part of the deal. He purchased it for next to nothing. No one thinks there's any value left in it. The owners were relieved to get rid of it. But me and Slim, we've been seeding it with silver."

Marcus fixed his eyes on the empty horizon behind his brother's shoulders. His mind felt nearly as blank as his surroundings. "Seeding it with silver? What the fuck does that mean?"

"We shave down and grind down cheap silver. Any kind we can get cheap from the pawn shops. We've spread that shit all over this abandoned mine. That's what you saw in the dirt I showed you."

"But why? What's the point?" Marcus asked, exasperation and anger welling up from his gut, lending his voice a sudden edge.

"So we can make a profit selling this shit piece of land. There are a million suckers walking up and down the Strip right now, just waiting for us to rope them in. We'll convince them there's still a lot of silver left in the mine. A lot! We'll sell them parcels of the land, or maybe the whole thing, and make a fortune. It's easy money, brother. Easy money."

Marcus stared at Mac, incredulous. Marcus didn't mistake himself for a shrewd businessman or a cunning grifter. Still, he trusted his first impression that the scheme Mac had just presented him with was the dumbest, riskiest, most farfetched idea he'd ever heard. He turned in a circle, his eyes darting in every direction until he faced his brother again.

"You can't be serious. You're telling me Slim—*Slim Daniels*—actually *owns* this land?"

"He told me he did."

"And you fucking believe him?" Marcus demanded.

"Slim's word is good with me. He wouldn't lie to *me*," Mac defended his childhood friend. "If Slim tells me he owns this land, then he fucking owns this land."

Marcus sighed. His shoulders sagged as he shook his head in bewilderment. "I can't believe this is happening."

"Look. This is the deal," Mac continued calmly. "Now that we've got the land seeded, Slim says all we need is like eighty grand to get things moving in the right direction. There's surveying to be done, land deeds, office space to rent, business cards to print up, shit like that. It's a long con. It's gonna take a little finesse to do it right."

Marcus couldn't imagine anyone with less finesse than Slim/Mac. "And you think you can pull that off?" he intoned sarcastically.

"I know we can. It's just a matter of getting the money together."

"And how are you going to do that?"

Marcus was surprised Mac hadn't punched his face in yet. If he kept questioning Mac's reasoning, he knew that powerful right hand would knock him down eventually. It wasn't something he looked forward to. But for the moment, Marcus was willing to risk the inevitable abuse if only to satisfy his own curiosity. *How long would it take before Mac snapped?*

"We're raising the capital now," Mac answered. "The copper mining's just a side gig. I'm hitting the poker tables. Slim's working the blackjack tables. We've got a system. We're going to take that ten grand from Mom and Dad and turn it into a hundred. We'll have that money in no time. You just wait and see."

"That's your plan? Gambling!" Marcus wailed. "You're going to piss our money away at the poker tables and let Slim burn through the rest playing blackjack?"

Mac moved in close to Marcus and shoved a finger in his face.

"You have no idea! You have no idea how much money I win at the poker tables!"

"That's the goddamn truth!" Marcus shouted. Shaking with rage and fear, he slapped Mac's finger out of his face. "You know what else I don't have a fucking idea about? I have no fucking idea how much of that ten grand you and Slim have pissed away already. I don't even know where that money is! You control it! You hand it out to me like it's my fucking allowance. Well, it's not! Half of that money is mine! It belongs to me. I fucking *earned* it!"

Marcus put a special emphasis on that word—"earned." He threw it into his brother's face, daring him to pretend he didn't know what it meant. He—not Mac—was the hapless kid who'd borne the brunt of their father's incoherent fury. If a small inheritance was a form of reparations, surely he deserved his fair share. Mac stood before him, his right fist balled, ready to strike, but Marcus didn't flinch. He stared up at his brother, angrily calculating in his own way how much his parents owed him. How much for every beating? How much for every verbal berating? How much for every night he lay awake trembling in his bed? How much for every time their father handcuffed him to a piece of furniture and their mother looked the other way?

"How much? Huh? How much do you think they owe me?" Marcus demanded. As the words left his mouth, his rage turned into impotent sorrow, sending waves of tears down his face. "It's not like five thousand actually covers the bill," he blubbered. "But it's something. I deserve at least that much, don't I?"

Mac punched his fist into the air rather than his brother's face. "Damnit, Marcus! I'm doing this for *us*! Don't you get it? Five thousand isn't shit! Of course, it's not enough! I want more! I deserve more. You do, too. But I *earned* that money, too. You know I did."

Marcus wiped snot and tears from his face with the hem of his shirt. He lit another cigarette and inhaled deeply before he spoke again. "We both got fucked. Even at the end. Fucking murder-suicide? Our mother handcuffed to a fucking chair, a bullet through her head? What're we supposed to do with that, huh?"

Mac had no answer to such a question.

"I don't want to take anything away from you," Marcus said. "I just want what's mine. That's all I'm asking you for. I want what's mine."

"And you'll get it! I promise!" Mac grabbed Marcus by his shoulders. "You just gotta give me some time. Me and Slim . . ."

"Slim! Give me a break!" Marcus shook off Mac's hands. "The guy's a fucking psycho."

"Maybe he is. Maybe he's not. But you underestimate him at your own risk. And you cut Slim a wide berth. You stay out of his way. You understand me?"

Marcus stared at the ground at his feet.

"Do you understand?" Mac repeated the question more forcefully.

Marcus glanced up at Mac and shook his head almost imperceptibly.

"No, no I don't understand," he whispered.

Marcus should have left it at that. The tension between the two brothers had crested and was starting to subside. He could have kept his mouth shut and ended the confrontation without taking a beating. But his curiosity made him reckless. He stared his brother down and spoke his mind.

"I don't understand why you're Slim's bitch," he said.

Marcus laughed hysterically as the blow from his brother's fist knocked him on to the ground. He continued to laugh, in between guttural, uncontrollable sobs, as Mac kicked him in his ribs. When the bulk of his rage was spent, Mac got down in the dirt next to his brother.

"You'll get what's yours," he promised, spittle flying from his lips. "If it takes me a hundred fucking years, you'll get your money, plus interest. In the meantime, stay the fuck out of my way. And don't even look at Slim. You hear me?"

Marcus nodded, shaking snot and tears into the parched desert floor.

Mac stood and brushed red dirt off his knees. "Get up! And stop crying like a pussy! You'll get what you deserve. I'll make sure of that."

11

Life changed for Marcus after his trip to the silver mine. During his waking hours, often even in his sleep, his mind was plagued with a seemingly endless string of unanswered questions, all of them having to do with the get-rich scheme Slim/Mac had come up with.

How do you shave silver?

How much silver do you have to shave to litter an entire abandoned mine with silver shavings?

Did Slim actually own that land? Was that even possible? Slim? A landowner?

Assume Slim does own that land, how the hell are he and Mac going to attract buyers for it? Those two are going to set up an office and play at being wheeler dealers? Slim/Mac are going to pass themselves off as real estate agents?

How much money, really, was Mac winning at the poker tables? It was one thing to play in the charity poker tournaments at the Elks Lodge back home. Sure, Mac could win there now and again. But could he really win in Vegas, like all the time?

Could Slim really cut it as a professional blackjack player? He had a hair-trigger temper and got into all-out brawls over nothing. How's he going to keep it together at a Vegas blackjack table?

Assume Slim/Mac are killing it at the tables. Even so, how long will it take them to raise eighty thousand dollars? And where did that figure come from? Did they just pull it out of their joint Slim/Mac ass? Or was it based in some tangible reality?

The questions piled up so high, so fast, Marcus wished he'd played a different, smarter, game with his brother. He imagined things would be different for him if he'd agreed to go in on the scheme, or if he'd even pretended to go along with it. He'd be a partner then. He'd be one of them. Then they'd have to answer his questions.

Marcus was swishing his feet in the swimming pool and thinking along those lines one night when Slim/Mac stood and snubbed out their cigarettes as if preparing to leave.

"Hey, Mac, I need a little cash," Marcus said, casually, not even bothering to turn and face his brother.

"Fuck that little cunt!" Slim said to Mac. "How long are we gonna let this little pussy live off our seed money, huh? Let him get his own damn money if he's not gonna help out with the business."

Marcus's stomach knotted as he pulled his feet from the water and sat cross-legged on the concrete deck, letting his feet and legs dry. He glanced up at Mac feeling like a whipped puppy.

"Come on, Mac," Marcus pleaded. "Half that money is mine and you know it. Besides, I'm working on getting a job. You know that, too. I'm scheduled to get my headshot done this week." Regret washed over Marcus even as the words left his mouth.

"A headshot? What the fuck do you need a headshot for?" Slim demanded.

Marcus rolled down his pants legs. "Every place on the Strip wants a headshot. Doesn't matter if you're waiting tables or pumping gas. You gotta submit a professional picture of yourself to get a job here. It's fucking insane."

"It's true." Mac came to Marcus's defense. "Glenn in Room 103 told me the same thing."

Slim looked from Mac to Marcus. "Fuck that bullshit."

Slim advanced toward Marcus and yanked him to his feet. "Are you telling me you'd rather put up with that bullshit than come in on the silver mine with me and Mac?"

Marcus shrugged. "Yeah, I guess I would. I met a girl who's helping me get something going."

Both Mac and Slim raised their eyebrows.

"You got a girl?" Mac asked.

"I don't 'got a girl,'" Marcus responded sharply. "I met a girl who's helping me out. That's all."

"Well, I'll be damned. The pussy's got some pussy," Slim sneered.

"She's nice," Marcus said, by way of defending Trina's reputation. Had he been a brave man, he would've made clear to Slim Trina wasn't "pussy," she was precious. As it was, he figured he'd already said too much.

"Any snatch must be nice for a pussy like you," Slim said.

"Come on now. Leave it be. You're embarrassing my brother," Mac said to Slim. He looked Marcus up and down, a flicker of big brotherly affection evident in his brown eyes.

"You want to borrow my truck some night?" he asked Marcus. "Me and Slim are hitting the tables most nights now. We can go in his car. You can take my truck, maybe take this girl out for a ride. What do you think about that?"

Marcus shrugged. The thought of driving that shiny red F-150 with Trina at his side sounded awesome. But he tried to play it cool. "Yeah, sure," he said. "I wouldn't mind having the truck now and again." Marcus swallowed his pride. "I still need a few bucks, just to get me by."

The two older men scoffed at Marcus in unison. They remained standing over him, bigger and stronger in countless ways.

"Give the little fucker some money," Slim said with a glint in his eyes. Mac fished a crisp fifty out of his wallet.

"Shove it down his damned throat," Slim ordered.

Marcus looked up at his brother, silently pleading for mercy just like he'd done his whole childhood.

"Come on, man," Mac said.

Marcus could tell Mac was hesitating. Slim could tell, too.

"Shove it down his fucking throat," Slim ordered again, his voice quieter and more menacing this time. "Make the little fucker eat our money until he learns how to feed his own damned self."

Mac hesitated for another second, just long enough for Marcus to see that flicker of sunshine in his brother's eyes cloud over. Mac was on him in an instant, throwing him to the concrete deck of the pool. He pinned Marcus under his body, held his face with one hand and pried open his mouth with the other. Marcus flailed in useless resistance, tearing up and gagging as Mac crammed the crisp fifty-dollar bill into his mouth.

"Chew it up!" Mac ordered.

Marcus chewed and compacted the bill, then tucked it into the pocket of his cheek.

"Make the little fucker swallow it," Slim said.

Marcus worked his jaw as if he were chewing and swallowed saliva in a series of big gulps.

"You got it down?" Mac demanded.

"It's gone," Marcus lied, nodding weakly. He knew Mac knew he was lying. He figured Slim knew he was lying, too. But the performance proved enough to end his ordeal.

"All right, then." Mac lifted himself off his brother's limp figure and hitched up his pants.

As Slim/Mac headed into the parking lot, Slim called back over his shoulder to Marcus.

"Shit that money out your ass and spend it on your new pussy."

Mac said nothing.

Marcus waited until he heard two car doors open and shut. Then he rolled over onto his side and nearly vomited the fifty out of his mouth. He took the filthy bill upstairs to Room 310, rinsed it off under the kitchen tap, smoothed it out, and pressed it between two paper towels. He cleaned himself up, too. Then he made the bed he shared with his brother and lay down on it with his hands clasped behind his head. He stared at the ceiling, blocking out the normal sounds of life at the Sandbar Suites—doors slamming, Cokes rattling out of vending machines, residents cursing one another in a variety of languages, moms yelling at their kids—and daydreamed about Trina until it was time for him to walk over to the Waffle House.

Marcus understood everyone at the Waffle House knew he was a lovesick puppy for Trina with no hope of ever attaining the object of his desire. But Marcus didn't care. He timed his nightly appearances to coincide with Trina's first smoke. A mere fifteen minutes standing alone with her outside of the Waffle House was enough bliss to make the rest of his miserable life worth living.

Trina's eyes lit up when he walked through the door. She poured him a cup of coffee, got her other customers taken care of as quick as she could, then motioned for Marcus to follow her outside.

He stood near her in the alley, excited but trying not to show it, as she set loose her cascade of curls, slipped a cigarette between her lips, and scrolled through her phone.

"Look!" She showed him a picture of Leonardo DiCaprio in a black tuxedo and bow tie, his hair cut over his ears and combed back to fully reveal his face. "A haircut like that would look really good on you."

Marcus liked the attention being given to him by Trina but also felt awkward, overwhelmed by someone scrutinizing his appearance so closely.

"Or this. This actually looks more like you." She pulled up an image of Joseph Gordon-Levitt, same basic hairstyle as DiCaprio, but Marcus did look more like Gordon-Levitt. "You're always hiding behind your hair, which is a shame because you have a really nice face. You don't have to hide it all the time. Show it off a little."

"You think so?" Marcus self-consciously brushed the bangs out of his eyes.

"I do. And that stubble isn't doing you any favors either." She held

Marcus's face with one hand, sending electricity shooting through him. She turned his head side to side as she examined him. "Yeah, I'd shave that."

Marcus blushed and grinned. "Any other suggestions?" he asked, pretending to be annoyed.

"Yes. Now that you mention it." Trina typed something else into her phone, scrolled for a bit, then presented him with a new image. "You'd look *soooo* good in a slim suit. You've got the body for it."

Marcus peered into the phone in Trina's hand. She'd pulled up an image of a strikingly handsome Black model posed in a sky-blue suit with a crisp white shirt buttoned at the collar. "I can't wear a suit like that!" he protested.

He'd worn suits before, for weddings and funerals, but he'd always gotten them used, from thrift stores. The sleeves were inevitably too long, the pant legs too baggy, and too long. He schlepped around feeling like a kid playing dress-up in his daddy's old clothes but it never occurred to him to do something about it.

"You can. And you should," Trina argued. "You have the perfect body type for it. You'd kill in a suit like that, especially if you got it fitted right."

"Fitted right?"

"Sure. You go to a department store, and you get the sales guy to help you find a suit off the rack that fits. But then you also have him measure you for adjustments, and they send the suit off to a tailor to make any alterations that need to be made so that the suit fits you perfect. Like a glove."

"I can't afford shit like that, can I? I mean, how much does something like that cost?"

"Depends. Hundreds. Maybe more."

Marcus's shoulders sagged.

"But a good suit is a good investment," Trina insisted. "Trust me on this. It's not like a T-shirt or a pair of jeans you're gonna throw away tomorrow. You get a good suit, and you can wear it for like forever. Real men get real suits."

"Maybe I'm not a real man."

"Hard to say," Trina said, blowing smoke in his face. "You haven't tried yet."

Marcus woke up before noon the next day, determined to at least try. He shaved his face smooth as a baby's behind. He found a Great Clips salon he could walk to and told the stylist he wanted to look like Joseph Gordon Levitt. She pulled up a photo on her phone.

"Like this?" she asked.

"Yeah, like that," Marcus said.

He turned pale and gripped the arms of the salon chair when the scissors came out and his hair started piling up on the floor.

"You'd think I was pulling a tooth. Without Novocain," the stylist quipped. "You're not going to pass out on me, are you?"

Marcus did not pass out. But he did leave the shop twenty minutes later positively lightheaded. He didn't think the face he glimpsed in the store windows he passed looked anything at all like Joseph Gordon-Levitt. What he saw was a buck naked, foreign face he'd hidden from the world for years. He didn't like the sensation of people actually *seeing* him. He half-expected passersby to back away in fright, as if they'd encountered a Frankenstein's monster or an Elephant Man.

It took about an hour on the Strip, with person after person walking by him with nothing but pleasant smiles before Marcus accepted nothing bad was going to happen. It was okay to be seen. In fact, it felt good. People could see him now, and in an odd way, he could see them for the first time too. Everything and everyone around him seemed suddenly clearer than they had before.

His confidence boosted, Marcus strode with his naked face into the Banana Republic at the Grand Canal Shoppes at the Venetian on the Strip. He was just going to look, assess how much a suit might cost, how much he would have to save up to purchase one. Instead, he landed in the hands of a middle-aged Black saleswoman named Jackie, ready to assist.

"Can I help you, sir?" Jackie asked, startling Marcus as he flipped through a rack of wool Italian suits, frowning at the price tags.

"My girlfriend tells me I would look good in a slim suit," Marcus half-lied.

"Your girlfriend is correct." Jackie pulled a dark blue suit off the rack and held it up against Marcus's body. "You'd look sharp in a suit just like this."

Marcus grinned uncertainly. "I don't think I can afford something like that, at least not today."

"You can't afford *not* to get it today," Jackie countered. "I'll get you set up with a store credit card that'll get you twenty-five percent off all your purchases in-house today. You'll walk out of here a new man, and it won't cost you a thing until next month."

"What about alterations?" Marcus asked, as if he knew anything about tailored suits.

Jackie took a step back and gave Marcus a professional once over.

"Honey, come with me. You're so regular, I can get you in a suit straight off the rack."

Marcus put himself under Jackie's command for the next ninety minutes, sweating nervously as he slipped in and out of the shirts, pants, and jackets Jackie kept bringing to him in the dressing room. She didn't release him from her care until she had him standing in front of a full-length mirror outfitted in a stylish blue suit with a crisp white shirt buttoned all the way up to his chin, or so it felt to Marcus, a plain but elegant (she assured him) tie, and a slim black leather belt.

"You look good!" Jackie declared. "But I can't let you walk out of here in that suit wearing those sneakers."

They both cast disapproving glances at Marcus's threadbare shoes.

Jackie delivered Marcus to Maureen, a skinny girl with long straight blond hair in the shoe department.

"Maureen knows her stuff. She'll take good care of you," Jackie assured Marcus as she winked at Maureen.

Marcus left Banana Republic more than a thousand dollars in debt. He stepped out into the warm evening air dressed to the nines, with his old clothes hanging off each wrist in a shopping bag. Between the haircut and the new duds, when Marcus caught a glimpse of himself in a store window, he was jolted by the sight.

Jake, at the Circus Circus bar, did a double take, as well. "Damn, Marcus! Is that you?"

"I think it is! Give me a beer, and I'll let you know."

Jake poured Marcus a beer and set it down in front of him. "So, what's with the new get-up?"

Marcus took a long drag on his beer. "Just trying to make some improvements. Trying to find a job. Trying to get ahead." He paused, then confessed to Jake, "I feel like a fool."

"You look good. You just look different, is all. Give it some time. You'll grow into it." Jake polished his highball glasses as he assessed the new and improved Marcus. "The change suits you. You keep it up, you might actually get somewhere."

Marcus had his doubts. He drained five more beers before he summoned the courage to head back to the Sandbar Suites and face the barrage of ridicule he was certain to receive from Mac and Slim. He timed his arrival at the poolside table so he could take his medicine in one big, humiliating dose.

Mac noticed him first.

"Jesus Christ, brother! What've you done to yourself?"

"I cleaned myself up is all," Marcus replied. "What? You don't like it?"

"You look like you're headed to a fag funeral, or a fag wedding," Slim commented. He got out of his seat, stood close to Marcus, and ran his hand across Marcus's clean-shaven cheek.

"Smooth as silk," he observed. "All the fag boys are gonna want to fuck that. Damn! I might fuck that myself." Slim grabbed his crotch and laughed.

"No. Seriously. What are you doing?" Mac asked, his brow furrowed with anger. "Where'd you get the money for this shit?"

"Credit card." Marcus took a seat on the concrete bench next to his brother. "Lady signed me up for one at Banana Republic. I got twenty-five percent off on everything. See?" He flipped his foot onto the table to show off his new black shoes.

"Yeah, I see," Mac commented dryly. "I see a big fucking bill that's going to come due."

"By then, I'll have a job," Marcus announced with false confidence. "I'll get my headshot scheduled this week. I'll get a job at a casino."

"You'll be turning fag tricks on the Strip," Slim said. "You and White Will can pair up and offer threesomes."

Mac shook his head in disgust. "Christ! I should've left you on the side of the road in Colorado."

"You should've pushed him down one of the old shafts out at the mine," Slim offered.

"Coulda, woulda, shoulda," Marcus said, trying to sound confident. "Don't worry about it. It's not your problem."

"You're always my problem," Mac said. "Fucking never changes."

Mac and Slim left, presumably for a night of blackjack and poker on the Strip. Marcus trudged upstairs to their room, put his bags down, took off his new clothes, and slept for the next several hours. He woke, as if he'd set an alarm, and dressed in time to make his way to the Waffle House for his regular visit.

Trina's jaw dropped when he walked through the door.

"You did it! You actually did it!" she exclaimed. "Becky! Look at Marcus! Doesn't he look handsome?"

Becky glanced over her shoulder. "He cleans up good," she agreed.

Trina stood across from Marcus with her hands on her hips,

nodding her head approvingly as he slid onto his regular stool at the counter. He blushed under her penetrating gaze.

"This is a good start," she said. "But it's not going to amount to shit if you don't take the next step."

"The next step?" Marcus looked up, startled.

"Tomorrow, first thing, you're going to the library."

12

Marcus had not been inside a library since high school. And it made no sense to him, at first, that the Clark County public library, located on Flamingo Street, just a hop and a skip away from the Sandbar Suites, was the logical place to go to look for a job.

"Computers, you dumb shit!" Trina had teased, knocking him on the head. "You're going to use the library's computers to apply for jobs. It's how it's done these days."

In its own way, the Clark County library was an even more intimidating place than the Banana Republic. From the outside, it looked to Marcus like a big behemoth of a building. Nothing about its exterior evoked memories of the old, cozy mustiness he associated with the small library back home: polished wooden card catalog drawers, stern old maid librarians who kept a sharp eye on the kids who loitered there after school, worn-out comfy chairs in corners, the narrow spiral metal staircase that led to the upper floor.

Marcus didn't have a clue where to start. But he was soon rescued by a young librarian named Ray, who spotted him wandering around a row of public computer terminals looking dazed and confused.

"Do you need to use a computer?" Ray asked. He was slender, with short, moussed blond hair, and dressed in what, to Marcus, looked suspiciously like a black slim suit.

"I'm supposed to use one to look for a job," Marcus admitted.

"Absolutely. Let me get you started. I'll have you up and running in no time."

Ray spent the next half hour getting Marcus logged in and set up with his own email account. He showed him some tips on using Google searches, walked him through a Microsoft Word program, showed him where he could find some sample résumés. Marcus couldn't thank him enough.

"No problem. Half the people here are doing the same thing," Ray assured him, gesturing to the dozen or so library patrons who were similarly peering into computer screens around the library. "Give a shout if you need anything. We're here to help."

It was a tidal wave of information overload that first hour in front of the computer screen. But with Trina's encouragement and Ray's guidance, Marcus went back the next day, and the day after that, and by the end of the week, checking in at the library was a part of his normal routine. He was there every day, typing and revising his résumé, learning how to store documents on a USB stick. Each day, he became a little more adept with his Google searches, and it took him less and less time to finish his job applications—an hour or more on the first day sped up to thirty minutes on the fifth day, then fifteen minutes thereafter.

Nothing came of it right away. But Trina assured him his efforts would pay off soon enough. Buoyed with newfound self-confidence, Marcus also returned to Banana Republic and put himself even deeper into debt updating his wardrobe. Jackie was always glad to help. She outfitted him in chino pants—two pairs of black, two pairs of tan—paired with a variety of button-down cotton shirts in an array of different colors and patterns. He discovered paisley and the color pink, and polka dots and bold geometric patterns that, as little as two weeks ago, he would've discarded out of hand.

"You want to stand out. You don't want to get lost in the crowd," Jackie advised him. "Try this!"

She handed him a long-sleeved black shirt that featured something like the outline of a dragon in white on the left side of the front and the left sleeve.

Marcus was wearing that shirt, paired with his black chinos, checking his emails on his phone—Trina had shown him how to do that—at the Waffle House counter when his cell phone rang.

"Where you at?" Mac asked.

"The Waffle House on Sinatra. Why? What's up?"

"Stay there," Mac ordered. "I'm on my way."

Marcus could feel the dark cloud that immediately engulfed him, and was aware both Trina and Becky noticed the sudden change. The two women exchanged concerned glances.

"You need anything else?" Becky asked as she topped off his coffee.

"No, thank you."

He stared numbly at his coffee cup, dreading the arrival of his brother. The Waffle House was *his* refuge. Trina was *his* girl. Becky was *his* friend. Mac breezed through the door and Marcus knew all that was about to get blown apart like a mobile home in a hurricane.

Mac slid onto the stool next to Marcus and looked his brother up and down. "Jesus! Slim was right. You *are* turning tricks on the Strip! What the hell kind of a fag outfit is this?"

Marcus forced a grin that probably came off like a grimace.

"All the girls are crazy about a sharp-dressed man," he said shakily, trying to quote the lyrics of one of his favorite ZZ Top songs and getting them wrong.

"Sharp? Is that what you call this?" Mac asked. "I'd call it fag boy fashion."

Trina appeared before them on the other side of the counter. "Hey, Marcus. Who's this stranger?"

"This is my brother, Mac," Marcus said. "I told you about him."

"So you did." Her eyes went from one brother to the other until a slight smile teased at her lips.

"He's not exactly what I expected," she said. "You don't look that much alike."

Marcus and Mac glanced at one another noncommittally.

"We don't ever give it much thought," Mac said. "He can't help it he's little and stupid."

The dig made Trina laugh.

"You must be the girl," Mac continued. "Brother told me he'd met a girl who was helping him out. He didn't tell me she was beautiful, though. Now I know why he's been keeping you to himself."

"He's not 'keeping me' anywhere," Trina corrected Mac. She tried to play it cool in front of Mac, but Marcus could see she was blushing.

"I like to help a stray cat when I can," she continued, her focus on Mac even as she talked about Marcus. "He needed a little sprucing up. He looks good now, don't you think?"

"You've definitely made some improvements," Mac complimented Trina.

Marcus wanted to punch his brother in the face. He and Slim had been riding him for weeks, ridiculing and undermining Marcus every chance they had for his appearance. Mac had just called him a fag boy.

Trina cast a warm gaze upon Marcus but he felt dismissed. "He's made real progress. It's nice to know it shows," she said with pride. She turned her gaze back to Mac and placed a menu in front of him. "You hungry tonight?"

"Starving!" Mac exclaimed. "And celebrating! Look at this!"

Mac stood and retrieved his wallet from his back pocket. He reached in and produced a check from Caesar's Palace, made out to Mac Brown for six thousand eighty dollars. "I won big at poker tonight, baby brother. I won eight thousand dollars. They automatically take out for taxes."

"And you're celebrating at the Waffle House?" Trina teased.

"Celebrating with my brother." Mac slipped an arm across Marcus's shoulders. "Steak and eggs and champagne!" he exclaimed for all to hear. The half-dozen diners in the Waffle House burst into cheers and applause.

Trina assessed Mac anew as she stared at the check in his hand. "You really won that playing poker? Can I see?"

Mac handed her the check. Her face turned serious, thoughtful, as she held Mac's gaze. They each held one corner of the check between them.

"Congratulations. That's impressive," Trina said, as she released the check.

"There's gonna be more where that came from," Mac said.

"That's what they all say," Trina said. "Everybody's gonna strike it rich in Vegas."

"Fuck everybody," Mac said. "I've got plans. I'm here to make my mark. You can take that to the bank."

Trina smiled as she gave her head a little shake and turned back to business. "So, steak and eggs and champagne it is," she said. "I can get you the steak and eggs, but you'll have to go across the street to EZ Liquor for champagne."

"Food first," Mac said.

Trina walked off to place Mac's order, neglecting to ask Marcus if he wanted anything. Not that he did. Marcus was, in fact, feeling sick to his stomach. But it would have been nice if she had asked.

"Why the long face, brother?" Mac asked. "I struck it big! And this won't be the last time, either. I know it! I can feel it!"

"That's great." Marcus was sincerely impressed with Mac's good luck, but also surprised Mac had opted for a check instead of cash.

"You have a bank account to put that in?" he asked.

"Yeah, I opened us a bank account weeks ago." Mac put the check back in his wallet just as Trina returned with coffee.

"You read my mind," Mac said. "Thanks!"

"No problem," Trina said. "You need anything, Marcus?"

"Nah, I'm good." Marcus was grateful for even that crumb of her attention.

As Mac sipped his coffee, Marcus tried to pick the conversation up where it had left off.

"You opened a bank account for us?" he asked.

"Yeah, to put our money in," Mac said. "You didn't think I was gonna stuff it under the mattress, did you?"

"No . . . I . . . I guess not." Marcus tried not to stumble on his words. "But this account is in both our names?"

"Well, no. It's just in my name. I opened it on my own. You weren't with me when I went to the bank," Mac said.

"So, I can't get to the money?"

"No, I guess you *can't*."

Trina appeared with Mac's meal then left the two brothers alone. As Mac concentrated on cutting his steak and dragging bits of meat through the runny yolks of his fried eggs, Marcus sat next to him in stony silence. After what seemed an eternity, he summoned the nerve to speak again.

"Am I going to *get* access to the money?"

Mac wiped his mouth on a napkin. "No, I don't guess you will, baby brother. Because now the money going into that account is me and Slim's winnings from the tables. It's our investment money. It's capital for the silver mine. Which you said you wanted no part of. You said it was a crazy idea, remember?"

"I remember," Marcus grumbled. "I just thought half of what it started with belonged to me. From Mom and Dad."

"Christ, Marcus!" Mac's voice rose to a holler. He slammed his fist so hard on the counter everyone in the Waffle House turned in his direction. He lowered his voice but the effect on Marcus was the same. "How many times am I gonna have to hear this shit from you? For fuck's sake! You'll get what's coming to you. How many times do you want me to say it?"

Marcus sat silent in his misery and shame while Mac finished his meal as if nothing had happened. It was like being at home around the family dinner table. Their father's fist came down, the dishes jumped, silence ensued, their mother stared off into the distance, and everyone went back to eating. The only difference now was they were in the Waffle House, and Mac was the man banging his fist, and Trina was the woman looking the other way.

Marcus was the same miserable child he'd always been. He felt as glued to his stool in the Waffle House as he had to his chair at the family table. He hadn't dared to move then, and he didn't dare move now, either. He watched glumly as Mac paid his bill in cash and left a twenty-dollar tip under his coffee cup for Trina.

Fool! Marcus thought. *Trina will pocket that money and never give you another look!*

That, at least, was what he'd seen happen with all the other men who left oversized tips for Trina. But tonight, when Trina picked up Mac's twenty, she turned her gaze to Mac, and they held each other's eyes for a long moment before she slipped the money into her apron pocket. She smiled and blew him a kiss.

13

Falling asleep lying next to the man who'd stolen his inheritance and was about to steal his girl was no easy thing. It took several hours before the image of Trina blowing a kiss to his brother faded from Marcus's consciousness and released him into the oblivion of sleep. The sun was rising over the Sandbar Suites before Marcus finally closed his eyes. But as much as he longed to bury himself in the mindlessness of sleep for endless hours, some part of him, perhaps the place where his pride resided, resisted that temptation.

He was up and dressed in his chinos and a pink shirt, heading toward the library with a couple hours to spare before the library closed. The words "faggot" and "fag outfit" still burned, but Marcus shook it off. He had, in fact, begun to approve of what he saw when he looked in the mirror. He liked the button-down shirts, the clean-shaven face, the dark hair combed back from his forehead, and the clear blue eyes. These days, what Marcus saw in his reflection was a young man who would not miss a day to check his emails, searching for more job opportunities, and submit another résumé and headshot. He also enjoyed the way he felt about himself when he was at the library. The clerks knew him by name now. They nodded and said, "Hi." They treated him with respect. They seemed to take an interest in what he was doing.

Tonight, Ray, who'd been assisting Marcus since he first stepped foot inside the library, paused while he was shelving books to inquire about Marcus's progress.

"Any luck?" he asked.

"Nothing yet," Marcus admitted. "I've never worked so hard to find a job in my life. I thought finding a job in Vegas would be a breeze."

"A lot of people think that," Ray commiserated. He turned back to his cart of books and seemed about to let the conversation end there. But then he set down the book in his hand and turned his attention back to Marcus.

"What kind of jobs are you looking for?" he asked. "If you don't mind my asking."

"Anything! Everything!" Marcus threw his hands up in exasperation. "Cashier. Stock boy. Waiter. Line cook. Bus boy. I'm not fussy. I'd take anything I could get."

Ray pulled up a chair and sat next to Marcus at his computer terminal.

"Have you thought about going to school?"

"Me? Go to school? I need a job. I don't have money for school. And I wouldn't know what to go to school for, even if I did."

"It might be the best thing for you to do," Ray said. "Especially if you have your heart set on staying in Vegas. Trade places with me and I'll show you something."

Marcus traded seats with Ray whose fingers worked their way across the keyboard.

"There are several schools in Vegas that basically serve as training grounds for the kinds of employees the casinos are always looking for. The one I'm most familiar with is the Kalman School of Gaming. I think they have two locations in the city. One of them is close to the library. See?"

Marcus leaned in over Ray's shoulder to peer at the images that popped up on the computer screen. In the middle were two boxes high-lighted in purple. Above the boxes, bold white lettering pronounced

"Professional Training in Casino Dealing and Bartending." In the background, videos showed good-looking, clean-cut young men and women mixing drinks at bars, dealing cards at gaming tables, and posing for class pictures.

Ray scrolled down to the next page, which listed Kalman's courses. Marcus leaned in even closer to the computer terminal.

"A three-week bartending course!" Marcus whispered, so as not to disturb other library patrons.

"Yeah, you could've spent the last three weeks learning a skill," Ray said. "And they'll help you find a job, too. They're tied right in with the casinos."

"I wonder how much it costs," Marcus mused aloud.

"That I don't know . . . But let's look." He scrolled to another page. "They have financial aid packages. They even have Pell Grants."

"What's a Pell Grant?"

"Government money for scholarships," Ray explained. "They're mostly available for low-income students, which I assume you would be."

"You got that right."

Ray clicked on a purple box that took them to another page, this one with more detailed information about the bartending courses.

"You can actually get the bartending course for free, if you roll it into the gaming course," he said, as he highlighted some text on the screen. "That's what the Pell Grants are for, the Comprehensive Casino Gaming course."

"What's it say about gaming courses?" Marcus asked.

Ray got out of his chair and motioned for Marcus to take his place. "Take a look. You might find something you like."

"Thanks! Thanks so much!"

"No problem. Happy to help. Good luck."

Ray patted Marcus on the shoulder then returned to his books.

Marcus hunkered down in front of the computer screen and tried to take in everything he was reading. "On-the-Job Training in our Simulated Casinos." "Classes start every Monday." "Courses in Filipino,

Spanish, Vietnamese, and Mandarin." A 350-hour gaming course. A 750-hour gaming course. Federal Pell Grants. Federal Stafford Loans. VA Funding. WIA/WIN Funding. FAFSA. Job Placement. "Assistance with arranging auditions and job interviews."

It was more than he could absorb in the few minutes that remained before the library closed for the evening. The one thing that registered clearly was how close the school was to where he lived. According to Google Maps, the East Las Vegas campus was located on South Sandhill Road, walking distance from the Sandbar Suites. The sheer proximity of the place struck a nerve with Marcus. It made something rise in his chest that felt like hope, like he might dare to do something, if only because the school was *right there*! It was so close. If Marcus hadn't made other plans for the remainder of the night, he would've let his feet take him down the road to the Kalman School of Gaming, just so he could look at it, to prove to himself it really was as close as Google Maps said it was.

As it happened, however, it was Trina's night off at the Waffle House, and Mac had told him he could borrow the truck while he and Slim were at the tables. It was those two facts coming together that allowed Marcus to take advantage of the opportunity before it passed.

He walked briskly back to the Sandbar Suites, hopped into Mac's truck, and headed to the Walmart Supercenter on West Charleston Boulevard. He found everything he needed—a large aluminum trash can, lighter fluid, a package of packing paper, matches, and a Louisville Slugger baseball bat. Then he headed for Trina's house on the northwest side of the city.

Marcus knew where she lived because a couple weeks before, he'd walked into the Waffle House to find Trina spitting mad. "Some asshole vandalized my car. Right in front of my own house! Drilled a hole in my gas tank to get the gas! Ben had to give me a ride to work tonight." Trina stopped talking while she wiped down the counter. "Anyhow," she sighed, "I could use a ride home this morning."

"You got it," Marcus had responded, before he'd even known for sure Mac would let him borrow the truck. He'd wolfed down his food at the Waffle House, headed out on foot to locate Mac at Caesar's, pleaded with Mac to lend him his truck, drove back home for a quick shower, and arrived back at the Waffle House right on time to deliver Trina safely home.

Now, as Marcus navigated his way out of the city and into the suburbs, he recalled that morning as the high point of his relationship with Trina. He'd loved every thrilling second of that ride—Trina sitting next to him, casual, relaxed, grateful for his help, chatting about nothing, lighting a cigarette, rolling down the window to blow smoke out of the cab. Every gesture, every word had been like an injection of pure joy mainlined into Marcus's soul. He'd do anything to experience that joy again.

Everything had gone to shit between Marcus and Trina with the arrival of Mac at the Waffle House. The instant Mac had come through the door Marcus had known his beloved Trina and the Waffle Hovel would never be the same for him again. Mac's mere presence in the room had effectively knocked him off his seat, lowering him from the status of Marcus in his own right to being Marcus, Mac's kid brother. From then on, Marcus knew in his gut every time he took his usual seat at the counter, he'd be seen by others as cowering in Mac's shadow. He was branded now. The small one, the quiet one, the weak one.

To make matters worse, Marcus knew something had sparked between Trina and Mac. It was bad enough an undeserving brute named Ben currently had the privilege of sleeping every night with his face pressed into Trina's magnificent head of hair. Soon enough, Marcus figured, that privilege would be transferred to Mac. And Mac would follow the same path Ben had cleared before him. Evidence of the violence Ben inflicted on Trina's body would fade, only to be replaced by the new wounds inflicted on her by Mac.

"Fuck 'em! Fuck 'em all!" Marcus said aloud as he pulled up in front of Trina's house.

The home itself—a tidy single-story stucco ranch with an attached

garage and a hedge-lined walkway leading up to the front door—
watered down his courage a bit. Marcus had nothing comparable to
offer the girl. Who was he to interfere?

But even as Marcus began unpacking his supplies from the back of
Mac's truck, he overheard the untidy commotion unfolding inside the
picture-perfect home Trina shared with Ben.

"You're a fucking whore! You don't make tips like that just by sling-
ing hash at a fucking Waffle House!" Ben sounded drunk and angry.
"You don't get a fucking twenty-dollar tip just for pouring a cup of
coffee. You think I don't know what's going on? You think I don't
know you're giving blow jobs behind the dumpster? You and that bitch,
Becky. The both of you are humping dicks. Don't think I don't know it."

Marcus cringed as he set the trash can on the walkway up close
to the house's front entrance. Lots of men gave Trina large tips. What
was she supposed to do? Put a sign on her chest that read: PLEASE
TIP RESPONSIBLY. MY BOYFRIEND WILL BEAT ME IF
YOU DON'T.

"Baby, I can't help it if dumbass drunk men stagger into the Waffle
House at three a.m. and think a couple of bucks is gonna turn my head
their way." Trina tried to defend herself. "You should be glad those
suckers are willing to part with their money like that. It's *our* money!
It's money in *our* pockets!"

"The hell it is!" Ben shouted.

Marcus heard glass shattering as he shoved wads of packing paper
into the trash can and doused it with a full bottle of lighter fluid.

"You think I don't know you stuff money away in a savings account somewhere?" Ben demanded. "That money isn't ours. You suck
as many men as you can, and you squirrel away as much of their money
as you can. You think I don't know that?"

Marcus heard the slap then heard Trina cry out.

"Stop it! You're insane! You'll regret this when you sober up in the
morning," Trina sobbed.

Marcus tossed a lit match into the trash can. Flames shot up to the height of the overhang that adorned Trina's front porch. Marcus strode up to the window to the right of the front door and smashed in the glass with the Louisville Slugger.

From inside, Ben muttered, "What the fuck?"

Ben swung open his front door to discover a small inferno burning on his walkway and a pile of broken glass littering his front porch. What he didn't see was Marcus with a sturdy Louisville Slugger, hyped up and coming down hard and fast on the back of his head. Ben was already sprawled out stone-cold on the porch when Trina came out the door behind him.

"Oh my God!" She rushed to Ben's side. "Ben, are you alright? Ben, can you hear me, baby?"

"Fuck Ben," Marcus said.

Trina turned at the sound of Marcus's voice. "Marcus?" she whispered. "What the fuck have you done?"

"I did what had to be done." Marcus tried to sound brave and confident, but his voice and his hands were shaking. "Get your things. I'm taking you away from this bullshit right now. Right now!" he added forcefully.

"Get my things? Are you crazy?" Trina looked around helplessly, then back to Ben.

Marcus took hold of Trina's hand, pulled her to her feet, and all but dragged her into the house. Past the living room and the dining room and kitchen, he pulled her along behind him toward the bedrooms at the end of a hallway. By sheer chance, the first door he opened was the bedroom shared by Trina and Ben. Marcus pulled open a closet door, spied a suitcase on a top shelf, dragged it down, and threw it on the bed.

"Grab some clothes. Get your personal stuff," Marcus ordered her in a surprisingly calm voice.

Trina stood motionless in the middle of the bedroom. "I can't just leave. We can't just leave Ben lying there."

"Yes, we can," Marcus said.

He opened the top drawer of the only dresser in the room and started pulling out handfuls of bras and panties and stuffing them into the suitcase. Trina still hadn't moved when he proceeded to the next drawer and picked up an armload of T-shirts.

"Come on!" he said gently. "You're leaving tonight. Right now. Get your things and let's get going."

Trina glanced over her shoulder, in the direction of the front door and Ben, then back at Marcus.

"Fuck!" she muttered under her breath. She hesitated another moment, watching as if from the sidelines as Marcus crammed jeans and sweatpants into the suitcase.

"All right! I guess I'm leaving." Trina grabbed a tote bag and ran into the bathroom. She emerged moments later with it crammed full of tampons, a huge bottle of Advil, washcloths, and towels. She swept earrings, necklaces, and bracelets off the top of the dresser on top of the other stuff in the tote.

Marcus had crammed as much into the suitcase as he could. Now he grabbed an armload of dresses and blouses from the closet and draped them over one arm.

"Anything else?" he asked Trina.

Trina's eyes darted around the room. "Shit! My cat!"

Marcus scanned the room for the cat while Trina moved toward the king-size bed and scooped up a black-and-white stuffed animal with ragged ears and dented whiskers. She squashed it into her tote bag, and now it was Trina pulling Marcus by the hand as she led them back down the hallway, Marcus pulling the wheeled suitcase with the other hand, Trina's dresses still draped over his arm.

"And my laptop! I need my laptop." She picked a silver PC up off the living room coffee table and tucked it under one arm.

"My purse! And my phone!" She grabbed a handbag hanging off a hook by the front door, looked inside and located her phone, then stepped out the front door.

"You good?" Marcus asked.

"No, not really." Trina snapped.

Her glance fell on Ben. She cursed under her breath as she stepped over him and Marcus followed behind her, hearing Ben moan. The fire in the trash can had dwindled to a cloud of black smoke as they rushed toward Mac's truck and tossed Trina's possessions into it. Trina opened the passenger side door with one last look toward Ben. She hesitated a moment.

"Come on. Get in," Marcus said in the gentlest of voices. "I'm taking you home."

"Is that what you're doing? Taking me home? Playing the hero all of a sudden?" Trina shot back. Still, she hopped into the passenger seat and slammed the door shut behind her.

As Marcus pulled away from the curb, a fire truck with its siren wailing and lights flashing rounded the corner toward Ben's house.

"Someone must've called in the fire," Trina said. "I guess the firemen will call an ambulance for Ben."

"Yeah, I guess," Marcus said. He stared straight ahead, his hands gripping the steering wheel so hard his knuckles turned white.

Trina shook her head at the sight of him. "Relax. It's over now."

Marcus loosened his grip on the steering wheel. But he couldn't stop grimacing. "I hope he's not hurt too badly," he said.

Marcus had never struck another human being, not with his fists, and certainly never with a baseball bat. The sound and the feel of the bat smashing the back of Ben's head churned in his gut now. He suddenly felt weak and lightheaded.

"He'll be okay," Trina said.

"You don't think I killed him?"

"No, slugger, you didn't kill him. You cleaned his clock, but he's not gonna die."

Tears pooled in Marcus's eyes. His body shook as the adrenaline rush that had propelled him into action drained from his system.

"You need to pull over. Pull over now!" Trina ordered him.

Marcus did as he was told, bringing the truck to a halt at the side of a busy two-lane highway. His head spinning, he draped his body against the steering wheel.

"Oh, for fuck's sake!"

Trina managed to get Marcus out of the driver's seat. He could feel her half-dragging him, half-carrying him into the passenger seat as he continued to swoon.

"Some knight in shining armor you turned out to be!" she spat out. As she steered the F-150 back into traffic, Marcus leaned against the door and closed his eyes.

"I'm sorry," he said.

"Yeah, you're sorry. Men are always sorry, aren't they?"

Marcus hid his face in the crook of his arm and sobbed. By the time Trina pulled Mac's truck into the parking lot of the Sandbar Suites, he'd run out of tears, but his humiliation was complete. He'd imagined returning to the Sandbar a conquering hero. He'd imagined tears of gratitude, eternal thanks, Trina at his side as he escorted her up the stairs to Room 310. Instead, Marcus had collapsed under the weight of his own actions. He labored feebly up the three flights of stairs, leaning on the handrail for support. When his shaking hands prevented him from unlocking his own door, Trina took the keys from him and opened it herself.

"There! We're home!" she announced as she deposited Marcus in a chair at the dinette table. She dropped her purse on the floor and took the seat opposite him, surveying her surroundings with what seemed a combination of familiarity and disgust. She lit a cigarette, inhaled deeply, and rubbed her eyes.

"I'm right back where I started." Trina laughed bitterly. "Ben brought me here, too. Not this same room. We were down on the ground floor. The fucking Sandbar Suites."

"It's not much," Marcus conceded. "But at least you'll be safe here."

"Safe? You think I'll be safe here?" Trina snapped. "I'm not going to be safe anywhere. And neither are you."

"What do you mean?"

"I mean Ben is going to fucking kill us both. Not tonight or tomorrow, maybe. But he'll come for us, you mark my words."

The idea that Ben would seek revenge had never occurred to Marcus. "I think everything will be okay," he said, without much conviction.

Trina blew a stream of smoke through her nostrils. "Nothing is okay," she said. "Not one fucking thing is okay."

14

The door to Room 310 opened and Mac's looming figure entered the apartment.

Marcus pressed his index finger to his lips. "Shhh," he whispered. "She's sleeping."

Mac squinted against the darkness and spotted Marcus sitting at the dinette table. "What? Who's sleeping?" he asked, also in a whisper.

"Trina," Marcus said. "She was tired. I told her to take the bed."

"Trina? From the Waffle House? She's here?"

"Yeah, she's here." Marcus stood and headed out the door. "Let's talk outside. I want her to get some rest."

Mac followed Marcus down the walkway and stairs. Marcus could feel Mac's icy stare on his back—he knew his brother was letting him stew. When they got down the pool, Mac didn't speak until he'd lit a Marlboro and smoked it down half-way. "What the fuck have you done?"

"I did something that needed doing," Marcus began.

He rubbed the palms of his hands with his thumbs, massaging his hands as if he were trying to work a cramp out of them. "I bashed in Ben's head with a baseball bat."

"The fuck you did. Who's Ben?"

"Trina's boyfriend. Probably ex-boyfriend now, I guess. I went to their house. He was hitting her. I hit him."

"With a baseball bat? You don't even own a baseball bat."

"I do now. It's in the back of your truck."

"Did you fucking damage my truck?"

"No, I didn't hurt your truck. Just Ben's head. And the front window. I smashed out the front window of the house, too."

"The fuck you did."

"And I lit a fire in a trash can, as a diversion, to get him out of the house. The fire and the glass breaking. That's what got him out of the house. I clobbered him on the front steps. He never knew what hit him."

"I bet he didn't." Mac rubbed his face. "You didn't kill the guy, did you?"

"No. Or at least I don't think I did," Marcus said, his voice cracking. "He didn't look dead to me."

"Seen a lot of dead men, have you?"

Marcus shrugged. "He looked like he was still breathing. That's all I'm saying."

Mac rubbed his face again. "I don't guess I'm lying down in my own bed this morning. I'm gonna catch some sleep in the truck. I'll talk to Slim about this later."

"Talk to Slim? Why do you have to talk to Slim?" Marcus asked, alarm rising in his voice.

"To figure out what to do next," Mac shot back.

"There's nothing more to be done."

"We'll see about that," Mac hesitated at the pool gate, looking back at Marcus, shaking his head. "Don't worry about it. We'll clean up your mess."

Marcus could feel Mac's disgust.

That night, the four of them—Mac, Slim, Marcus, and Trina— gathered around a table by the pool, sharing an order of McDonald's takeout, debating and planning their next move. Marcus listened as he put a few French fries into his mouth, barely aware of what he was eating.

"So, this little cunt left the job undone? Is that what you're telling me?" Slim addressed the question to Mac.

"I didn't leave anything undone," Marcus protested. "The guy was out. He was on the ground. He was finished."

"That don't mean the job is finished," Slim said between mouthfuls of fries. He pointed a greasy French fry at Trina. "You get all of your shit out of that house, baby girl?"

Trina shook her head then sipped a Diet Coke. "My car's still there if he hasn't destroyed it already. And my clothes. My shoes. Everything, really. We just tore out of there with what we could carry."

"That son-of-a-bitch gonna let you go back in there and take what's yours?" Slim asked.

Trina shook her head again.

"There you go," Slim said. "We gotta go back there and finish the job. It ain't over 'til it's over."

Marcus could feel that somehow he was being edged out and barely felt part of the group. The four continued to eat and drink in silence.

Finally, Trina turned her gaze to Mac, speaking directly to him. "I'm afraid of Ben. I'm afraid of what he might do to me, or to Marcus."

Mac placed a calming hand on Trina's arm. "We'll deal with it. We'll deal with it tonight. You don't have to worry about a thing."

Trina visibly relaxed in her chair. Marcus, on the other hand, spoke up nervously.

"I already bashed the man's head in. Isn't that enough?"

"No, it's not," Trina answered him sharply. "He needs to know I'm protected. He needs to know there's a line he can't cross."

"I'll protect you," Marcus said.

Trina rolled her eyes. Slim and Mac guffawed. Marcus could feel his face turn hot.

"Look," Trina turned to Marcus. "I appreciate what you did for me last night. It was a nice . . . gesture. But where are you gonna be when I'm on my own at the Waffle House and Ben comes in looking for me? What are you gonna do to protect yourself when he comes looking for you?"

Marcus stared at Trina. He had no answer to her questions.

"This shit is beyond you. You're a nice guy, but you can't handle it," Trina said. She reached across for Mac's hand. "I need to feel safe. I need Mac to finish this for me."

The ground seemed to lurch beneath Marcus's feet as he looked into the faces of his three companions. Slim shoved the remainder of a carton of French fries into his mouth. Trina squeezed Mac's hand and scooted over to be closer to him. Marcus looked from one face to the other like a man lined up in front of a firing squad. It was over for him, and he knew it.

"Fine," Marcus muttered. "Let Mac take care of you. I'm done."

"Not yet, you're not. We need you in the truck," Mac said. "We need you to drive us away."

"Fuck you!" Marcus sputtered half-heartedly.

"No, fuck you, baby brother!" Mac stood and towered over his younger brother, his voice rising in anger. "You created this mess, and it's me and Slim that are gonna clean it up. So, you'll damn well do your part and drive the truck. Get your lazy ass out of that seat, and let's get this thing done."

Marcus followed Mac, Slim, and Trina to Mac's truck, climbing into the back seat with Slim while Trina took her place in the front next to Mac. It stung Marcus to his core to see Trina was lost to him now. He wanted to hate her, to hate Mac, too, but he couldn't, because he knew they were right. He wasn't the right man for the job. He couldn't think about the blow he'd delivered to Ben's head last night without a wave of nausea rising from his stomach to his throat. He knew what he'd do if he were ever faced with Ben's wrath. He'd run if he could. Most likely, though, he'd just stand there and take whatever he had coming. That was the story of his life. That was who he was. Last night's heroics had been a fluke. The real Marcus was once again the whipped puppy he always was and always would be.

Marcus stared out his window while Trina gave Mac directions to the house. Mac pulled up to the curb and shifted the truck into park. Mac turned to the three of them and handed out everyone's marching orders.

"You got your keys?" he asked Trina.

Trina fished her car keys out of her purse and dangled them in front of Mac's eyes.

"Good. You get in your car and drive home," Mac commanded. "Just go. You understand? Don't wait for shit. We'll get the rest of your stuff. But you don't need to see what's going down here."

Trina nodded.

"Marcus, you take the wheel. Keep the engine running," Mac said. "Me and Slim will do the rest. You got it?"

"I got it," Marcus said.

"All right," Mac said, and Slim added a "Let's get her done," as everyone opened their doors and piled out of the truck

Sitting in the driver's seat of his brother's truck, Marcus gripped the steering wheel as if he needed to hang onto something to keep himself from being ripped out of the cab by a tornado. Trina's car, a little blue Toyota Corolla, was parked in the driveway. Marcus heard her turn over the ignition and the engine start up just as the front door of the house swung open, and Ben stormed out. He made it down the two front steps and a couple of paces down the walkway before Mac doubled him over with an elbow blow to the gut. Ben was Mac's size, big and brawny, certainly capable of facing him as an opponent, but Mac had struck without warning, hitting the big man so hard he'd stopped him in his tracks.

Marcus turned his gaze to Trina. The Toyota hadn't moved. Trina's hands were on the steering wheel, but her eyes were focused on Mac and Ben. She watched as Mac pinned Ben's arms behind his back and forced him to his knees. She watched Mac grab a fistful of Ben's hair and lift his head up, giving Slim a clear shot to kick him squarely in the face.

Marcus couldn't read the expression on Trina's face, but he half-expected her to run screaming from the car and beg Mac and Slim to stop the vicious beating they were giving to the man she'd presumably loved twenty-four hours ago. But she didn't intervene. She watched intently until she saw Mac and Slim haul Ben by his arms back into the house. Ben's head hung down to his chest, bobbing grotesquely as they dragged his limp body up the front steps. With that, Trina calmly backed her car out of the driveway and headed, Marcus assumed, for the Sandbar Suites.

Moments dragged by like hours as Marcus waited alone in the driver's seat of Mac's truck. He could hear and see nothing of what was going on inside the house. It was left to his imagination to picture how Ben's punishment was being meted out behind that closed door. Were they beating him? Torturing him? Stringing him up? Setting him on fire? Various scenarios played out in Marcus's mind. When he couldn't stand not knowing any longer, he slid out of the truck and made his way into the house.

When Marcus entered the living room, he found Ben on the floor with Mac kneeling on his chest, a jackknife pointed at his neck. Slim was perched on an arm of the living room couch, his eyes gleaming with excitement as Mac slapped Ben's face to bring him back to a semi-conscious state. He pushed the tip of the knife deeper into his throat. Ben whimpered as tears rolled down his bloodied cheeks.

"Is our business here done now? Are we done?" Mac demanded of him. "Am I gonna have to come back here and fuck you up again, or are we done?"

Ben muttered something indistinguishable.

"Speak, you motherfucker! Are we done here or not?"

"We're done," Ben whispered. "We're done."

"Damn straight we are!" Mac said. "That girl is no longer your concern. You got that? I know where you live. You come anywhere near her or my brother, you're messing with me. You got that?"

Ben barely nodded his head before losing consciousness.

"Yeah, I thought so," Slim grinned from the sidelines. He noticed Marcus just as Mac pulled himself up from Ben's body.

"What the fuck are you standing there for?" Slim demanded. "I thought we told you to stay in the truck."

Mac wheeled around, his eyes blazing at the sight of his younger brother. In the next instant, Mac pulled Marcus up by his shirt collar, lifted him off the floor and hurled his slight frame against a living room wall.

Slim cackled. "He's coming in for the kill now! Boy, you don't know who you're messing with!"

There was no place for Marcus to run, no place for him to hide as Mac bore down on him, his face a mask of contorted rage. He grabbed a terrified Marcus by his throat, pinned him against the wall, and spewed hatred into his face.

"You little shit! You worthless cunt! What good are you to me, huh? When have you ever done anything useful in your entire worthless fucking life? You're fucking worthless! You can't do a damned thing on your own! I've always had to carry you! Always!"

Trembling, Marcus managed to speak. "I came in to see if I could help," he whispered. "I wanted to help."

"You wanted to *help*?" The sheer absurdity of the idea seemed to suck the fury out of Mac's body. He loosened his grip around Marcus's throat and dropped his hand to his sides. "You've never been any help to me, not once in your entire fucking life. It's always me helping you."

Mac turned his back on his brother. Marcus, plastered to the wall, surveyed the living room—Slim grinning from the archway between the living room and the dining room, Ben a bloody unconscious mess on the floor.

"You wanna help?" Mac sneered as he turned back to face Marcus, still backed into the wall where he'd left him. "Let's get the rest of Trina's shit and get the fuck out of here."

Marcus led Mac and Slim down the hallway into the master bedroom. Mac loaded his arms with the rest of Trina's dresses. Slim emptied the contents of the dresser into a single drawer and carried the whole drawer out to the truck. Marcus desperately collected shoes from the closet floor, stuffing them into a JCPenney shopping bag he spotted under the bed.

Marcus, the last one out of the house, turned off all the lights and shut the front door behind him, taking one last look over his shoulder at Ben. He wasn't proud of what he'd done, either last night or tonight. He'd spent a lifetime watching other men—his father, his brother, Slim, and others—lash out in violent ways and never seem to give the damage they'd done a second thought. Marcus wasn't built that way. The bloody events of the last two nights left him feeling sick and uncertain. He hadn't proved his manhood or won Trina's love. The whole sordid affair seemed utterly pointless to him now. He crawled into the back seat of Mac's truck, cradling the bag of Trina's shoes in his lap.

"Well, that's one less thing we have to worry about," Slim announced as they pulled away from Ben's house. Then he winked at Mac.

"That bitch is your problem now, buddy."

15

All the way back to the Sandbar Suites, Marcus stared gloomily out the window and wondered if they'd even find Trina waiting for them there. He loved the girl. He wanted her to be there. He wanted the chance to watch over her a little, to have her in his life just a little, even if she'd never belong to him. It would just be nice to have her around.

But he also wanted her to go. *Just go!* he urged Trina as he imagined her in the little blue Corolla. *There's nothing here you need, nothing to hold you down. You're free now! Leave all this shit behind you and just go!*

And take me with you!

That thought circled around inside his head, too. Marcus imagined her car stuffed to the gills with shoes and shirts and her laptop and blue jeans, Trina driving, the two of them laughing in triumph as they sped out of the parking lot of the Sandbar Suites and headed . . . Where? Anywhere! California. Oklahoma. Canada. Mexico. It wouldn't matter where they went, as long as they left Mac and Slim choking on dust and exhaust fumes as they made their escape.

Or she could leave on her own. That was okay, too. He imagined a scenario where Trina escaped alone, and he caught up with her later. That was kind of sweet. He liked the idea that Trina, out in the world on her own, would reach back for Marcus. She'd realize she missed him, that he was the man she'd wanted—no, needed—all along. That would work, too. Marcus liked that idea a lot.

Trina's car, of course, was in the parking lot of the Sandbar Suites, just as Marcus had expected it to be. When Marcus and Mac walked through the door of Room 310, Trina looked up from her place at the dinette table and immediately reached out for Mac. That was what Marcus had expected as well. Her eyes zeroed in on Mac with an intensity that essentially blocked Marcus from her view. He might as well have not even been in the room.

"Is it done?" Trina asked Mac.

"It's done," he answered.

Trina got up out of her chair and threw herself into Mac's arms. She clung to him as if he were a life raft in a turbulent ocean.

"I was so afraid!" Trina sobbed, her entire body trembling. "I didn't know what might happen. I didn't know if you'd be hurt!"

Mac buried his hands in her loose hair and held her even closer.

"Nothing's going to happen to me," he said soothingly. "And nothing's going to happen to you, either. I won't allow it. End of story."

Marcus, slumped at the dinette table, looked up to see Trina, eyes closed, in Mac's embrace. Her sobbing slowly subsided and her body stopped shaking. Her cheek was still pressed against Mac's chest when she opened her eyes and they immediately landed on Marcus, who was watching at her.

"Oh, Marcus! Are you okay?" Trina asked. She eased out of Mac's arms and placed a hand on Marcus's shoulder.

"Yeah, just a little tired," Marcus lied. He thought he was prepared to lose Trina to Mac, but he wasn't. Seeing Mac's hands in her hair was like a gut punch. He was trying not to faint at the kitchen table right there in front of everyone, right there in front of Trina.

"You're not looking so good, Marcus. You should go to bed." Trina turned to Mac for confirmation. "I'll sleep in the recliner, or on the floor. You take the bed."

"Not gonna happen," Mac said. "I didn't snatch you out of your own house so you could sleep on my floor. You'll take the bed, isn't that right, baby brother?"

Marcus wanted to scream. *No! No, that isn't right! I took Trina out of that house! I did it, not you!* Instead, he lifted his head and nodded weakly. He made eye contact with Trina through a cloud of tears.

"You get the bed," he said to her.

He was grateful for the smile she bestowed upon him in return.

Mac opened the refrigerator and pulled out a six-pack of Bud Lights. He popped the cap off a bottle and handed it to Trina, did the same for Marcus, and one for himself.

"Cheers!" he said before he tipped back his head and nearly drained the bottle.

"Cheers! To new beginnings!" Trina clinked her bottle against Mac's then Marcus's.

Mac chugged the rest of his beer and belched loudly.

"Come on, kid," he said, kicking Marcus's chair. "Let's get this lady's shit out of the back of my truck before it goes missing. I don't trust these fucks around here for a minute."

"My things!" Trina exclaimed, a smile of genuine happiness lighting up her face. "I'd totally forgotten about them!"

For the next couple of hours, the three of them hung out together in the apartment, drinking beer and smoking joints as Trina unpacked her worldly possessions. She greeted some of the items as if they were long lost friends.

"My jewelry box!" she exclaimed. She set it on the dresser and opened the lid. "I love these earrings!" She held up a pair of beaded black earrings and showed off how they dangled from her earlobes almost to her collarbone. "I got them to go with this dress." She pulled a long, black, sleeveless lace dress from a pile of dresses on the bed. "See?" She held the dress up to her body.

"And these shoes." She pulled a pair of black, patent leather high heeled shoes out of the JCPenney bag.

"Gorgeous," Marcus said.

"Very practical," Mac said.

Trina shrugged them both off. "Yeah, I know," she said. "What do I need anything like this for? Can't exactly wear it to the Waffle Hovel. But it makes a girl feel better when she has something beautiful to wear, even if it's only for once in a while." She twirled in a circle with the dress pressed to her body.

"Besides," she said, as she found a place for her dress in their now overcrowded closet. "I found all these things at thrift shops. I never pay full price for my clothes. Never! It's a total waste of money. Well, except for panties and bras. I get those new."

"Rightly so," Mac said.

"I thought you said good clothes were an investment," Marcus piped up, suddenly self-conscious in his full-price outfit from Banana Republic.

Trina looked Marcus up and down, assessing his attire.

"You paid full price for those clothes?" she asked. "Oh, Marcus! A good suit is an investment, not casual wear. You'll have to come with me to Goodwill someday. I'll teach you how to shop. I can't let you waste your money on retail prices for clothes. Oh, speaking of money!"

Trina crossed the room and picked her handbag up off the kitchen counter. "I need to pay for my share of the rent, until I can find a place of my own. A third is two hundred, right? Or have the rates gone up since I was here last time?" She was counting money out of her wallet.

"Put your money away," Mac said. "You don't owe us a thing. And you can stay here as long as you want, or as long as you can stand the company."

Trina walked up to Mac at the dinette table and handed him a stack of bills. "That's two hundred dollars. You take it, or I leave right now. That's non-negotiable. I. Don't. Freeload."

Mac folded the bills in half and slipped them into his pants pockets. "All right," he said. "You're paid up for a month. Welcome home!"

"Thank you."

Trina went back to sorting through her things, pulling items out the bags, holding them against her body. Stoned and drunk, Marcus watched her every move with a fool's grin plastered across his face. She held up a lacy red negligee with matching high heels and garter belts.

"Victoria's Secret via thrift shop," she explained. "It's amazing what you can find at the second-hand stores in Las Vegas."

Marcus knew she was openly, brazenly flirting with Mac, with no regard for his own wounded pride. *So be it!* was his attitude. He smoked more weed and drank more beer and enjoyed the view until he nodded off to sleep right there at the table.

He woke up when Mac kicked his chair. He didn't know how long he'd been asleep. But the room was dark, and he spied what he assumed was Trina under the covers in the bed, her back turned to the two men.

"Go sleep in the truck, baby brother," Mac whispered. "I'll take the recliner."

The recliner. Close to the bed. Close to Trina.

Marcus staggered to his feet and stumbled down the three flights of stairs, clinging to the handrail the whole way. When he got to Mac's truck in the parking lot, he got the door unlocked, and climbed in.

He fell asleep thinking about the curve of Trina's hip underneath the blankets of the bed he used to share with his brother. He wondered how long Mac would stay in that recliner, wondered if he hadn't left it for the bed already.

16

It was just a matter of days before Trina started to remind Marcus of their mother. Whatever else their mother had been, she was a woman who liked things done around the house in the proper way. Fred could go off on a drunken tear and handcuff Marcus to the boiler in the basement, but by God, she'd still fold T-shirts just so and stack them neatly in drawers; she'd still hand wash and towel dry dishes after each and every meal; she'd still wash sheets every Saturday and press her husband's shirts every Sunday.

Trina was the same, only bossier. The day after the brothers had moved her in, Trina came back from the Goodwill with two used laundry hampers. While the brothers watched, she taped a handwritten label on each hamper—one "dark," the other "light"—and picked up all the dirty undershorts, pants, socks, shirts, and bath towels scattered around the apartment.

"That's where dirty clothes go," Trina announced. "I'll wash it all. That can be my job 'cause I don't want you guys ruining my delicates, or throwing dark shit in with my whites. But don't leave shit all over the apartment. Okay?"

"Yes, ma'am," Mac said.

Trina shot him a look. "Are you being sarcastic with me?"

"No, ma'am, just following orders."

"Good."

Trina placed a small bowl on the dresser. "That's for loose quarters, to pay for the washer and dryer. You empty your pockets into that every day, and I'll always have quarters on hand when I get a chance to wash clothes."

She looked at them expectantly.

"Oh, you mean now." Marcus fished the change out of his pants pockets, sifted out the quarters, and dropped them into the bowl. Mac did the same.

"We got us a live one," Mac whispered to Marcus, but loud enough for Trina to hear.

"You don't know *what* you got," Trina teased back. Then she tidied up the kitchen, made the bed, dusted the furniture, wrote up a shopping list for the grocery store, and handed it to Mac.

"Let's go," she said, turning toward the door as she spoke.

"Let's not," Mac said.

Trina stopped in her tracks and turned back toward Mac.

"Excuse me?" she said.

Mac looked up from the shopping list in his hand and cleared his throat.

"You do what you want," Mac said, "but I can get ninety percent of the stuff on this list for free. So, I'm not going to the supermarket and wasting my money on shit I don't need to spend money on."

Trina stood with her hand still on the doorknob, staring at Mac in disbelief.

"It's groceries," she said. "Bread, milk, butter, sandwich meats, cereal. It's basic stuff. You can't get it for free."

"I can," Mac countered.

Trina came back into the room. She stood before Mac with her purse slung across her shoulder, her arms folded across her chest.

"What are you doing?" she scoffed. "Taking handouts from food banks?"

"Sometimes," Mac said, without an ounce of shame.

Trina's eyes widened and a skeptical grin crossed her face as she turned to Marcus.

"Is he serious?" she asked. "You guys are pulling my leg, right?"

"'Fraid not," Marcus said. "We get a bunch of stuff from a food bank around the corner on Flamingo Road. I usually go. It's open every Wednesday."

Trina looked from one brother to the other, her grin replaced with a slight frown. "For real?" she asked, directing the question to Marcus.

Marcus shrugged. "For real. I can't find a job. I don't have any money."

"You have money! I watch you spend it every night at the Waffle House."

"That's Mac's money. He give me enough to get by."

Trina pulled up a chair opposite Marcus at the dinette table and folded her arms across her chest, lit up a cigarette and laughed as she exhaled. "You guys, that is fucked up. It would never occur to me to go to a food bank unless I was absolutely desperate. And you guys are not desperate, not by a long shot. What else don't I know about you two con artists?"

"You go to the grocery store if you want to, baby girl," Mac said as he handed Trina's shopping list back to her. "But you come with me tonight and I'll show you how to eat like a king in this town and never spend a dime."

"Bullshit!" Trina laughed. "He's shitting me, right?" she said to Marcus.

"Not really," Marcus said. "He and Slim make out pretty good, actually."

"We toss our table scraps to the dog." Mac winked at Trina and jerked his thumb at Marcus. "Tell her, brother! Tell Trina what I got for you the other night."

"Lobster tails," Marcus said.

"No fucking way!" Trina wadded up her shopping list and threw it in Marcus's face. "You're lying! Both of you are taking me for a fool!"

"No, ma'am." Marcus tossed the balled-up shopping list right back at her. "I opened the refrigerator door two days ago and ate lobster for breakfast."

"Fuck me!" Trina laughed. "I knew you weren't coming to the

Waffle Hovel for the food. But I didn't think you were eating fucking lobster for breakfast!"

"Put on your fancy dress and come out with me and Slim tonight." Mac pointed to the closet where Trina had hung up her lacy black dress. "Me and Slim will find you the best food in town, and it won't cost us a cent!"

"You and Slim? Slim?" Trina let the name of Mac's best friend hang in the air. "I'm not putting on my best dress for Slim."

Mac pointed a scolding finger at Trina. "You underestimate Slim at your own peril. You could learn a thing or two from him."

"I'm sure he could teach me something," Trina scoffed as she stubbed out her cigarette. "As it happens, I have to work tonight, so I'll have to take a rain check on that dinner invitation."

She stood and headed toward the door. "In the meantime, if it's all the same to you, I'm gonna go to the store like a normal person and buy some normal food. I'm not in the habit of taking handouts, or eating other people's garbage."

"Suit yourself," Mac said lightly.

Trina hesitated at the door, once again looking from one brother to the next. "Is he shitting me?" she asked Marcus again. "Have you ever gone out with those two clowns and seen what they get up to?"

"No," Marcus said, shaking his head. "I eat what they leave in the fridge. And it's not half-bad. To be honest, between what I get from the food bank and what Mac brings home from, well, from wherever, we only spend money on beer and cigarettes. Everything else is free."

Trina stared at the two brothers, her hand on the doorknob. She let her gaze wander over to the closet, where her dress waited for her, then back to Mac and Marcus. She took her hand off the doorknob and sat back down at the table.

"All right," she said. "I'll bite! The Waffle Hovel can get along without me for one night. Me and Marcus will come out with you and Slim, and you two can show us how it's done. Maybe we'll learn something, after all."

17

"**T**he fuck is this? Prom night?" Slim looked Trina up and down as she, Mac, and Marcus each took a seat at the poolside patio table where they tended to meet up each evening. Marcus thought she looked great. Smelled good, too. Trina was dressed in her lacy black dress, a tiny, sequined evening bag slung over her shoulder. She'd made up her face, sprayed on some perfume, and stepped into her high heels.

"Trina wants to further her education," Mac replied. "She don't believe you and me know how to feed ourselves. I told her you'd teach her."

"The fuck you did," Slim said. He looked Trina up and down again, then side-eyed Marcus. "And I suppose this little pussy needs schooling, too?"

"He needs something," Mac joked.

"Fuck me," Slim griped. "This ain't a game, you know? We're supposed to be working, not fucking around with these two."

"I don't need this shit." Trina stood to leave. Mac grabbed her hand and pulled her back down into her seat.

"A couple hours won't kill us," Mac said to Slim. "You're the master. You showed me, now you can show them."

"All right. All right," Slim stubbed out a cigarette and stood. "You ready for your first lesson?"

"Sure. I'm game," Trina said.

"All right. First thing is," Slim said, "you're dressed all wrong for the job. We could maybe use you for a distraction with the get-up you're in tonight, which is useful, don't get me wrong. But that fancy dress and that little thing you call a handbag aren't proper *work* clothes."

Slim picked up a loose-fitting sport coat that had been draped across the concrete bench and slipped his arms in. He opened the sport coat, as if he were drawing back the curtains on a stage, revealing two large, hand-sewn pockets on the interior of each side of the coat.

"*This* is work clothes," he announced.

Trina leaned forward to examine the pockets more closely. She put her hands inside the pockets, testing the strength of the stitching. "You did that? That's good work." She glanced up at Slim, looking him directly in the eye for the first time.

"Outfitted Mac's coat, too." Slim let the coat hang loose on his wiry frame and patted both pockets from the outside. "I call these my 'fruit bins.' Apples. Bananas. Grapes. You slip that shit in there and no one ever knows the difference."

Marcus had wondered how they got all the food home.

Trina smiled appreciatively and turned her face to Mac.

"You ready?" Mac asked.

"I'm ready!" Trina said.

They all stood to leave, except Marcus, who wasn't entirely certain he was part of the group.

"Come on," Trina said. "You don't want to miss the adventure!"

Marcus got up, but only because Trina was the one doing the asking. They all got into Mac's truck, drove to Wynn Hotel and Casino, and followed Slim inside to the buffet. With its vaulted ceilings, upholstered chairs, prime rib carving stations, and mounds of chilled shrimp, it was about as far removed from a charity food bank as a person could get.

"We can't go in there," Trina said. "There's no way."

"Time to put your game face on," Slim said, as Marcus stood back to watch, and Mac wandered down the mall.

***

Slim put his arm around Trina's waist and swept her into the over-the-top opulence of the Wynn buffet before she could protest and blow their cover. She looked almost giddy as Slim breezed her right by the hostess station and guided her to a two-seater table another couple had vacated mere moments before. Marcus saw Slim play the part of a perfect gentleman, helping Trina into her chair before he slid into his own seat across the table from her. Trina's eyes got big with excitement as Slim picked up a fork and knife and started shoveling the scraps that remained on the plate into his mouth.

Trina glanced at the food on her own plate, but hesitated.

Slim slipped a roll from a breadbasket into his coat pocket and drained the last swallow of a nearly empty glass of red wine down his throat and said something to Trina Marcus couldn't hear.

Trina picked up a dirty fork, examined it dubiously, then stabbed a leftover piece of chicken breast smothered in some kind of white sauce. She closed her eyes and delivered the morsel to her mouth.

Her eyes popped open. In her excitement, she whispered something to Slim and scooped up indiscriminate forkfuls of food from her plate. She paused for a second for a sip of water, then followed Slim's lead and wiped her mouth with a cloth napkin as they stood to go. Slim slipped his arm back around Trina's waist and waltzed her back by the hostess at the front of the restaurant. Slim caught the woman's eye, gave her a thumbs up—"Excellent!" he said—and guided Trina back out into the mall where Marcus was waiting.

"Oh my God! What a rush!" she exclaimed to Marcus. "And the food! I mean, it's kind of gross, but it's also *really good!*"

"Damn straight it is," Slim said.

Mac wandered back to the group.

"What's next?" Trina asked Mac.

"What's next is I'm finding me a blackjack table," Slim responded. The remark was directed to Mac. "You working tonight or not?"

"Don't abandon me now!" Trina pleaded as she slipped her hand into Mac's. "I called out for the whole night."

Mac looked from Slim to Trina, then back to Slim. "Looks like I'm calling out tonight, too."

"Suit yourself." Slim turned to leave, but Trina grabbed his coat sleeve and held him back.

"Take the night off," she urged. "Come on! Teach me the tricks of the trade. I'm a quick study, I promise!" She looked over at Marcus. "We can all learn."

Trina inched closer to Slim. She held the lapels of his suit jacket in her hands, her breasts nearly brushing against his chest. Marcus could see Slim glance down at her cleavage, pause, then take a step back.

"Big Mac here can teach you anything you need to know," Slim said, making eye contact with Mac. "I'm out of here. You can catch up with me at Caesar's later if you decide to go to work."

Trina sighed as she, Mac, and Marcus watched Slim head back out to the Strip.

"Well, that was fun while it lasted, right?" Marcus said, trying to make the best of Trina's exuberant mood.

Trina slipped her arms through each of the brother's arms as they started to make their way out of the Wynn. "Where's there another buffet we can hit up?" she asked Mac. Where should we go next?"

"Anywhere you want," Mac said. "It doesn't have to be a buffet. You can run the same kind of game at the finest restaurants in town."

"Name one!" Trina challenged him playfully.

"Mott Thirty-two. You ever hear of that place?" Mac responded immediately.

Both Trina and Marcus shook their heads no.

"It's Chinese food, but it's one of the fanciest places on the Strip. You can drop hundreds of dollars on a meal there. Drinks start at eighteen dollars a pop! I can get you in and out of there for nothing."

"With an eighteen-dollar cocktail in my hand?" Trina teased.

"Not exactly," Mac conceded.

"I'll settle for a little paper umbrella," Trina said.

Mac steered Marcus and Trina into the Venetian Resort and led them through the complex web of gaming rooms, shops, restaurants, and bars until they came to the threshold of Mott 32. It was even more opulent and elegant than the Wynn buffet.

Trina stopped walking. "I can't go in. I'm too nervous. I'll give you away."

"What about you, baby brother?" Mac asked Marcus.

"I'll stay with Trina," Marcus said.

"Brave of you!" Mac snorted. "Watch and learn, children."

Marcus and Trina huddled together outside the entrance of Mott 32 as Mac patted his pockets while he approached the young woman at the hostess stand.

"I think I left my phone at the table," he said. He pointed toward a table that had yet to be cleared.

"Please, take a look," the hostess said. She waved him in ahead of customers who were waiting in line.

They watched Mac head straight for the table, make a show of looking underneath it and around the booth benches for his allegedly missing cell phone, in between bites and sips of whatever remained of the meal on the table. He was there for less than a minute when he fished his phone out of his coat pocket.

"Ah! Got it!" he exclaimed with feigned relief, loudly enough for the hostess to hear. He slid out of the booth and waved the phone triumphantly at her on his way out the door.

"Oh! Thank goodness!" she said. "I'm so glad."

"Me, too!"

Outside the restaurant, Trina fell into Mac's arms, laughing. "I can't believe you just did that!"

Marcus was laughing, too. "What did you actually eat?" he asked.

"Damned if I know! Duck, I think. Maybe a little crab meat. It was good, though."

Mac positioned himself between Marcus and Trina, draping an arm across each of their shoulders as they strolled through the Venetian.

"That's a good ploy. I like that one," Trina said appreciatively. "But don't you ever get caught?"

"Yeah, sometimes," Mac admitted. "But what are they going to do? Call the cops? You're there for a minute, then you're gone. The most they're going to do is give you dirty looks on your way out the door. Who gives a shit?"

"I think I would," Marcus offered. "I don't think I could do it. Could you, Trina?"

The question brought a broad smile to Trina's face. "I don't know." She gave a quick shrug. "I think I *could*, but I don't know if I *would*. I'd have to be desperate. Or drunk. Or both."

"You've already done it!" Mac said. "You did it with Slim at the Wynn fifteen minutes ago."

"That's true," Trina conceded. "I just don't know if it's worth it. It's so hit-or-miss. Bites and sips. It's not like you're getting a real meal. It's not like you've actually *eaten* at Mott Thirty-two."

"You want a real meal?" Mac said. "I can get you a real meal. I can get you a steak dinner, if you've got the patience for it, and if you can swallow your pride."

"What do you mean?" Trina asked.

Mac steered the group back outside and pointed them north on the Strip. "Gallagher's Steakhouse is right up the road from here," he explained. "If you hang around outside looking pitiful enough, like a homeless person or something, somebody—usually a woman—will hand you their leftovers. Best damn steak you'll ever eat."

"That sounds like a lot of work," Trina said. "Like it could take a long time."

"It is a lot of work. That's why I usually check trash cans or dumpsters."

"You don't!" Trina slapped his arm.

"Damn straight I do. How do you think Marcus was eating fucking lobster tails for breakfast? I pulled that shit out of a trash can."

"You did?" Marcus screwed his face up in disgust.

"Yeah, I did. Come on!"

Trina and Marcus trailed after Mac. Marcus was picturing the dumpster where his breakfast had come from, as Mac led him and Trina not up to the entrance of Gallagher's but to a trash can stationed on the sidewalk several paces removed from the restaurant. Without skipping a beat, he removed the lid from the trash can and poked aside discarded plastic drink cups, cigarette packages, and napkins.

"We're in luck tonight!" he announced.

He fished a large Styrofoam takeout container out of the trash. He opened the lid and displayed the contents to his companions. Trina and Marcus peered inside, glanced at one another, then shrugged in unison.

"It looks like filet mignon, asparagus, and mashed potatoes," Trina said.

"It probably is." Mac closed the lid of the takeout container and handed it to Trina. "Bon appétit!"

Trina accepted the free meal and rewarded Mac with yet another broad smile. "This may be the strangest night of my life," she laughed.

Mac placed his arms back across the shoulders of his two companions, and the three of them strolled back toward Mac's truck in the parking lot of the Wynn casino.

"The world is my fucking oyster," Mac said. He kissed Trina on the head and squeezed Marcus's shoulder.

"Now all I need is a good night at the poker tables."

18

The sun was shining, it was mid-afternoon, yet Marcus felt as if he'd only just closed his eyes and succumbed to sleep when he heard a solid tapping on the window of Mac's truck. *Now what?* he wondered. Because there was always something going on in the parking lot of the Sandbar Suites—hookups, fist fights, drugs, arguments, uncontrolled sobbing—it was hard to get a good night's sleep.

He turned the key in the ignition, pressed the button, and the window slid down to reveal Trina standing outside his door, holding a cup of coffee.

"Today's the day." She handed him the cup through the open window.

"I can't," Marcus said blearily.

"You can. Come upstairs and get ready."

Marcus returned his seat to an upright position and sipped the hot coffee. He hoped Trina might just go away, but she didn't. She stood there as if she expected him to do something, so he opened the door and followed her up the stairs into the apartment. There were croissants—a little worse for wear, Marcus suspected they'd been slipped into a coat pocket—waiting for him on the kitchen table.

"Where's Mac?" he asked before biting into one.

"No clue." Trina shrugged. "Off somewhere with Slim."

She watched Marcus eat and drink with the same expectant look on her face she'd shown him at the truck. So, he did as she expected.

He shoved the rest of the croissant into his mouth, showered, dressed, and followed Trina back downstairs to her car. She drove him to the Kalman School of Gaming and Bartending on South Sandhill Road and walked him through the front door as if she were his mother.

When they re-emerged several hours later, Marcus fell into the passenger seat of Trina's car drained of every last ounce of energy.

"What have I done?" he asked, both dumbfounded and elated.

"You signed up for classes, like you said you wanted to do. There! It's done!" Trina held up her hand for a high five. Marcus complied weakly.

"Yeah, but really, what have I *done*? Did I sign up to go to school for free?"

"No, you didn't." Trina laughed. "You signed up for a federal loan and a grant. The loan's for nine thousand five hundred dollars. You'll have to start paying that back six months after you graduate—"

"If I graduate," Marcus cut in.

"*After* you graduate, you start paying back the loan. Grant money is free. So, that's two thousand four hundred fifty you don't have to pay back—ever."

"That's good, I guess."

"It's great!" Trina said. "Your academic advisor—"

"I have an academic advisor?"

"Yeah! Whitney, the younger woman, the one with the purple hair and the face piercings. She said once you learn your first game, you can get a job, earn some money, and still take classes part-time. Hell, I might go back on Monday and sign up for the course myself! I'd sure rather work in the casinos than at the damned Waffle Hovel. That job's not exactly a dream come true."

"Kind of expensive, though," Marcus said. He told Trina how much he owed Banana Republic, plus what he now owed the federal government. The figure made him feel queasy.

"Yeah, debt's no laughing matter," Trina said. "I got myself in over my head with credit cards once. I'll never do that again. I was paying so much in interest! It ruined my budget for years."

Marcus looked at Trina with fresh eyes. She seemed so pretty and soft, almost ethereal, with her hair floating around her head like an unruly halo. But she was tough and practical, too, as if the whole gauzy appearance of the girl was built up around a backbone of steel.

"You keep a budget?" Marcus asked, genuinely surprised.

"You bet I do." Trina came to a stop in the Sandbar Suites parking lot and turned her full attention to Marcus. "And you should, too. If I hadn't stuck to a budget when I was in debt, I never would have gotten myself back on track. Every spare penny I had went to paying down that debt. And once that debt was paid off, every spare penny I had after that went to savings."

"You have a savings account?" Marcus remembered when he had wanted to go back to Vermont and open a savings account with his share of the inheritance.

"You don't?" she shot back. "You have to save. You have to set money aside just as regular as paying rent. You'll never get ahead if you don't."

They got out of car, walked up the steps to their apartment.

"I don't have enough money to put into a savings account," Marcus said.

"Yes, you do. Everybody does," Trina said. "It may not be much at first. Five dollars a week. Ten dollars a month. The amount doesn't matter. All that matters is you do it, so it becomes a habit. Savings add up. They really do."

As they entered the apartment, Trina tossed her handbag onto Marcus's bed, a cot set up against the half-wall partition that separated the bedroom from the rest of the apartment. That's what they all called it—"Marcus's bed"—despite the fact he'd only slept in it a few times. Trina had insisted on buying it for him (from Goodwill) since she'd displaced him from the bed he'd formerly shared with his brother. Marcus had abandoned it for Mac's truck after he awoke one morning to the telltale moans and sighs of a sexual liaison between Trina and Mac. By all rights, the cot should've been known as *the place where Trina puts her purse*. Still, they all called it "Marcus's bed."

Marcus felt a pang in his heart every time he looked at the little cot. The sight of it reminded him that Trina had melted into his brother's arms, not his. He pushed aside the pain that always came along with those images and grabbed two beers from the fridge, then sat across from Trina at the dinette table.

"But I can't start saving until I pay off that loan, right?" Marcus said.

"Wrong," Trina corrected him. "You start saving now, and you keep saving even as you pay off that loan."

They sipped their beers in silence for a moment, each lost in their own thoughts.

"I love saving money," Trina admitted after a while. "I love seeing that figure go up, slow and steady, always going up. It's weird, though, you know? When I don't have money, that's when I want things I don't need. I want that dress. I want those shoes. I want that bracelet. Stupid shit, you know?"

Marcus nodded, although he'd never experienced anything like that himself.

"Then once I have the money," Trina continued, "the desire goes away. It's like I can take a step back and realize the dress, or whatever, isn't what I really want. It's not what I need."

"What is it you actually need?" Marcus asked. He relished any opportunity to get closer to Trina, and in this moment, he felt closer to her than he ever had before.

"Security," Trina announced without hesitation. "Certainty. Power! Knowing I have, like, this army of money behind me, that it will be there for me when I need it. It's *mine*. It's there for *me*. I can do with it what I want. No one can take that away from me."

Trina shrugged and sipped her beer. She averted her eyes from Marcus's rapt attention.

"I don't know," she said, looking suddenly embarrassed. "I like my savings account. What can I say? It makes me feel . . . safe."

"That's good," Marcus said. "You should feel safe. You deserve to feel safe."

Another awkward silence hung between them. Then Marcus shyly asked the question they both knew was dangling between them.

"How much have you saved up? I mean, I don't want to pry. But how much have you saved?"

Trina took a moment to consider her answer. "I would say I feel safe-ish. Like if my car goes to hell tomorrow, I can pay cash and get at least something to replace it. Or, if I wanted to, or if I had to, I could afford to live in some kind of shitty place of my own. I don't have to stay with you and Mac. I can leave if I have to. So, I'm not in the worst situation possible. Things could be worse. I feel safe-ish."

"Seriously? You're choosing to live here? Why?" Marcus couldn't imagine anyone with the means to do otherwise opting to live at the Sandbar Suites, least of all with the likes of him and Mac.

"Because it's so much cheaper," Trina responded as if her reasoning were obvious. "Me and Ben were paying two thousand a month rent, plus utilities. Two hundred a month here, with no utilities? That saves me a lot of money."

"Yeah, but . . ." Marcus's words trailed off as he gestured around the cramped space the three of them shared together. "I mean, why settle for this?"

"I'm not settling," Trina stated firmly. "I'm saving. I'm building toward something better. I wasn't 'settling' for what I had with Ben, either. I was biding my time. Waiting for the right moment when I had enough money to move out on my own without winding up at the Salvation Army. Vegas is expensive. It's hard to store up enough money to pay first and last month's rent, get the electric turned on, pay an application fee at a decent apartment complex. I don't have any family or friends here, not really. I only have myself to depend on. I had a plan. Then you came along and fucked everything up."

"I really did, didn't I?" Marcus grinned and shook his head.

"Yeah! You really did!"

They were both laughing when Mac opened the door.

"What the fuck is going on here?" he asked, half-joking, half-serious.

He leaned down to Trina to touch his hand to her hair and kiss her on the lips.

"We're discussing budgets and savings accounts," Trina chirped. "I'm gonna help your brother get on the right track with his finances."

"Is that so?" Mac got a beer for himself from the fridge.

"Yeah, it is. And he starts gaming school on Monday, too."

"The fuck he is." Mac scowled at Marcus and took his first swig of beer. "You're going to school? When the hell did that happen?"

"This afternoon," Marcus said. "Trina took me over there. You should've seen her. She's good at getting shit done. I don't think I could've done it without her."

"Really." Mac slid Trina out of her seat, took the chair for himself and pulled her back down onto his lap. They still only had two chairs among the three of them.

"And how much does this so-called school cost? And how the fuck are you gonna pay for it?" Mac demanded.

"Loans and grants," Trina answered on Marcus's behalf. The light-hearted atmosphere in the room had suddenly turned dark. Trina kissed Mac's cheek, trying to coax the scowl off his face.

"A loan? For how much?" Mac's eyes bored into Marcus's skull.

"It's a Stafford loan for nine thousand five hundred," Trina said. Mac tossed her off his lap.

"Let the little shit speak for himself," Mac snapped. He glared even harder at his brother. "And where do you think you're going to get nine thousand five hundred dollars? Do you think you're getting that money from me? Or Slim? Is that what you think?"

Marcus felt the blood drain from his face as Trina backed up from Mac, retreating into what passed for a kitchen. Marcus's first thought was to admit he wasn't thinking at all. That would've been the truth, because he felt as if his brain had shut down and his body was shrinking smaller and smaller. This was what he'd always done, make himself go numb and small, anything to make the verbal assaults and the physical blows less painful.

But Mac turned his ire on Trina. "This is your doing," he said, taking a step toward Trina, glaring at her instead of Marcus. "You can't keep your nose out of other people's business? You gotta take him down to that school and get him hooked up with God knows what? A loan, my ass! That fucking school is going to cheat him out of everything he has!"

"The loan is an investment in his future." Trina parroted the words the financial advisor had used while Marcus had signed the loan paperwork.

"An investment?" Mac spat the words in Trina's face.

She tried to back farther away from Mac, but she was already pressed up against the kitchen sink. There was no place else for her to go.

"He had a chance to make an investment, a real one, and he fucking turned it down. I brought him out here so he could take a chance on something real, something big. Me and Slim are doing all the work. All he has to do is keep his mouth shut and tag along. Does he do that? No! He stirs up trouble and pisses my money away on worthless shit. He'll fuck everything up for me. I know he will."

"How?" Trina pointed toward Marcus, still glued to his seat at the kitchen table. "How exactly is Marcus fucking things up for you?"

Mac took one more step toward Trina before Marcus found his voice.

"Back off! Leave her alone!" Marcus shouted. "It's my money! It's my decision! I'll pay the loan back when I get a job. It's got nothing to do with you! Why can't you just leave me the fuck alone?"

Mac wheeled on his brother. The blow he delivered to Marcus's head knocked him out of his chair. Curled on the floor, Mac looming over him, Marcus could feel the rage radiating off Mac like a heat wave.

"I should have left you alone. I wish the fuck I had," he snarled. "I should've left you alone with the old man and let him beat the shit out of you for as long as he wanted. I should've left you in Florida and let you find your own way back home. I should've left you in Colorado.

I should've left you to your own devices to deal with Ben. You'd be a dead man by now, and we'd all be the better off for it."

"Mac, stop it!" Trina pleaded. "He's your brother, for God's sake. Let him go."

Mac got down on one knee and leaned over Marcus's body, bringing their faces close together. Marcus, still crumpled on the floor, tried to look up at his brother. Mac leaned in even closer, addressing his brother in an angry hiss.

"All I've ever done is look out for you. It's *all* I've ever done. But I swear to God, Marcus, if this deal goes sideways for me here, if you cause any more trouble for me *or* Slim, I'll fucking kill you. You got that?"

Marcus nodded his head.

"Good!"

Mac rose and hitched up his pants, scorn for his younger brother etched into every line of his face.

"Who the fuck do you think you are anyhow, going to school?"

19

Marcus had no doubt about who the fuck he was. He was nobody. He was nothing. Always had been. Always would be.

And yet, when Monday morning rolled around, Marcus somehow found the wherewithal to climb out of Mac's truck, tiptoe into the bathroom, wash his face, brush his teeth, shave, comb his hair, and set out for his first day of classes at Kalman. He didn't expect much to come of it. Having survived high school by sitting at the back of the class and keeping his mouth shut. He'd taken the easiest classes available. He'd doodled and daydreamed for four years, and neither his teachers nor his fellow classmates had paid him much mind.

The very real possibility his instructors and classmates at Kalman might actually expect something of him—might notice him; might expect him to answer questions, maybe even to ask questions; might expect him to learn something—tied his stomach into a knot. Fool that he was, Marcus had dared to believe Trina might be there offering encouragement on this first day of the rest of his life. He'd imagined her staying up after her shift at the Waffle House, delaying getting into bed next to Mac, so she could make sure Marcus had a notebook and pens, that he knew where he was going and he'd get there on time. He'd pictured her packing a sack lunch for him! He'd hoped she'd take him by his shoulders, look straight into his eyes and declare: "You can *do* this!"

But as Marcus stepped out of the bathroom, Trina merely gazed at him through sleepy eyes, gave him a wan smile, then nuzzled her face against Mac's shoulder and went back to sleep.

The almost-sure prospect of failure churned in Marcus's guts. Even as his feet walked him in the direction of the school, he thought about quitting. He rehearsed a line-up of the lame excuses he'd use to cover his ass and explain why gaming school hadn't worked out for him. *The student loan money didn't come through. The teachers sucked. He couldn't get the classes he wanted.* As if he needed an excuse. As if anyone cared. Did Mac care? Did Slim care? Did Trina?

He was pathetic, and he knew it. Always had been, always would be. Still, he turned himself in the direction of the Kalman School of Gaming and put one foot in front of the other until he arrived at the school. It was a long enough walk for him to smoke two cigarettes and take a couple of tokes of weed as he made his way to school.

As he slunk through the front door, walked hesitantly down a short hallway, located his classroom, and took a seat at the back of the room, he wasn't sure he gave a flying fuck, either. He found himself seated next to a barrel-chested, heavily tattooed, middle-aged man whose right leg bounced up and down in a fit of nervous energy. The man stuck out his right hand.

"Al McMinnis, long-haul trucker," he said, giving Marcus a firm handshake.

"Marcus Brown," Marcus replied, adding, "just Marcus," since he had no occupation to attach to his name. Al didn't seem to notice.

"You done this kind of thing before, taken classes, I mean?" Al asked.

Marcus shook his head.

"Yeah, me neither." Al leaned in close to Marcus and talked almost in a whisper. "I don't know that I might not have the aptitude for it, as they say."

"Me neither," Marcus admitted.

"Well, we'll give it a try, right? It doesn't hurt to try, right?"

Marcus nodded. In fact, however, he strongly suspected trying had the potential to be extremely painful, if failure and humiliation counted as pain. For those things not to hurt, Marcus knew he'd have to make himself go numb. Trying *did* hurt, but you could find ways to pretend it didn't.

More students found their way into the classroom, including a plump girl with long blonde hair who took a seat in front of Marcus and Al. She immediately spun around in her seat and started talking to them.

"I don't know what the fuck I'm doing here!" she blurted out. Her eyes were rimmed with tears.

"That seems to be a catching thing," Al commented dryly.

It made both Marcus and the girl laugh at the very moment the instructor, a slim young man with a bald head and an athlete's build, walked into the room. He introduced himself as Mr. Williams, and after he took roll, he told the twenty or so students to pair up with a buddy and spend the next five minutes finding out as much about that person as they could.

"Be prepared to report on what you learned," Mr. Williams warned them. "Good luck! And go!"

The blonde girl whipped back around to Al and Marcus with a look of panic on her face. "Let's us three do it! I don't want to buddy up. I like you guys. Us three can do it."

Without waiting for her fellow classmates to agree, she launched into speed-dating director mode. She fired questions at the two men— *Where are you from? Are you married? Kids? Job? Education? Hobbies? Girlfriends? Where do you live?*—barely giving them time to answer one question before she raced on to the next. She didn't give either of the guys a chance to ask her a single question. The second she finished interrogating them, she spit out the details of her own young life in less than a minute.

When it was their group's turn to present their findings to the rest of the class, she stood up and got the ball rolling with her snapshot of Al.

"This is Al McMinnis." She put a hand on Al's shoulder. "He's fifty-two years old. He's been a long-haul trucker for the last fifteen years. He's tired of being on the road all the time 'cause he misses his wife and his two teenage daughters. He lives here in Vegas, so he figures he might as well work here in Vegas, too. And that's why he's here this morning."

The girl sat down and motioned for Marcus to stand. He blushed and stammered through his introduction.

"This is . . . this is, uh, Jessica . . ."

"Duvall," Jessica whispered to Marcus.

"Duvall. Jessica Duvall. She's, uh, eighteen years old. She grew up in Idaho and she, uh, said she was having nightmares about turning into a white potato."

Everyone in the room tittered appreciatively.

"Uh, that was about, um, a month ago," Marcus continued. "And one day Jessica, uh, packed up her Ford Focus with whatever she could fit in it, and she left. And, uh, now she's here."

Marcus resumed his seat with his face burning, but he was pleased nonetheless to have made it through the presentation without totally embarrassing himself. He stared at his feet as Al stood to present his introduction of Marcus.

"This young man is Marcus Brown. I forget how old he is. But he grew up in Vermont and he's come to Vegas by way of Florida. He just recently suffered the loss of both his parents in some kind of tragic accident, and he and his older brother have come to Vegas to start a new life together."

As Al took his seat, he patted Marcus on the back. To Marcus's astonishment, the entire class burst into a heartfelt round of applause. When Marcus lifted his eyes from the floor, he found Mr. Williams gazing at him with kind and serious eyes.

"We're all sorry for your loss, Marcus," Mr. Williams said. Other students nodded their heads in sympathy. Then Mr. Williams took in the whole class with his compassionate eyes.

"Anyone else show up here this morning looking for a fresh start?" he asked the class.

Ten or more students tentatively raised their hands. Mr. Williams pointed at one of them in the back row.

"You, sir! Tell me about that young lady sitting right next to you," he said. "Is she looking for a new lease on life?"

Mr. Williams went around the whole room. Marcus listened intently as each student in turn stood to give their outline of the person who just happened to be sitting next to them that morning. They were a motley crew, to be sure. Old and young. Male and female. Some looking for career changes, others looking for ways to pass their days with part-time work in retirement. There were single mothers struggling to put food on the table for their kids; divorced homemakers striking out on their own for the first time in twenty years; former salaried executives tired of the bullshit of their corporate lives; line cooks determined to get out of the nerve-wracking, fast-paced environment of restaurant kitchens. Waitresses who wanted to become dealers. Dishwashers who wanted to become bartenders.

When it started, the introduction exercise had seemed corny to Marcus. If he could've hid in the back and avoided the public exposure, he would have. But by the time the last student finished his report and sat back down at his desk, the cascade of personal details had the cumulative effect of making Marcus feel at home in the classroom. His story was not much different from anyone else's, and neither were his prospects for the future.

He'd started the day certain of failure. But as he looked at his classmates and included himself among them, it struck Marcus as unreasonable to assume everyone in the room was destined to fail. Surely, not every one of them was a loser. Surely, some of them, maybe even including himself, would succeed.

At the end of that first class, both Jessica and Al offered Marcus a ride home. He declined. "I think I'll walk. Clear my head."

Marcus was, in fact, lost in his own thoughts at the end of that day. But he was also in no hurry to arrive home if that's what Room 310 at the Sandbar Suites was supposed to be. He knew what awaited him there. Mac's hostility. Slim's scorn. Trina's betrayals. The neighbors fighting and whoring, dealing and stealing. Why rush?

He made his way to the library instead. He nodded hello to Ray, the librarian who had helped him, and was about to log in to a computer to check his emails, when it occurred to him that Ray, unlike everyone at home, might actually be interested in knowing he'd survived his first day of school. So, Marcus ambled over to the circulation counter.

"Just came from Kalman. The gaming school," he said bashfully. "First day of class."

"Seriously? That's awesome!" Ray turned to a colleague, a red-haired girl Marcus had seen there before. "Marcia, Marcus just finished his first day at Kalman."

Marcia peeked around the edge of her computer screen and offered Marcus a thumbs up.

"Cool! You gonna be a card dealer?" she asked.

"Maybe." Marcus shrugged. "I signed up for gaming and bartending. Kind of leaning more toward the bar thing, to be honest. Can't quite picture myself running a table."

"Not yet maybe. But you never know," Marcia said. "Learn some skills. Gain some confidence. You might really enjoy being at the head of a table. It's kind of sexy."

"Like I said, I'm leaning more toward bartending." Marcus laughed.

Marcia smiled at him. "That can be sexy, too. Girls fall in love with bartenders all the time. Or at least I do. There's something about them, mixing up drinks behind the bar. They just look so cool."

"Hey! Come with me for a second," Ray interjected, rescuing Marcus from Marcia's flirtations.

Ray came around the circulation desk, and Marcus followed him to the section of the library that featured books about travel. He pulled out a copy of the latest *Fodor's: Las Vegas* and handed it to Marcus.

"You should study this, especially if you're tending bar. People are always asking for tips about where to go, what to do, where's the best steak in Vegas, that kind of thing. I've heard people say it really increases their tips when they can just rattle off useful information about the Strip. You can never know it all, but I bet even a little information goes a long way."

Marcus thanked Ray for the advice. After he glanced at his emails and applied for another job (pool attendant at the Tropicana), he checked out the book with his new library card and set himself adrift among the constant flow of humanity along the Strip. He wandered in and out of bars and casinos, nursing beers while he flipped through the pages of *Fodor's: Las Vegas*. The book overwhelmed him at first, page after page of maps, information about hotels, restaurants, vintage clothing stores, cannabis shops, bars, casinos, golf courses, shopping malls, spas, racetracks, walking trails, airports, taxis, rail lines . . .

No kidding, I'll never learn it all!

Moments later, however, standing at the corner of Las Vegas Boulevard and Reno Avenue, holding a beer in one hand and *Fodor's* in the other, looking at the tram line on his left and the Tropicana to his right, something clicked.

"South Strip," he mouthed. He tucked the book into the shoplifting pocket Trina had sewn into the inside of his sport coat, and resumed his walk. Heading south along the Boulevard, he sipped his beer and paid attention to every sight he passed.

This is the South Strip, he said to himself. *The Tropicana. The Luxor. Mandalay Bay. The Four Seasons Hotel. Hershey's Chocolate World.*

For the first time since he'd arrived in Las Vegas, the city started to make sense to him. He wasn't exactly at home in it, but neither was he totally lost.

Marcus timed his Fodor's tutorial and his journey back to the Sandbar Suites so he could pass by the Waffle House in time to see Trina. Not that he imagined she actually cared about him. But, if any place in Vegas felt like home to him, it was the damned Waffle House.

He'd been going there regularly for weeks. Why shouldn't he be welcome there now?

He got his answer: Mac. Marcus's heart sank as he stood across the street from the Waffle House and spied Mac sitting at the counter where Marcus had once sat. Trina was refilling Mac's coffee cup, smiling at him, taking care of him. He wondered if Mac was stuffing his face with steak and eggs again and bragging about his big winnings. He wondered if Mac was selling his bullshit story about the silver mine. He wondered if Trina was buying it. He wondered if Trina loved Mac, or if Mac loved Trina. He wondered if any of that mattered anymore.

Then he had had enough. "Fuck 'em!" Marcus said aloud.

He made his way to the Sandbar Suites, where he stretched out on the big bed in Room 310 and continued flipping through *Fodor's: Las Vegas* until he fell asleep.

20

With Kalman as his base point, Marcus settled into a new routine. Roll out of the truck in the morning. Shower and shave. Go to school. Go to the library. Walk the Strip. Study Fodor's. Watch TV. Crawl back into the truck.

He didn't reckon it was much of a life. But with Al and Jessica and Mr. Williams seemingly on his side, and with Mac and Slim and Trina to be avoided, it suited him, nonetheless. He was still jittery. He still smoked and toked as he made his way to the corner of Flamingo and South Sandhill every day. But it was a new kind of nervous, one born of hope and excitement rather than dread and anxiety. It might not amount to much, but he was at least doing *something*.

Without anyone of them saying a word, Marcus, Al, and Jessica became their own little Kalman family—Al the world-weary dad, Marcus and Jessica his adopted kids. All three of them had signed up for the dual program, learning to tend bar and run all the different gaming tables Vegas had to offer. Both Marcus and Jessica said they hoped they wouldn't have to start with poker first.

"How many different versions of poker do they have, anyhow?" Jessica whispered to Marcus on the second day of class.

"I don't know," Marcus whispered back. "My brother's the poker player, not me. I don't know a royal flush from a full house. But I can count to twenty-one, so I'd rather start with blackjack."

"Me, too," Jessica said.

Al grinned as he eavesdropped on their conversation. "Y'all are pitiful," he whispered. "Stick with me. I can teach you to play poker."

And stick together they did. They sat together at the front of the class. They ate their lunches together. They always had a deck of cards at hand, and they played blackjack and various games of poker every chance they got.

At the end of their first week, they hopped into Jessica's Ford Focus and treated themselves to a round of beers at Circus Circus. Marcus introduced Jake to his new friends. They sat at a high-top table and took turns dealing cards. Then they cruised through the casino itself. Marcus watched the professional dealers through newly-opened student eyes. The three compared notes on what they saw, and talked about what it would be like to control tables of their own.

When Jessica dropped Marcus off at the Sandbar Suites that Friday night, she surveyed his surroundings with knowing eyes.

"I sure hope we're doing the right thing," she mused as Marcus slid out of the car. "There's gotta be something better than this, right?"

"I sure hope so."

As Jessica pulled away, Marcus heard a ruckus boiling over somewhere among the upper levels of the apartment complex. Sleeping in the truck, he'd adjusted to the raised voices, the slamming doors, the hands slapping faces, as if they were the normal ambient sounds of a nearby highway or railroad track. He'd learned to block them out. But these voices grabbed his attention.

"It's my money! I'll do whatever the fuck I want with it!" Mac yelled loud enough from behind the closed door of Room 310 for everyone in the complex to hear him.

"The hell you will!" Slim roared back. "Do you know what the fuck we're up against here? The bill is coming due, buddy. And these motherfuckers are gonna get what's owed them one way or another."

"I can handle them," Mac bragged.

"The fuck you can!" Slim countered. "This ain't like back home.

This here is real business, with real consequences. You fuck this up, you'll be on your own. I'll be damned if I take the fall for you again."

Those last words from Slim struck fear in Marcus's heart. Marcus had never been able to unravel the mystery of what had happened between Mac and Slim back home when they were teenagers, and he was just a boy. He knew a man had been killed. He knew Slim had been held responsible for the man's death. He knew Slim had gone to prison, while Mac stayed home and finished high school.

It had seemed to Marcus a safe assumption back then that Slim was the more dangerous of the two older boys. Mac was a hothead and a brute. But Slim wasn't just volatile, he was literally lethal. To question that assumption now made Marcus's heart race but question it he did. Were Mac's fits of rage really less dangerous than Slim's? And if they weren't, what did it mean when Slim said he'd be damned if he took the fall for Mac again? *What exactly had Mac done back then?*

The thought crossed Marcus's mind just as he spotted Trina. She was alone, smoking a cigarette and drinking a beer at the patio table next to the pool. He joined her, took a deck of cards out of his shirt pocket, and started shuffling them as Mac and Slim erupted out of Room 310 onto the third-floor walkway.

"That's your fucking problem, not mine!" Mac spat in the face of his oldest and closest friend.

"Motherfucking coward!"

Slim pushed Mac in the chest. Mac answered with a fist in Slim's face, forcing him to his knees. But only for a second. Slim shot back up and landed a powerful blow to Mac's gut.

Men, women, and children appeared on every walkway and gathered in small groups in the parking lot, gawking at the two combatants as they slugged out their differences on the walkway. This being Vegas, bets were made, and Marcus heard most folks put their money on Mac. *Rookie mistake, betting against Slim in a slugfest*, Marcus thought. He shuffled his cards to calm his nerves and glanced cautiously at Trina.

"What's that about?" he asked.

"The silver mine. What else?" Trina flicked ashes off the end of her cigarette and sipped from the bottle of beer.

"What's the problem?" Marcus asked.

"Money! What else would the fucking problem be?" Trina responded angrily, as if Marcus were responsible for the violence taking place outside their apartment.

"Sorry!" Trina stubbed out her cigarette. "All I know is they need like eighty grand for this deal to go through. And they don't have it. They were doing good for a while. They were on track, or so Mac thought."

"What happened?"

"I don't know for sure." Trina lit a new cigarette and lowered her voice. "Mac thinks Slim is losing money at the tables. Money's gone missing from the account. Mac's not sure he wants to bankroll Slim anymore. It's a mess."

Marcus inched closer to Trina's side of the table as they, along with all their neighbors, watched Mac and Slim continue to do battle. Panting for breath, Mac was backed up against the door of Room 310, prepared, it seemed, for a killer punch. Instead of finishing Mac off, however, Slim spat a stream of blood out of his mouth. Gripping the rail with one hand, he pointed dramatically toward Trina and Marcus at the pool.

"Get the whore to help you!" Slim shouted, deliberately loud enough for Trina to hear. "She's got the money! If you weren't such a pussy, you'd get it from her and this fucking deal would be done! We're this close! This close!"

All eyes turned to Trina. Marcus reached across the table to hold her hand, but she brushed him off. She sat up straighter in her chair, lifted her arm above her head, and flipped the world a middle finger.

"Not gonna happen. Not in a million fucking years," she said under her breath to Marcus.

Then Slim delivered the blow to Mac's head that made his knees crumple beneath him.

A chorus of "Fuck!" "Damn!" "Can you fucking believe that?" rang out from the good people of the Sandbar Suites.

"Fuck you all!" Slim bellowed. "Fuck you all to hell!"

"Yeah, fuck you, too!" came back from the crowd.

Slim slipped an arm around Mac's waist and pulled him back to his feet. Their rage apparently depleted, they held onto one another as they dragged themselves back into Room 310, slamming the door behind them.

Marcus stared at Trina, imploring her with his eyes to talk to him.

"What? What exactly do you want from me?" she snapped.

"I don't want anything from you," he said, raising his voice, "but they sure as shit do!" Marcus pointed up to the third-floor, to the empty space that had been occupied by Mac and Slim. "And they'll get it, too. You understand that, don't you?"

Trina jabbed a finger in Marcus's face. "They'll never get my money."

"They got mine!"

"That's because you're *you*! You let Mac walk all over you. Don't think I don't see it. I'm *me*! That's not going to happen to *me*."

Marcus bolted from his seat, raked his fingers through his hair as he paced back and forth in front of Trina. The last of the setting sun was at her back, turning her loose reddish hair into a glowing halo of fire around her small, pale face. She was, to Marcus, both a heavenly creature from another planet and an infuriatingly earth-bound stubborn girl.

"I love you," Marcus declared. He pointed again to the third-floor walkway. "They don't! And if you had any sense at all, you'd leave. Now. Tonight. Before it's too late. You have no idea what those two are capable of . . ."

"Those two?" Trina fixed Marcus with a steely, unwavering gaze. "I just hope they don't beat each other to death before they pull things together with the silver mine."

Marcus sighed and sat back down opposite Trina at the table.

"You don't actually think that's a real thing, do you?" he asked.

"I think it's a real *scam*," Trina said. "I have my doubts about whether those two can pull the thing off. But there are bigger men than them involved in this thing. I don't know who they are. I've never seen them come around. But I promise you, Slim and Mac are pawns in someone else's game. Either way, I'm going to stick around until I see how this thing plays itself out."

"Why? What's in it for you?" Marcus pleaded.

"Money, maybe." Trina looked up at the closed door of Room 310.

"It's too risky," Marcus said. "It's dangerous. Mac doesn't treat you right. He hurts you."

Trina met Marcus's gaze directly for a second, startled by the insinuation that Mac was abusive. But just as quickly, she snorted and looked away, flicking ashes from her cigarette as she did so.

"I can take care of myself just fine. I never asked you to barge into my life and rescue me, if that's what you think you've done. You'd do well to look after yourself. Mac beats on you, not me. Slim, too. Slim's never laid a hand on me. You can't say the same, can you? You're the one who ought to leave, not me."

"I'm working on it." Marcus laughed grimly. "But I don't have any money yet."

"Well, don't look at me. You know where I stand on that."

They smiled at one another like friends.

"But seriously," Trina said. "Mac treats you like shit. Why *do* you stay?"

Marcus shrugged. "He's my brother."

"And?"

Trina's blue eyes were somehow both kind and unsparing at the same time. It wasn't much of a question, really. Still, Marcus didn't seem to have an answer for it.

"And . . . he's my big brother," Marcus said with another shrug.

"Brotherly love? That explains everything?" Trina said dismissively. "'Blood is thicker than water.' 'Family is everything.' That shit is what keeps you hanging around?"

"I guess," Marcus said, with no conviction.

They shared a moment of silence, as if an unbridgeable chasm existed between them. Marcus knew Trina wasn't the angel he'd once thought her to be. She was harsher and more calculating than he would've ever imagined. But he loved her still.

"We should both leave. Together. You and me," Marcus blurted.

"You're such a dope!" Trina laughed. "You know that, right?"

The two dissolved in a spasm of giggles just as Mac swung open the squeaky pool gate and approached them. "What the fuck are you two laughing about now?"

They laughed even harder as Trina reached for Mac's hand and kissed it. "Life! We're laughing about life. It's all one big fucking joke. Now sit down and let me get you a beer."

Trina kissed Mac on a bruised cheek as he folded his battered body into a seat at the table, then she headed off with her car keys in hand to make a beer run.

Marcus watched her go, glowing in the warmth of their shared laughter, grateful for whatever remnants of friendship, or love, remained between them. When he turned his attention back to Mac, his brother leaned across the table and gripped his forearm.

"That pussy belongs to me now. And don't you fucking forget it."

21

ussy. The word burned a hole in Marcus's brain as he trudged off to school the next day. He was a pussy. Trina was a pussy. Hell, everyone in Vegas was a pussy. Whatever optimism he'd clung to about himself and his classmates vanished as quickly as it had appeared. *What a bunch of fucking losers*, he thought as he took his accustomed seat between Al and Jessica. Mac was right. Like everyone else who comes to Vegas, he was being played. He was just getting played at a different kind of table. Kalman was no different than a blackjack game or a poker tournament. They'd lured him in with federal loans and grants and the promise of a jackpot in the form of a decent job, and now he was learning he'd bet all his money on a losing hand.

"Anyone know what the average starting pay is for a Vegas dealer?" Mr. Williams asked the class that morning. "Fifteen an hour? Twenty? Ten? Anyone care to take a guess?"

"Twenty," someone called out.

"Less," said another. "More like fifteen."

"Unfortunately, you're both wrong," Mr. Williams informed them. "Most casinos start dealers at minimum wage."

"What the fuck?" Jessica muttered under her breath. Then she spoke up for the entire class. "Are you serious? I signed up for an education that's going to keep me earning minimum wage? How's that a fresh start? No one gets ahead making minimum wage. How are we supposed to live?"

"Tips," Mr. Williams announced, for which he received a shared groan from his students. Marcus shared a looked with Al and Jessica.

"Don't despair. There's a ton of money to be made at the tables, I promise. The real money isn't in your paycheck. The real money is in your tips. Which is why just knowing the rules of the game, just showing up and putting in your time, isn't the only thing you need to work on. If you want to get ahead, if you really want to succeed, you need to develop a public persona as well. You need to develop a style, a personality, a way of working with people that makes them want to give you their money." The class fell into a dismal silence.

"They might have mentioned that before we signed on to the program," a dejected female student said. "I'm not exactly Miss Congeniality."

"Me, neither," Jessica said as she shifted uneasily in her seat and pulled her long shirt almost down to her knees. She seemed to be self-conscious about her weight.

"You're not Miss Congeniality *yet*," Mr. Williams said.

He was one of the younger instructors. Lean and fit, he'd gone bald early, but he had a megawatt smile and an easy confidence. He'd told the class he'd been a successful dealer. The students trusted him. Or they had.

"Just like you're not a dealer yet," Mr. Williams continued. "Interacting with the public is a skill you learn like any other. You need to identify your strengths and weaknesses. Develop your strengths, minimize your weaknesses. In other words, be yourself, but better."

When the class broke for lunch, Marcus, Jessica, and Al gathered outside around a battered picnic table. They ate their lunches with a gloomy air of defeat.

"I'm fucked," Marcus said, breaking a long silence that had ensued. "I don't have any strengths."

"What're you talking about?" Jessica seemed genuinely surprised. "You're adorable! Women are going to love you. Heck, they'll tip you with the keys to their hotel rooms. I'm the one who's fucked."

Now Marcus and Al were the surprised ones.

"What're *you* talking about?" Marcus asked.

"What do you think?" Jessica shot back. "Look at me. I'm fat!"

"You're not fat," Al said, not looking up from his ham and cheese sandwich. "You're full, like Marilyn Monroe, curvy in all the right places. Guys will be all over you."

"Look, no one is fucked," Al continued. "It's like Williams said. People come to Vegas to spend their money. It's literally what they come here to do. We just have to find a way to get them to toss some of it our way."

Al balled up his empty brown paper bag and scored a three-pointer as he tossed it into a trash can several feet beyond Jessica's shoulder.

"How?" Marcus asked.

"By deciding who we're going to be and working on it, just like Williams said. Like right now," Al turned to Jessica. "Who do you want to be?"

"Anyone but me, the potato girl."

Marcus sympathized. He'd like to be pretty much anybody other than himself, too.

The conversation seemed to have reached a dead end. The three friends sat in silence. But after a few moments, Jessica found her voice again.

"When I think about it," she said tentatively, not looking at either of the men. "When I actually think about myself running a table, I almost picture myself like I'm a person in an advertisement. I don't look like I do now. My hair is done. My makeup's done. My nails are done. I look good in my uniform, put together. Still fat, but more like heavy, because I look good. I'm smiling. I'm enjoying myself. I look like a girl who likes what she's doing." She laughed self-consciously when she met Marcus's attentive gaze.

"I picture myself with shoulder length, curly blond hair," she continued, "instead of this straight hair I've had since I was a kid. Like that curly blonde hair would be the new me."

Marcus and Al studied Jessica in silence, both nodding their heads.

"That's not a bad idea," Al said. "Change your appearance. Assume a new identity. Create a new character for yourself. I need to stop being a truck driver. Stop dressing like one, too."

Now they turned their attention to Marcus.

"What about you? Who do you want to stop being?" Jessica asked him.

A pussy came to Marcus's mind. Jessica and Al didn't know he'd already changed his hair and his clothes, and he still felt like the same loser he had always been and suspected he would always be. Jessica seemed to sense the depth of discomfort this turn in the conversation was causing Marcus.

"Who do you need to stop being?" she asked again, gentle, but more persistent than the first time.

Marcus knew the answer, but he found it intensely difficult to say aloud what he knew to be true. He'd known it for years, and especially over the last couple of months, the truth had been drilled into him more than ever. But he had never actually *said* it. Until now.

"I need to stop being Mac's baby brother. I need to fucking grow up."

"There you go." Al patted Marcus on the shoulder. The three friends sat quietly for another moment. Then Jessica piped up.

"So, it's settled? We're doing this? We're all in this together?" she looked each of the men in the eye. "I'm not the Potato Girl anymore? You're not the truck driver anymore? You're not the kid brother anymore?"

Marcus and Al nodded.

"You swear?" she asked.

"Scout's honor," Al said.

"Promise," Marcus said.

"Good," Jessica said. "Because I don't think I can do this on my own."

Nothing has changed, Marcus told himself as Mr. Williams directed him to train at a roulette wheel for the remainder of that class period. *Or has it?* When Marcus glanced across the way at Jessica dealing blackjack to their classmates, he was startled to realize he was, in fact, already seeing her differently. He couldn't point to any one thing that was different over the course of the thirty-minute lunch break. But she struck him as suddenly seeming more capable and confident. Same with Al. Marcus looked at him dealing cards at a poker table, with his baseball cap off for the first time, and Al, too, seemed suddenly more in tune to what he was doing.

Marcus imagined a change had come over him, too. Something in his mind clicked. The layout and rules of the roulette table that had once been incomprehensible now seemed easy and familiar. Inside and outside bets. Columns and dozens. Straight up pays thirty-five to one. Split pays seventeen to one. Corner is eight to one. Street. Double street. Top line. As his classmates placed their bets and the roulette wheel spun around and around, Marcus ran the table without a hitch. He felt relaxed, comfortable, almost cool. A girl flirted with him. He almost flirted back. *Give me a few more days,* he thought, *and I'll actually do it.*

Marcus carried that new-found confidence with him when he checked his emails at the library Friday afternoon. He'd come to not expect much from the countless job applications he kept sending out. But when he opened an email from Circus Circus and read a bar manager there wanted him to come in for a job interview the next morning, he wasn't nearly as shocked as he'd expected to be. Only scared and anxious to the point he hesitated about what his response should be. He considered ignoring the email altogether, or deleting it outright, or lying and saying he wasn't available—anything to avoid another inevitable humiliation, the look of disappointment that would cross the bar manager's face the second he saw Marcus in person.

That was a possibility, for sure. But as Marcus pushed back from the computer screen and looked around himself at the Clark County library, he knew it wasn't a sure bet. Mac and Slim could call him a pussy all they wanted. But that wasn't the way Ray and Marcia at the library saw him. That wasn't the way Al and Jessica, and Mr. Williams at the gaming school saw him. It might not even be the way Trina, who'd sent him in this direction in the first place, saw him. It might not even be the way he saw himself anymore—the inevitable sure loser.

Marcus's fingers hovered over the keyboard. *Christ! Don't be such a pussy!* he told himself. He typed in his response—*Yes, I would be happy to meet the bar manager at Circus Circus for a job interview tomorrow morning*—and pressed SEND.

22

With two hours to spare before the library closed, Marcus settled into a cushioned chair in a reading room and opened *Fodor's: Las Vegas*. He'd purchased his own copy, one he kept with him all the time. He no longer browsed through its pages as if he were a tourist, searching for nuggets of information he'd soon forget. He read it, repeatedly, from cover to cover, underlining things that interested him, and scribbling notes in the margins. He absorbed as much about Las Vegas in the abstract as he could before he had to leave the library.

Then, as had become his habit of late, he headed out into the night and made his way to the Strip to experience some of what he'd read about firsthand. Some things remained beyond his grasp. He would never have enough money to reserve himself a seat for dinner on the patio at the LAGO, which *Fodor's* said provided one of the best views in town of the fountain show at the Bellagio. But he knew where it was, and he knew the chef's name, and he knew the menu specialized in small plate Italian fare, and you needed to make a reservation, probably months in advance, and not show up in a tank top or open-toed shoes.

Other experiences were more accessible. He could afford the twenty-dollar price of admission to see for himself the two thousand species of aquatic life on display at the Shark Reef Aquarium at Mandalay Bay. But, it didn't cost him a thing to make his way over to Fremont

Street and marvel at the free LED light show that played out each night in the enormous canopy overhead. He'd tasted the frozen custard at Luv-It and had a slice of pizza at Evel Pie. He'd ridden the Big Apple Coaster at New York-New York, watched the volcano erupt at the Mirage. He'd even received a small stipend to watch a preview of a new sitcom at CBS Television City. Things he hadn't done but he knew about included a pool at the Wynn that allowed topless bathing, ditto for the Liquid Pool Lounge at Aria. It didn't cost a cent to walk down the Strip and recognize the Aria, the Golden Nugget, the oyster bar at Palace Station, the Ghost Donkey tequila bar at the Cosmopolitan.

That's where Marcus stood, in front of the Cosmopolitan, looking at the brilliant lights of Las Vegas Boulevard and drinking a can of beer from his six-pack of Bud Lights. Feeling buzzed, he turned away and noticed three men emerging from a tunnel in the concrete viaduct set down from the sidewalk. Marcus stared. Two of the guys, both young, skinny and covered in tattoos, walked up the slanted cement sides to street level and slipped through a hole in the chain link fence. A few people pointed, others moved away in fear or headed off blindly in the opposite direction. Marcus remained fixed where he stood, unable to look away. The third man noticed Marcus staring and walked over.

"You okay, buddy?" the man asked. "You're not looking so good."

"Is this real? Did you just walk out of the sewer?" Marcus asked.

"Yeah," the man said, laughing. "I did just walk out of the . . . they're not sewers exactly, more drainage tunnels. Name's Dan."

Dan shook Marcus's hand.

Marcus was bewildered but took Dan's hand. "Uh, I'm Marcus."

"Nice to meet you, Marcus."

"Do you work down there?" Marcus asked, looking Dan up and down. He didn't look like he was dressed for dirty work. He was wearing a nice T-shirt and clean jeans, and he seemed different than the other two guys Marcus had seen emerge from the tunnel.

"In a way, I do," Dan answered. "I'm a lay minister of sorts. Most people don't realize it, but there's miles and miles of storm and flood tunnels right underneath our feet. People live down there. I look after them a little. Try to get them living back above ground if I can."

Marcus had seen the Sandbar Suites as a dead end. He was both intrigued and horrified to imagine living conditions that were even worse.

"People actually live underground?" he asked.

"They do. Was that not included in your guidebook?" Dan asked mischievously, pointing to Marcus's copy of *Fodor's*.

"Not a word," Marcus said, understanding the guy was joking with him.

"I suppose storm drains and sewage tunnels are not exactly tourist destinations," Dan conceded. "But it's a fact people live down there. I lived down there once myself if you can believe that."

Marcus wasn't sure he could believe it.

"You want to experience a part of Vegas that's not included in your book?" Dan challenged him. "You want to see the tunnels for yourself? I'll take you down there. Come on! Once in a lifetime opportunity."

Marcus hesitated. The thought occurred to him Dan might've picked him out of the crowd as the perfect mark for a bizarre mugging operation. But as he looked at his surroundings—the people, the lights, the cars, the flashing electronic billboards, the restaurants and hotels, all of it in a constant state of frenetic motion—the possibility of burrowing into someplace dark and quiet held an odd appeal.

"Yeah, I want to see it," Marcus decided.

"Follow me." Dan led Marcus down the cement embankment.

He pulled a silver pen flashlight out of his back pocket as they walked into the pitch-black tunnel. Darkness enveloped Marcus but as his eyes adjusted, he spotted the orb of light from Dan's flashlight in front of him. He followed the light.

As Marcus carefully walked behind him, Dan retrieved a larger flashlight from a backpack he'd slung across one shoulder. He pointed the wide beam of light down a wide, empty tunnel that seemed to extend into the darkness forever. They began to walk into the tunnel.

The ceiling was tall enough for them to stand without stooping. The concrete floor was dry.

"Are we in a sewer?" Marcus asked.

"Storm drains," Dan said. "It's dry right now, but when it rains, these tunnels fill with water from the streets. The Strip would turn into a river without them."

"And people live down here? They don't drown? Their stuff doesn't get washed away?"

"Flash floods claim a few people now and then, I suppose. But drowning really isn't a major concern. Your shit getting washed away, or wet, that happens pretty regular. But people down here are just like people up there," Dan observed, pointing to the ceiling over their heads. "Flood carries your house away. What do you do? You rebuild! It's the same thing, only without insurance."

Marcus stared at Dan in disbelief.

"You'd be surprised how many folks live down here," Dan continued.

"Why did you live in these tunnels?" Marcus asked, sincerely curious.

"Didn't have any place else to go, I guess," Dan said. "I was a junkie, addicted to heroin. Heroin was my whole life. All I wanted was to be left alone, just me and my habit. I hid down here. This is where I felt safe. Tell you the truth, I made myself pretty comfortable down here."

Marcus found that hard to imagine. But as if to prove Dan's point, Marcus spotted a large dome of greenish light glowing in the distance of the tunnel. He realized, with a start, that he was looking at a green nylon tent illuminated from the inside with a light of some kind. As they approached, Marcus made out the silhouette of a man sitting cross-legged on a mattress inside the tent.

"Hey, Teddy!" Dan called out. "It's me, Dan!"

A gray-haired head poked out from the opening of the tent.

"Who's that with you?" Teddy asked in a gruff voice.

"A friend," Dan said.

"Like hell," Teddy countered. "Why you be bringing folks down here like it's a tourist attraction, huh? You know better than that. This is where I live, man. I'm trying to sleep."

"We'll only be a minute," Dan assured Teddy. "I scared this guy when I walked out of the tunnel below the Cosmopolitan. He looked like he'd seen a ghost. I'm just showing him a slice of reality, is all."

"Well, shit," Teddy grumbled as he emerged from his tent. "I ought to start charging admission."

But he stuck his hand out to Marcus, all the same. "What's your name, son?"

"Marcus."

"Where you from?"

"Vermont."

"Yeah? I'm from upstate New York myself. Now I live here. Viva Las Vegas!"

Teddy swept his arm over his encampment. In the play of Dan's flashlight, Marcus noticed a few shirts and a jacket hanging neatly from coat hangers on a rolling metal clothes rack. A board laid across two plastic milk crates held an assortment of canned and packaged goods— SpaghettiOs and ramen noodles, Raisin Bran and Thomas' English muffins. There was a small saucepan sitting on an electric hot plate, which was plugged into a string of extension cords, which plugged into an outlet located in the ceiling of the tunnel.

Teddy invited Marcus into his tent to get a better look. Marcus peeked his head in and to his surprise, the set-up didn't seem half bad. Teddy's space included a plywood platform, elevated off the ground with a collection of milk crates and cinder blocks for Teddy's twin mattress, a sleeping bag, and a pillow. His clothes were stored in plastic totes, which also served as tables. There was a battery-operated camp light on one, plus a bag of potato chips and a two-liter bottle of Diet Coke.

"It ain't much," Teddy observed as Marcus pulled his head back out of the tent.

"The storm waters don't flood you out?" Marcus asked.

"Hell, yeah, they do," Teddy said. "You save what you can. You start over. It ain't like I got a lot to lose."

"But don't you want more?" Marcus asked.

"I've had more. I've had less." Teddy shrugged. "This suits me for now. I didn't do so well living up there." Teddy pointed to the ceiling, to the aboveground world that seemed as if it were a million miles away. "I do better down here."

"It's rough up there," Marcus said.

"It's rough everywhere," Teddy retorted. His brown eyes and furrowed face suddenly turned hard.

"I'll take one of those beers," he said, pointing to the two cans Marcus was still carrying, dangling off their plastic ring packaging. Marcus handed both of them to Teddy.

"Thank you, son," Teddy said. But he stood there expectantly, as if there should be more forthcoming. Marcus looked to Dan.

"It's called money," Dan said breezily.

Marcus pulled out his wallet and handed Teddy a twenty.

"It's all I've got," Marcus said.

"I'll take it," Teddy said. "Mighty kind."

Teddy turned to retreat into the privacy of his tent, then suddenly swung around to face Marcus. "Don't come down here again, son," he said. "You're not cut out for this kind of life." He gestured to the book in Marcus's hand. "You stick to your guidebook and stay above ground, you hear?"

"Yes, sir," Marcus nodded.

Teddy popped open one of the beers and disappeared inside his tent.

"Where to next?" Dan asked. "You want to go in deeper, or are you ready to go home?"

Marcus looked both ways, as if he were checking for traffic before he crossed a busy street. Then he looked at Dan.

"Why did you bring me down here?"

"I don't know. I just did. Why'd you come?"

"Confused, I guess," Marcus shook his head. "I really don't know what the fuck I'm doing."

"Most people don't. But you can't let it get you down," Dan advised. "Believe it or not, in the long run, most things turn out okay."

"Do you really believe that?"

"I really do."

Dan rested his hand on Marcus's shoulder.

"Come on. I think you've seen enough for one night. Let me take you back the way we came in."

As the two men retraced their steps, they walked through the tunnel in companionable silence. Marcus stuck close to Dan's side, fearful of the dark and alien world. Dan, on the other hand, seemed entirely at home. He led them back to the entrance if he were returning to the front door of his apartment.

Emerging from the dark and the stillness of the storm drains into the garish, sensory overload of the Strip left Marcus dazed as he followed Dan back up the slanted concrete walls, through the hole in the fence, and back onto the sidewalk.

Dan grinned at Marcus's reaction.

"It's wild out here, my friend. You take care. I think Teddy's right about you," he said. "I don't think you'd make it down below. You need to find your way up here."

Then Dan disappeared into the crush of people that thronged Las Vegas Boulevard.

23

arcus bought himself a new six-pack and smoked a joint as he made his way off the Strip and headed toward the Sandbar Suites. It took the weed for him to shake off the feeling he was being pursued by ghosts. Teddy had seemed like a decent-enough guy, and Dan was certainly likable and friendly. All the same, Marcus walked the now-familiar streets of Las Vegas with a definite case of the jitters. He looked twice at every shadow, his mind plagued with images of Teddy and Dan back in the tunnels.

Between class at Kalman, the job interview invitation at the library, his sightseeing homework, and the descent into the tunnels, it had been quite a day. As the Sandbar Suites came into view, Marcus imagined a scenario where he found Trina alone in Room 310, bored with what she was watching on TV, turning to him with smiling eyes as he opened the door, eager to hear stories about his eventful day. It was farfetched, he knew, but not inconceivable. Marcus knew tonight was Trina's night off from the Waffle House. It was late enough that Mac and Slim should've already departed for the gaming tables on the Strip. It was entirely possible Trina was in the room alone. It was entirely possible she was bored and lonely. It was entirely possible she might welcome his company. Stranger things had happened.

It was with such optimistic thoughts Marcus turned the key in the door of Room 310. Peering around the partition between the kitch-enette and the bedroom, he saw the television was turned on with the sound muted, and in the glow of the bluish TV light, he imagined he spotted Trina dozing alone on the bed. He shut the door quietly be-hind him, and tiptoed closer to the bed, tentatively calling her name.

"Trina? Are you awake? I brought us some beers."

Marcus detected a rustling of linens. He smiled with anticipation, his fingers searching for the switch to a small bedside lamp, when he suddenly realized, to his horror, there wasn't just one figure in the room but two. He jumped back in alarm, sputtering apologies and trying not to trip over his own feet as he spun around to avert his eyes and make his way back to the front door of the apartment. He would've bolted then, he would've made his escape relatively unscathed, were it not for what he saw the split second before he turned his head—wild desper-ation in a pair of familiar blue eyes set in the small, pale face turned toward him from the bed. He knew that look, he knew the feeling. When Marcus was a child, he had pleaded wordlessly for his mother to intervene against his father's cruelties. She never had.

Time stood still for Marcus as he turned back around, straining in the dim light of the television to make sense of what lay before him. Mac stood at the edge of the bed, his erect penis poised like a sword over Trina's exposed breasts. Marcus's eyes moved from Trina's breasts to her face, then up her arms to her hands, her two slender wrists bound together in one ring of the silver handcuffs, the other ring at-tached to a rung of the wooden headboard of the bed.

Marcus lifted the beers over his head.

"Marcus, don't!" Trina pleaded, struggling against the cuffs.

Marcus slammed the six-pack into Mac's back. The blow simul-taneously seemed to take Mac's breath away and fill him with rage. Breathless and amazed by what he'd done, Marcus dropped the beers and staggered away from the bed as Mac turned toward him.

"Stop it! Stop it!" Trina cried, her face tear-stained, her wrists bleed-ing as she pulled against the steel of the handcuffs.

Mac grabbed Marcus's throat in both hands and hurled him face-up onto Trina's flailing body. They were all three in the bed, Trina trapped on the bottom, Marcus trapped in the middle, Mac triumphant on top, his fingers tightening around Marcus's throat.

"I fucking hate you!" Mac whispered. "I've always fucking hated you."

He tightened his grip around Marcus's neck.

"Let her go!" Marcus wheezed. "I don't care what you do to me. Just let Trina go."

"She's a fucking whore, for Christ's sake! Why do you fucking care?" Mac spit the words out, his hands still clamped around Marcus's throat as he searched his brother's eyes as if looking for an answer.

Marcus couldn't breathe. His chest and throat burned, and his vision had begun to darken around the edges, but still he managed to speak.

"I love her."

Mac stared into his brother's eyes for another second, then his face turned blank, his fingers relaxed around Marcus's throat, his head dropped into the curve of Marcus's neck, and his body collapsed in a heap on top of Marcus's slender body. For an awful moment, Marcus lay stock still under Mac's weight, imagining Mac was dead, the victim of a fatal heart attack or a stroke. But in the next moment, Mac groaned and stirred. He lifted himself up from the two bodies beneath him, turned, and collapsed into the recliner.

Marcus gasped for air, but it was only then, when the weight of his brother was off him, that he fully realized he was lying across the naked figure of the woman he loved. He felt he was floating on Trina's skin. Her hair was in his face. Her breasts brushed against his left arm. Blood from her wounded wrists trickled down her arms. He loved her so much! Marcus moved to cover her nakedness with his body, to embrace her, to protect her, to cover her with all his love.

"Get the fuck off of me!" Trina screamed. "Get the fucking key and get me out of here!"

Marcus staggered to his feet. He glanced helplessly around the room.

"On the dresser!" Trina shouted. "It's on the dresser!"

Sure enough, there it was—the key to the handcuffs. Years ago, Mac had fished that same key out of their father's pants pocket and released Marcus. Now Marcus picked the key up off the dresser and fumbled with shaking hands and tear-blurred eyes as he released Trina.

"I'm sorry. I love you so much. I'm sorry. I love you," spilled from Marcus's lips.

Trina clenched her teeth and turned her head away from him. The instant the key clicked in the lock, she brushed past Marcus and threw herself into Mac's arms in the recliner. Mac buried his hands in Trina's hair. Marcus looked on aghast as tears flowed down both their faces. Trina kept whispering she was sorry. Mac kept assuring her it would be okay. Mac and Trina were still crying, apologizing, and comforting one another when Marcus collected his Bud Lights from the floor and staggered back out into the night.

He made his way to a chaise lounge by the pool, where he systematically popped open and drank all six of the Bud Lights, one right after the other. The last drop of beer was racing down his throat when he rolled off the chaise lounge and lay sprawled out face down on the concrete. He found himself eye to eye with his little family of ducks, which made him smile.

"Guess what?" he said to the ducks. "I have a job interview tomorrow."

Then he passed out.

24

rina and Mac were still asleep, dead to the world late the next morning when Marcus crept by them on his way to the bathroom. He showered and shaved, put on the best of his casual Friday clothes, and walked down the stairs of the Sandbar Suites, his mouth dry and pasty, his head throbbing, his guts churning.

He grabbed a hot coffee from the 7-Eleven and made himself walk to Circus Circus at the other end of the Strip. He fully expected the bar manager to take one look at him and send him back to whatever hole he'd crawled out of.

It was to Marcus's great surprise, almost to his dismay, when Howard, the bar manager, offered him the job. A squat, rotund man in his mid-forties, Howard showed Marcus around the bar and the kitchen, his belly leading the way, then hoisted his girth onto a bar stool and asked Marcus if he could start on Monday.

"Me?" Marcus asked.

"Yeah, you." Howard laughed. "Jake says you're a standup guy, says we should give you a chance. Is there some reason I shouldn't?" Marcus could think of a million reasons not to take a chance on him.

"No, not really," Marcus lied. "Except I've never tended bar before."

"Good! I'll train you myself," Howard said. "That way I won't have to break you of all the bad habits you would've picked up from someone else. Come back Monday morning with a social security card and a photo ID and we'll get you started. We won't let you loose on the public right away. You'll be with a whole group of new hires, watching company training videos, getting the corporate culture lectures, shit like that. We'll ease you into it. Sound good?"

"Sounds great," Marcus said. "How much will I get paid?"

"Minimum, plus tips. You okay with that?"

"I just need a job," Marcus said. "I'll take whatever you give me."

When Marcus broke the news of his employment to his classmates and Mr. Williams at Kalman later that day, the class erupted in a round of applause and whistles. He blushed from head to toe from the attention, but that, too, felt good. When the celebration subsided, everyone in the room, including Mr. Williams, fell to calculating how much Marcus might earn with tips added in.

"I usually tip at least one dollar a drink," Jessica said. "So, if you served twelve drinks in an hour, that's an additional twelve bucks. You're already making decent money."

"Howard's going to start me on the slower shifts," Marcus said. "He told me not to expect too much from tips at first."

"Maybe so," Mr. Williams said, addressing the entire class, "but those slower shifts are a great time for you to bone up on the skills that will definitely increase your tips further on in your career."

"Like what?" Jessica asked, ready to take notes on the legal pad she now kept with her.

"Like learning how to be friendly but not too friendly. Knowing when to talk and when to keep your mouth shut. It's always a balancing act behind the bar," Mr. Williams explained. "And there's no place to hide back there. You're always in the public eye."

The idea of being watched for the entirety of a four-hour shift filled Marcus with dread. He'd spent a lifetime hiding, trying to make himself small, to go unnoticed.

"You'll get the hang of it," Mr. Williams said, addressing Marcus directly. "But the good news," he shifted to the class at large, "is one of the easiest things you can do to increase your tips has nothing to do with your personality at all. And that's simply knowing as much about Vegas as you can."

Jessica wrote that down on her legal pad: *Know Vegas.*

"Where's the best place in town for a steak dinner?" Mr. Williams threw the question at Marcus.

"On the Strip or off?" Marcus challenged him.

"On!" Mr. Williams responded.

"SW Steakhouse at the Wynn," Marcus answered confidently. "It's one of the only places in the country where you can get true Kobe beef."

"Good Lord, Marcus!" Jessica laughed. "What's Kobe beef?"

"It's real fancy beef from Japan," Marcus explained. "It's only been imported outside of Japan since 2012."

"And how much will a serving of Kobe beef at SW set me back?" Mr. Williams asked.

"Hundreds," Marcus said. "They have a four-ounce steak that costs three hundred dollars."

"Someone's been doing his homework." Mr. Williams grinned at Marcus. "You been studying the guidebooks?"

Marcus held up his well-worn copy of *Fodor's: Las Vegas.*

"I Google a lot of stuff, too," he added.

"And he's out on the Strip, like for hours every night," Jessica chimed in.

"That's good. That's impressive." Mr. Williams nodded. "You all could learn a thing or two from this man."

Marcus again walked the Strip for several hours after class that day, but he wasn't so much learning the tricks of his new trade as he was avoiding Mac and Trina. He was haunted and disgusted by the things he'd seen and experienced the night before—his lovely Trina hand-cuffed to a bed, his brother Mac enjoying her being powerless, Mac's hands tightening around his throat, Trina throwing herself into Mac's arms . . . It was all more than Marcus could comprehend, and each time the ugly images came to his mind again, unanswerable questions backed up on him like cars stuck in a traffic jam.

Was Trina a willing participant, or was she forced? Was Mac hurting Trina, or was Trina somehow hurting Mac? How could Mac, after all we've been through as kids, use those handcuffs against a woman he loved? Does Mac love Trina? Has Trina made up her mind about loving Mac? Why can't she love me? Why does my brother hate me? Why don't I hate him?

Marcus had no answers to any of those questions, but there weren't enough flashing lights in all the Vegas Strip to distract him from his worries. He pushed the thoughts aside as best he could with a combination of beer and weed and continued his aimless wandering on the Strip until he found himself among the multitudes watching the fountain show at the Bellagio.

The waters were dancing to the beats of *Uptown Funk* when a flash of black lace on exposed white flesh riveted his attention. It was Trina, in the black lace dress and the black high heels she'd shown off to him and Mac her first night at the Sandbar Suites. She was laughing and dancing to the music, holding Mac by one hand and gamely trying to get him to dance along with her. Marcus watched Mac make a few awkward dance steps before he let go of Trina's hand and stood off to the side as Trina lost herself in the music alone. When the music stopped, she pirouetted back to Mac, threw herself into his arms and kissed him. He saw her mouth the words "I love you," watched Mac pulled her closer to his chest and bury his hands in her loose flowing hair.

Heartsick and bewildered, Marcus was still watching the couple when Mac looked up from Trina's hair and spotted his younger brother. His face went dark, and when their eyes met, Trina must have felt the tension in Mac's body, because she suddenly looked over her shoulder to see what had caused Mac's alarm. When she spotted Marcus, the smile left her face, and Marcus waited for the inevitable—Mac and Trina turning away, leaving him wallowing in his loneliness.

When Trina instead took Mac firmly by the hand and started guiding him through the crowd directly toward his younger brother, it was

Marcus who tried to flee. Had he not been penned in by a group of selfie-taking Japanese girls, he might've gotten away. As it was, Trina and Mac caught up to him, and his flight stopped when Trina grabbed hold of his arm.

"Wait! Just slow down, will you?" she pleaded.

"Wait for what?" Marcus grumbled. His heart pounded wildly in his chest.

"We need to talk, we need to work this thing out," Trina said.

Marcus glanced cautiously at Mac, who nodded his head grimly in agreement.

"Come on," Mac said, gruffly but not unkindly. "Let's grab a beer. Let's be brothers again."

Marcus still had two Buds hanging from the plastic rings of his six-pack. He ripped one can out of its ring and handed it to Mac, took the other one for himself and shoved the plastic into his back pants pocket. Trina fell in at Mac's left side as the two brothers popped open their beers and headed away from the Bellagio fountains, back out onto the Strip. They walked and drank in silence for several minutes, neither of them looking at the other. Trina nudged Mac in the arm several times, whispering, "Say something," but to no avail. The two brothers continued to walk in silence until they reached Caesars Palace.

"Let's go in here," Mac said.

Marcus tensed a little as Mac slipped a muscular arm across his shoulders. Mac opened the casino doors ushering them in, with Trina trailing behind. Stepping from the relative quiet of the outdoors into the throbbing golden gaudiness of Caesars, Marcus let Mac guide him toward a secluded booth at a bar far removed from the main casino floor. A waitress came and went, taking their orders and delivering drinks.

Marcus was the first to break the silence.

"Come Monday, I'm gonna be working in a place like this," he announced.

"What?" Mac sat up straighter in his seat.

"You got a job?" Trina asked excitedly. "Where? Doing what?"

"Jake pulled some strings for me at Circus Circus," Marcus said. "They hired me as a bartender. I start Monday morning."

"That's amazing! Congratulations!" Trina reached across the table and patted Marcus's hand, then turned to Mac. "Isn't that great? Aren't you proud?"

Mac settled his eyes on Marcus's face. He sipped his Jack Daniel's and gave his head a slight nod.

"Took long enough," Mac said. "Maybe now you'll start chipping in on rent."

Marcus stared at the tabletop. "It's just Circus Circus. It's not Caesars Palace." He looked up at the gilded glory of their current surroundings.

"It's a start. It's your foot in the door. It's fantastic," Trina reached for his hand again.

Marcus looked from Trina's hand to her face. "I owe it all to you. You're the one who dragged me into that school. I never would've done that on my own."

"Sure, you would have! Eventually," Trina teased. "All right. Come on, now, you two. Cheer up. I propose a toast! To Marcus and his new job!"

She raised her glass of Chardonnay in the air, and kept it poised there until first Mac and then Marcus reluctantly clinked their glasses against hers and made normal eye contact for the first time.

They each took a sip of their drinks.

"And now we let bygones be bygones, right?" Trina raised her glass in the air again. "The past is the past. Today is a new day. Am I right?"

The three clinked their glasses together and drank again.

"There. Now. Is everything all right?" Trina looked from Marcus to Mac and back again. "Are we good?"

The two brothers looked at one another across the high polish of the table, neither of them knowing what to say. There was a mutual recognition of something profound between them, but neither man could express in words what it was beyond Mac asking Marcus, "Are we good?" and Marcus responding, "We're brothers."

"Fuck, yeah! We're brothers!" Mac exclaimed, breaking the tension between them. "Let's drink to that!"

Mac ordered a round of tequila shots for the three of them, and then another. They tossed the liquor down their throats in a determined effort to pretend all was well between them and they were having a great time. But the second shot was still burning a fire in Marcus's gut when Mac gave in to his restlessness.

"I need to find a poker game," he announced.

"No, not tonight! Stay with us!" Trina pleaded. "You said we needed a night out. I called in sick and now you're going to go to the tables?"

"I know! But tonight's going to be a good night. I can *feel* it! I'm so close!"

Mac edged Trina out of the booth and stood. He pulled a wad of bills out of his wallet and handed them to Marcus.

"Look after her for me tonight. Show her a good time, okay?"

As Marcus accepted the cash, Mac kissed Trina on the forehead.

"Be good," he said. "I'll catch up with y'all later."

Trina and Marcus watched Mac make his way through the crowds gathered around the game tables and then disappear.

"Asshole." Trina muttered and then turned her attention back to Marcus. "Now what?"

Marcus finished counting the bills Mac had given him.

"We've got nearly three hundred dollars," Marcus announced. "What should we do with it?"

Trina rested her chin in her hand and smiled coyly. "Put it in savings, of course."

Marcus grinned. "That's not a celebration."

"No, it's not, is it?" Trina laughed. "But it's your celebration, not mine. You're the one with a new job. What do you want to do?"

"Spoil you," Marcus responded without hesitation. "Come on! Let's go window shopping. I've read there are some really good shops around here, but I've never actually seen them. Let's go look."

Trina's face broke into a smile. "That's the best idea I've heard all night!"

She tossed back the rest of her wine. Marcus did the same with his beer, then they walked together out of the bar in search of the shops. Marcus followed Trina since she seemed to know where she was going—she guided him into the Forum. He'd read about the famous mall at the Forum in *Fodor's* but seeing it for real was a trip just the same. An enormous, enclosed space with an artificial blue sky overhead and open spaces designed to replicate ancient Roman streets, the mall was unlike anything he'd seen in Vegas before.

"This is fucking unreal!" Marcus exclaimed as he gawked at his surroundings. "It's amazing what they come up with in Vegas. I mean, look at this place!"

Trina laughed at his amazement. "Pretty far removed from the Sandbar Suites, isn't it?"

"It's a whole different fucking world," Marcus said still gawking. "I honestly had no idea. You've been here before?"

"I come here once in a while." Trina shrugged. "Just to look, just to see how the other side lives before I schlump over to Goodwill."

"We've got three hundred dollars tonight," Marcus reminded her as they passed a Gucci shop. "You should spend it here. You should get yourself something. That would make me happy. That would be a celebration for me."

They strolled side by side, close enough so their shoulders touched, and Trina's hair spilled over onto Marcus's arm. He was smelling the scent of her shampoo when she stopped walking and faced Marcus.

"You don't hate me?" she asked, looking as if she was holding back tears. "After last night, I mean?"

"Never!" Marcus said. "I'm never going to hate you."

"What about Mac? Do you hate him?"

"Yeah, sometimes I do. And sometimes he hates me. It's always been that way," Marcus admitted. "We hate each other so much sometimes. We'll drift apart for a while, go our separate ways. But we always end up back together, usually at a bar. We get drunk and life goes on. I don't understand any of it."

They resumed their walk past diamonds and designer handbags, Italian shoes, leather coats, gold Rolex watches, sequined evening gowns, silk ties, crystal wine glasses, emerald bracelets—a whole world of opulence they could only look at. In the midst of all this splendor, Marcus's memory of Trina handcuffed to the bed in Room 310 of the Sandbar Suites seemed even more grotesque, his brother's lust even more revolting.

He shook his head to clear the images from his mind and opened his arms as if to embrace the consumer wonders that surrounded them on all sides.

"What would you do if you had all the money in the world? What if you didn't have to worry about money at all?" he suddenly asked Trina.

"You mean if I won the jackpot?"

"Yeah! Say you win the big Mega Bucks. What would you do with all that money? And don't tell me you'd put it all in savings!"

"But I would put a lot of it into savings!" Trina slapped his arm playfully. "I'd also buy a house. And a new car. And maybe start a business, make something of myself, be my own boss. My dream shop would sell lingerie, chocolates, and champagne. It would be *the* place to go for anniversaries and Valentine's Day. What would you do?"

"Me?" Marcus was surprised she'd asked. "I'd go home. Buy a house, settle down. I don't have any big ambitions. I just want a quiet, normal life. A wife and kids."

He nudged Trina with his elbow.

"Don't look at me!" she warned.

Marcus did look at her, just the same, happy and relaxed for what felt like the first time in months. They were standing in front of the

Versace shop when Marcus took Trina by the hand and started pulling her back in the direction of the casino.

"Where are we going?" Trina asked.

"To the slot machines! You can't win a jackpot just standing around talking about it!"

25

Trina protested all the way back to the Caesars casino and was still arguing against the plan when Marcus pressed a fifty-dollar bill into her hand.

"I've never gambled in my life!" she protested. "All I'll do is piss the money away!"

"So what if you do? It might be fun," Marcus countered. "Didn't you come out to have some fun?"

"I guess. But I feel like I'm wasting Mac's money."

"It's as much my money as it is Mac's." Marcus folded her fingers around the fifty. "I'm giving you fifty dollars of *my* money. And I'm ordering you to play the slots with it!"

"Ordering me?" Trina laughed giddily as she accepted the money. "I don't even know what to do! You have to come with me!"

"You've been in Vegas how long, and you've never played slots?" Marcus teased her.

"Never! I've never flushed my money down a toilet, either."

She slipped her hand inside Marcus's as they wandered among the flashing lights, ringing bells, and carnival-like music pouring forth from the Palace's slot machines.

"How am I supposed to know which one to try?" Trina shouted over the noise.

An older woman with a halo of silver hair and huge round black bifocals overheard Trina and Marcus laughed.

"Here, sweetie! Try this one!" she said. "Maybe you'll have better luck than me."

"See. It's just waiting for you!" Marcus pulled her over to the slot.

"I don't know what to do!" Trina protested.

"Feed your money into the machine and push the button," the old woman instructed her. "What've you got to lose?"

"I've never done this before!" Trina hesitated.

"Stop stalling! Play the game!" Marcus cheered.

"You got nothing to lose," the old woman advised as she walked away.

Trina took her place in front of the 5 Dragons. With Marcus's help, she fed the fifty-dollar bill into the machine and laughed nervously as the screen came to life, indicating a credit of *5000* in the top left corner. The bet column was set at *150*. The win column showed *0*. She pushed the red button to make her first bet and jumped back from the screen and into Marcus as the electronic sounds blared and colorful cartoon images of fish and dragons, playing cards, turtles, numbers and letters whirled round and round on the reels then stopped in place.

"Oh look! I'm down to four thousand eight hundred and fifty already," she said.

"Come on! Push it again!" Marcus ordered, smiling and enjoying her exuberant mood.

She pushed the button again. The images spun and stopped. Her credit went down to forty-seven hundred. "Oh, I get it." She laughed. "I lose a dollar fifty of your money every time I push that red button. I should have that fifty gone in no time!"

Marcus encouraged her as she pushed the button again and again and again. Sometimes the spinning images clicked into place and for reasons that totally eluded them, her credit notched up. But mostly it went down. One bump up, two bumps down. Two bumps up, five bumps down.

"Told you I'd just piss your money away," Trina teased Marcus as her credit slipped down to five hundred just a few minutes into the game. As she pushed the red button again, and the images on the screen whirred and clicked into place, both she and Marcus watched for the credit total to slip down again, but this time, the screen of the 5 Dragons game seemed to explode in a cacophony of carnival sounds, flashing lights, and a credit score rocketing into the thousands of dollars. The two of them took a step back from the slot machine.

The color drained from Trina's face as she looked back and forth between Marcus and the game.

"What's happening? What did I do?" she asked under her breath.

Before Marcus could answer, other slots players abandoned their own games to crowd in behind Marcus and Trina. They watched with bated breath as the figure in her credit column continued to soar.

"What's happening? Am I winning?" Trina asked a young man, a casino employee who appeared at her side.

"Miss, you are winning!" he exclaimed.

In her excitement, Trina kissed the man on his lips, then turned to Marcus and kissed him, too.

"We're winning!" she squealed. "I can't believe it!"

It seemed to Marcus as if the numbers spinning around and around in the credit column might never stop. When they did, Marcus and Trina were transfixed by the figure presented to them on the screen.

"Did I just win a hundred thousand dollars?" Trina asked of no one in particular.

"You just won one hundred thousand six dollars and fifty cents, to be exact," the young casino employee informed her.

Trina covered her face with her hands and squealed again, then threw herself into Marcus's arms. The crowd cheered and clapped as Marcus hugged and jumped up and down with her in front of the 5 Dragons slot.

"I can't believe it! I can't believe it!" Trina cried again and again.

She stopped jumping and held Marcus's face in her hands as she looked him straight in the eye. "Is this real? Tell me the truth! Is this really happening?"

Marcus couldn't stop grinning and picked Trina up in his arms. "I think it's real." He laughed. "I mean, it sure seems to be!"

Trina wrapped her arms around Marcus's neck, then pulled back away from him with wide, astonished eyes.

"We have to find Mac! He's not going to believe this!"

Marcus wasn't sure he believed it himself, but a trio of Caesars employees who now parted the crowd to reach them seemed to indicate something, at least, had happened. He felt as if he'd done something wrong and squelched an urge to run until he noticed the Caesars people—two men and a woman—were all smiling as they made their way through the cheering throng.

"Who's the lucky winner?" the woman asked.

"Me! It's me, or at least I think it's me," Trina gushed, holding Marcus's hand. "I mean, it was your money, but I pushed the button. So, I don't know. Am I the winner?"

"I gave the money to you!" Marcus said to Trina, then addressed the Caesars employees. "The winnings are all hers!"

Trina buried her face in Marcus's chest, crying and laughing at the same time.

The Caesars woman, a handsome, matronly blonde, put her arm around Trina's shoulders and started guiding her off the casino floor.

"Come with me, dear. Everything's going to be okay. You just won a whole bunch of money!"

The two Caesars men shook Marcus's hand and told him congratulations. Then they posted themselves on either side and guided him off the floor as well, trailing behind the two women. All along the way, people high-fived Marcus and slapped him on the back. People did the same to Trina, with a few men calling out, "Marry me!" or "I love you!" as she passed by.

It was a relief when they were removed from the noise and the

DEATH VALLEY   193

attention and found themselves standing before another Caesars employee, a thin, youngish Black man set up within a metal cage and
surrounded by security cameras.

"Hey, Mary," the caged man called out as the blonde woman approached with Trina and Marcus in tow. "You bringing me more winners tonight?"

"I sure am! This young lady just won one hundred thousand six
dollars and fifty cents on a 5 Dragons slot machine."

"Verified?" the man asked.

"Verified." Mary handed the caged man a printout of some sort.

"All right, then. I'll take it from here," the man said.

Mary shook both their hands and wished them good luck. Then
she left them alone with the caged man.

"I'm Brent," he told them. "And who might you be?"

Flushed and giddy, Trina introduced the two of them, stum-
bling over both their names. "I'm Trina. Catrina, I mean, Catrina
McPhearson. And this is Marcus Brown, right? That's your last name?"

Marcus nodded.

Brent grinned. "Just breathe," he said soothingly to Trina. "We've
got everything under control here. I'm gonna need to see some ID.
You're gonna fill out a tax form. The hotel's gonna comp you a suite for
the night. All you have to do is sit back and enjoy."

"I just can't believe it! None of this seems real yet," Trina gushed.

"I hear that a lot," Brent said. "You got any ID with you, Miss Trina?"

Trina slipped the small, sequined handbag off her shoulder and
snapped it open. From what Marcus could see, there wasn't much in
it—some loose cash, a lipstick tube, a squashed package of cigarettes,
a lighter . . .

"It's not here!" Trina gasped and turned startled eyes to Marcus.
"My ID! It's not here!"

"Are you sure?" Marcus asked, also alarmed. "Here, let me look.
You're too nervous."

"Don't panic," Brent advised. "Just relax and take your time."

Marcus rifled through the few items in Trina's purse. He took each item out one at a time and placed it in Trina's hands until the small bag was empty.

"No ID," he said.

Trina grabbed the empty bag from his hand, shook it, as if her absent ID might come tumbling out. Tears spilled from her eyes.

"Oh no! No crying. Come on now, Miss Trina." Brent got up from his chair and came closer to the metal bars that separated him from Trina.

"There's no need to cry. Everything's gonna be okay," he said. "I bet you left your ID at home, or back at the hotel, in your regular purse, don't you think?"

Trina nodded and wiped tears from her face. "I bet that is what happened," she agreed. "I bet I left it at home. Or lost it!"

Her tears started flowing again.

"That's okay. Even if you lost your ID, you're not going to lose your money. Your winnings are going to be right here. They're not going anywhere," Brent reassured her. "I can't give you anything tonight, because you can't present us with a valid ID, but it's all going to be right here when you do. You can come back later tonight. You can come back tomorrow. Hell, you can come back in two weeks, your winnings will still be here. Okay? Trust me, Miss Trina?"

Trina managed a weak smile. Marcus put his arm around her shoulders, and she leaned against him for support.

"Yeah, I trust you," she said. "I'm just mad at myself. So stupid!"

"Don't be mad. It'll work out." Marcus reassured her.

Brent addressed them both. "I'm gonna call up front, hook you up with a VIP suite, free booze, free meals. You're a big winner! This is your night! Isn't that right, Marcus?"

"That's right!" Marcus squeezed Trina's shoulders and wiped the last of her tears off her cheeks with the palm of his hand. "Let's go find Mac. Let's get this party started!"

26

"**S**hould we go home for my ID? I want to claim my winnings," Trina said. "Let's walk home and get it."

"But what if your ID really is lost? What if you go home and you can't find it? Then you'll feel like the whole night is ruined," Marcus noted. "Let's find Mac first. Then if you really want to run home to look for your ID, he can take you there in the truck."

Trina agreed it was a reasonable plan. But they were distracted from locating Mac by a Caesars attendant who appeared with a key card and insisted on escorting them to the Forum Classic Suite. They followed the young woman onto an elevator, rode with her up to the nineteenth floor, and followed her down a hallway and through a door that gained them entrance to a suite easily ten times larger than their apartment at the Sandbar Suites. Marcus was awed. With Trina, he checked out the two bedrooms and four beds, a full kitchen and a bar, a balcony overlooking the Strip, and a hot tub in a separate room attached to the bathroom.

"I'm never going to want to leave," Trina whispered to Marcus as a waiter wheeled in a bottle of chilled champagne with a couple of glasses.

"Yeah," was all Marcus could come up with as he gawked at the swanky opulence of the huge suite.

They postponed looking for Mac again, this time to pop open the champagne and take the bottle and two glasses out to the balcony.

Marcus poured the bubbly, laughing as the golden liquid rose up over the rims of their glasses. He licked champagne off his fingers and toasted to Trina's good fortune. "Here's to you! You did it!"

Trina held up her glass and looked out over all the lights of Las Vegas, as if she were a queen surveying her kingdom.

"I can put down a deposit on a house," she mused aloud. "I can get my own damned place! I can have something that's all mine."

"You can quit the Waffle Hovel," Marcus said. "Or don't even bother to quit. Just never show up again. Or show up as a customer and leave big tips for everyone. Show off a little bit! You can do whatever you want."

The desert breeze brushed the hair back from her face and rustled the hem of her long dress, and Marcus smiled at this vision of Trina. They drank the bottle of champagne, just the two of them.

"Fuck Mac," Trina declared after her third glass. "This was supposed to be our night out on the town. He wanted to apologize, make things up to me in a way, you know? And he ditched me to play poker."

"He doesn't deserve you."

Trina emptied the last drops of champagne into her glass and poured the sparkling liquid down her throat.

"No one deserves me. What's a girl to do? Should we go find him?"

"Yeah, I guess we should," Marcus answered.

They made their way back down to the casino floor on unsteady feet, laughing at their stumbles then standing in stunned silence once they entered the Palace Poker Room, located between the Coliseum theater and the race and sports book area.

"Jesus! It's huge," Trina noted under her breath. "Do you see him anywhere?"

The enormous floor was packed with poker players gathered around tables, throngs of onlookers, and cocktail waitresses. Marcus scanned the room for some sign of his brother. He jumped when he heard Mac's voice behind him.

"Where have you two been? I've been looking for you every-where," Mac said.

Trina jumped, too, and fell giggling into Mac's arms.

"We've been drinking champagne and enjoying the view from a balcony on the nineteenth floor. In a suite the size of a house," Trina said, swaying unsteadily. "How's your night going?"

"Not great. I lost a little," Mac admitted. "Who do you know has a suite here?"

"Nobody. I mean, me, us. We have a suite," Trina said.

Mac placed his hand at the small of Trina's back and guided her to the bar where they'd first started the night. Marcus sighed, knowing his special time with Trina was over, and trailed behind.

"We have a suite for the night on the nineteenth floor. See?" Trina fished the key card out of her handbag. "They gave it to us. It's amazing. So big and clean. You'll see. But first you have to take me home so I can find my ID."

Mac turned his attention to Marcus.

"What the fuck is she talking about? What the fuck have you done to my woman?"

"Nothing! She did this all herself!" Marcus laughed. "She won at the slots! Big! A hundred thousand dollars!"

"Are you fucking with me?" Mac looked from Trina to Marcus in bewilderment verging on rage. "Do not fuck with me, baby brother! I'm not in the mood!"

"No one's fucking with you." Trina leaned in close to Mac and kissed his cheek.

She retrieved the printout Brent had given her from the cashier's cage and showed it to Mac. "Look! I won! My first time ever to play the slots, and I won. A hundred. Fucking. Thousand. Dollars. I'm never touching a slot machine again!"

A waitress appeared at their table, but Mac was too confounded to order. Trina took charge of the situation.

"He needs a Jack Daniel's, double, straight. I need a double vodka tonic. This young man needs a Bud Light."

The waitress caught a glimpse of the document Mac was holding and smiled knowingly. When she returned with their drinks, she announced they'd be on the house, per Caesars big winners' policy.

"We're big winners." Trina raised her glass in a toast to herself, smirking at Mac. "Well, I am, at least. I'm a big winner. I don't know about you two losers."

Mac let the dig slide, choosing instead to hold Trina's face in his large hands and kiss her hard on the mouth.

"Oh sure! Now you love me," Trina teased.

"Damn straight I do," Mac said.

Did Trina not care, or did she not notice, Marcus wondered, when Mac folded the cashiers' printout into quarters and slipped it into his back pocket.

"You should kiss Marcus, too," Trina offered. "He gave me fifty dollars and made me play the game. I wouldn't have done it without him."

"Oh, yeah?" Mac raised his eyebrows as he studied his brother. "So, it was actually my money that won big?"

"No. You gave that money to me, and I gave fifty to Trina, so it's Trina's money," Marcus corrected.

"But I need my ID," Trina interrupted. "I can't get my money until I find my ID."

"You lost your ID?" Mac asked.

"I don't think so." Trina held up her tiny evening bag. "I think I left it at home when I switched out my handbags. That's what Brent thinks, too. So, we should go home, and come back, and then I'll be rich."

"Damn, girl!" Mac swallowed the double shot of Jack Daniel's in one gulp, shook his head from the shock to his system, and slammed his glass on the table. "You want me to take you to the Sandbar Suites when a Caesars suite is waiting for us on the nineteenth floor? Fuck the Sandbar Suites. Am I right?"

Mac turned to Marcus for confirmation.

"I think he's right," Marcus said to Trina.

"But what about my ID? And my money?" Trina sucked up the last of her drink. "I can't stop thinking about it."

"It's not going anywhere. We'll get it first thing tomorrow," Mac reassured her. "But let's enjoy tonight first. Okay?"

Trina hesitated with a small sigh. But then her face brightened again.

"Do you want to see the suite?" she asked.

"I want to see you in the suite," Mac replied.

The pair slid out of the booth holding hands and moved away.

Trina glanced back over her shoulder at Marcus. She blew him a kiss and mouthed the words, "Thank you!"

27

Marcus watched Trina as she walked away from him until he lost sight of her in the crowd. Figuring he'd never see the inside of the suite on the nineteenth floor again, he had the waitress bring him another Bud Light. He sat alone at the bar, contemplating his next move.

A normal person, he thought, could go home and go to bed. But his life wasn't normal. He didn't want to go home and rest in the same bed where the woman he loved had been degraded—by his brother, no less. He had no appetite for his cot at the Sandbar Suites, either. And he supposed his backup bed, Mac's truck, was parked somewhere out on the Strip. He had no idea where to find it. There was always the chaise lounge and the ducks down at the pool, where he had passed out last night. But that prospect didn't exactly beckon him away from the bar, either.

Marcus finished one beer; the waitress brought him another without asking. He emptied that one and she brought him another. And so it went. Marcus drank and ruminated. Images of recent events flashed by in his mind but it all made no sense. His father killing his mother. His father killing himself. The wild cross-country trip with Mac from Florida to Nevada. Their fleeting joy that first night in Vegas as they cruised the Strip. Seeing Trina at the Waffle House. The vicious beatings of Trina's boyfriend, Ben. The silver mine. The school. The job offer. Trina shackled to a bedpost. Trina winning one hundred grand at a slot machine. Trina sipping champagne on the balcony of a suite at Caesars Palace.

Marcus lost track of time and the number of beers he drank as he sat on a bar stool at Caesars Palace and doubted if any of what he remembered was even real. That couldn't possibly be his actual life, could it? But then he was afraid it was, so he drank even more. He was nearly asleep, his body draped across the bar like a wet towel, when he heard Trina's voice approaching him from behind.

"There you are! You've been sitting here this whole time!"

Trina edged herself between Marcus and a man on the stool next to him. Mac was right behind her. Slim was behind Mac. She grabbed Marcus's arm and pulled him away from the bar.

"Come on! We have stuff to do," she said. "We're getting married!"

"What?" Marcus looked from Trina's flushed face to Mac's somber mug. "Are you serious?"

"It's what the girl wants," Mac said. "Who are we to argue?"

"That's crazy!" Marcus said.

He pulled on Trina's hand, trying to slow her down as she dragged him through the crowded room. She tripped and fell into Mac's arms, giddy, obviously intoxicated. Mac propped her back up on her feet. Slim sneered from the sidelines.

"It's Vegas! It's what people do!" Trina exclaimed. She succeeded in dragging her three male companions out to the covered entrance to the casino, where they could talk without shouting over the crowd inside.

"It's all arranged," she told Marcus, since he was the only member of the group who appeared to need convincing. "We have a reservation at Chapel of the Bells. We just need a license. And a ring. Like right now! Will you get me a ring, please?"

Trina teetered on her high heels.

"You should go to bed. Get some rest," Marcus told her.

"I already went to bed. With this guy." Trina jerked her thumb toward Mac. "Now I'm going to get married at the Chapel of the Bells.

Kelly Ripa got married there. If it's good enough for Kelly, it's good enough for me! It's too good for you!" She brayed the last words at Mac.

"Come on, man! Don't do this!" Marcus pleaded with Mac. "Take her back to the hotel. Let her sleep this off."

"They kept bringing us champagne! As much as we wanted!" Trina giggled.

Mac shoved a fistful of dollar bills into Marcus's front shirt pocket.

"Go to a pawn shop and buy a couple of rings," he instructed. "Then meet us at the chapel by ten o'clock."

"And flowers! I should have some flowers," Trina added. "Lilies. I want white lilies. They're my favorite."

Marcus's mouth hung open.

"Go with Slim," Mac ordered him. "I gotta get me and Trina to the county clerk's office when it opens at eight."

"Eight in the morning? What time is it now?" Marcus looked around in bewilderment.

"Seven thirty," Slim snapped. "Time's wasting. Let's get going."

Slim separated Marcus from Trina, pushing him toward the Circus Circus parking lot. Marcus tried to look back to keep Trina in his sight, but he immediately lost track of her. Just before Slim shoved Marcus into the passenger seat of his car, he slipped Mac's cash out of Marcus's shirt pocket.

"I don't even know why I'm bringing you along," Slim muttered under his breath. He slammed one car door shut and yanked open another. "Worthless piece of shit. Worthless fucking cunt!"

Marcus closed his eyes and leaned his head against the car door. His head spun. He could understand his brother fucking Trina in a big, paid-for bed in a fancy hotel. But marrying the woman, the same woman he'd referred to as his pussy, that was something else altogether. He didn't believe for an instant Mac wanted to spend the rest of his life with Trina, settle down and have some kids with her, grow old together. The quick wedding was connected to Trina winning the money; he just couldn't figure out what the angle was.

Marcus would've been suspicious of the wedding even if Trina had been stone cold sober. The fact she was more intoxicated than he'd ever seen her aroused his concerns even more. On top of that, the presence of Slim on the scene and what his involvement implied made Marcus feel sick. He might vomit in Slim's car at any moment, and if he did, Slim would surely kill him. But Marcus figured Slim had wanted to kill him since he was a kid, and in his drunken state, this was hysterically funny. He doubled over with laughter. When he lifted his head, Slim punched him in the side of his face.

"Who the fuck do you think you're laughing at, bitch?"

Marcus nestled against the car door again with his eyes closed and a smile on his lips, thinking, *I'm laughing at you, fucker.* He stayed curled up, lost in drunken oblivion as Slim parked the car and came and went. He emerged back into the real world only when Slim yanked open with passenger side door without warning, and Marcus tumbled out of Slim's Shit Mobile.

"Fucking Christ!" Slim complained. "Get up, will you? It's your brother's fucking wedding day."

He helped Marcus to his feet and dragged him into a building, depositing him like a bundle of dirty laundry on a bench. Marcus was startled into semi-consciousness when he realized he was propped up against Trina, the two of them sitting on a two-seater white pew decorated with gold trim. Marcus marveled that they were sitting inside what appeared to him to be the world's smallest church, built to hold a congregation of about ten people. Mac and Slim were a couple feet away at the front of the chapel, conversing with a man in a dark suit, showing him documents, pointing at Trina, laughing and winking.

"Isn't it romantic?" Trina murmured as if she were talking in her sleep. "A whirlwind romance."

Marcus slipped his arm around Trina's waist and kissed her forehead.

"He's going to buy me a diamond later, after we get my money," she murmured. "I'm going to have a house *and* a diamond. Small ones, but still . . ."

Marcus pulled her closer to his chest.

"You don't have to go through with this," he whispered to her. "You can leave right now, before it's too late. I'll help you. I'll get you out of this."

Marcus tried to pull Trina to her feet, but she slapped his hands away, causing enough of a flurry for the three men at the front of the chapel to turn in unison toward her.

"Get your hands off of me!" she slurred. "You're just jealous! You just wish it was you getting married rather than Mac. Like that was ever going to happen!"

"You got everything under control over there, baby brother?" Mac asked. "We're set to go if she's ready."

"I was born ready!" Trina announced.

She tripped on the hem of her dress as she took her first step toward the podium, and it became Marcus's job to keep her steady on her feet throughout the brief ceremony that followed.

Tears rolled down his cheeks as he watched Trina and Mac exchange gold wedding bands. But when the man in the dark suit pronounced them husband and wife and the newly married couple kissed, there was a fleeting moment, despite his own sadness, when Marcus almost felt happy for them. *Who's to say they won't be good for one another? Who's to say they won't make it?* He found himself smiling as he remembered an old Chuck Berry song. *Yup*, Marcus thought, *you never can tell.*

Following the ceremony, the newly minted husband and wife stumbled out of the Chapel of the Bells into the bright light of a Vegas morning, with their wedding party of Marcus and Slim in tow. Slim retrieved his car, slammed on his brakes, and got out to open the back door for Mac and Trina to slide in among discarded McDonald's bags, beer cans, and empty cigarette packages.

Marcus deposited himself in the front passenger seat, cringing to the sounds of Trina and Mac making out in the backseat. But the kissing and groping didn't go too far before Trina announced she was going to be sick. Slim pulled the car over. Trina slid out of the backseat and vomited on the sidewalk of Las Vegas Boulevard.

"Are we still going to Caesars?" Trina asked shakily as she crawled back into the car. "We aren't going back to the Sandbar right away, are we? Do we still have the suite?"

"We still have the hotel," Mac reassured her. "Honeymoon in Vegas, baby!"

Trina blinked against the glare of sunlight coming in through the car windows. "We don't have to check out?" she asked.

"I took care of it," Slim spoke up curtly from the driver's seat. "Don't worry about it."

Marcus wasn't so far gone he failed to notice the exchange that took place between Mac and Slim just before Slim pulled away from the hotel. Mac had leaned in through the open window of the front seat. Their eyes had met in a meaningful gaze. Slim had said, "Get her done." Mac had nodded solemnly, like a man making a profound promise. Then he straightened back up and turned his attention to Marcus and Trina.

Marcus was in rough shape, but he knew there was something sinister about Slim making sure Trina still had the fancy hotel suite at her disposal. And, he wasn't so far gone he didn't realize what a spectacle they were, even by Vegas standards, as they made their way across the lavish Caesars lobby. He saw people smirking at them—Trina the bedraggled drunk bride in a torn black dress, her magnificent hair now a magnificent mess, accompanied by two men, one very drunk and struggling to keep up, the other tall, sober, and muscle-bound, moving them quickly toward the elevators.

Marcus was still too drunk to know what any of this meant or to protest when Mac ushered him and Trina into the hotel suite on the nineteenth floor and started popping more bottles of champagne.

"I can't!" Trina protested.

But it turned out she could, and Marcus could, too. Mac cajoled them to drink up, and when cajoling failed to get the job done, he insisted. Mac kept the wine flowing, and Trina and Marcus kept drinking it. The last thing Marcus remembered of that morning was Trina rolling off the living room couch in a fit of hysterical laughter. She'd spilled her glass of champagne, and Mac was dutifully refilling it as she crawled back onto the couch, laughing through her tears and pointing at Marcus.

"Oh my God! We're related now! You're my brother-in-law!"

Trina was still drinking and still laughing when Marcus's world went black.

28

When next he opened his eyes, Marcus felt as if he were facedown on a raft of white linen, set adrift in the middle of a white ocean. When he mustered the strength to raise himself up on one elbow, he deduced he was, in fact, in the bedroom of the suite on the nineteenth floor of Caesars Hotel. He crawled to the bathroom on his hands and knees so he could vomit into the pristine white toilet.

"Mac? Trina?" Marcus called their names as he staggered out of the bedroom. He found Trina sitting alone at the dining room table. She was clothed in a white hotel bathrobe, her auburn hair spread out around her head and shoulders like an electrified halo. She glanced up from the phone in her hand when she heard him approach. She looked as haggard as he felt. It was clear she'd been crying, although her eyes seemed dry at the moment.

"Do you know where Mac is?" Trina asked.

Marcus dropped into the chair opposite her at the glass-topped table and shook his head. Trina scrolled slowly on her phone.

"What are you looking at?" Marcus asked.

"My wedding night." Trina turned the phone's screen toward him. "You were there, remember?"

Marcus took the phone from her and scrolled through the images. They were familiar and foreign all at the same time. Bits and pieces he remembered—the smallness of the church, the tiny white two-seater pews, the man in the dark suit, the four of them lined up in front of him, Trina and Mac in the center, flanked on either side by Marcus and Slim. But he had no recollection of the bright gold podium the minister stood behind, or the gaudy bouquet of silk sunflowers Trina held primly in her hands, which Marcus now saw were lying on the table between them.

"You asked for lilies," he said, remembering, as if that were a salient point.

"Who took these pictures?" Trina demanded.

Marcus shrugged. "I have no idea."

"Christ! What have I done?" Trina shook her head and sipped from a cup of coffee.

"There's coffee?"

"In the kitchen." Trina pointed behind her.

Marcus fetched himself a cup and returned to the table.

Trina took her phone again and scrolled through the images again, groaning.

"I can't believe I did this," she groaned. "I can't fucking believe I let this happen."

"Don't worry about it." Marcus tried to console her. "You were caught up in the moment. Things like this must happen all the time. I mean, it's Vegas, right? If you don't want to be married, you don't have to be married. You can get an annulment, or something, right? Quick marriage, quick divorce, right?"

"Yeah, right," Trina agreed without much conviction. She nervously turned the gold band on her ring finger. Marcus reached across the table and held her hand.

"How drunk was I?" Trina asked.

"Pretty far gone," Marcus answered. "You said something about them bringing you champagne, like as much as you wanted. And there was more when we came back here. Lots more."

"Christ!" Trina closed her eyes and massaged her forehead. "I never drink like that. I can't hold my liquor. I must've been drunk off my ass."

"You were celebrating. You'd just won all that money. It was all in fun," Marcus said encouragingly. "I bet Mac doesn't want to be married, either. You'll see. He'll walk through that door, and you'll both be embarrassed, and the whole thing will be forgotten."

"Where is Mac anyhow?" Trina asked. "Have you seen him today? Or Slim?"

"Nope."

"Fuck me!" Trina lit a cigarette, filled her lungs with smoke and exhaled.

"What about my ID? Have you seen my ID?" she demanded.

Marcus shook his head.

"Fuck! Fuck! Fuck!" Trina cursed all the way to the larger of the two bedrooms. She was slipping into her bra and panties with the door open when Marcus had an idea.

"Maybe you already have your ID," he called to her from the dining room. "Don't you need your identification to get married, even in Vegas? You got married, so you must've had your ID then. Are you sure you don't have it on you?"

Trina emerged from the bedroom, pulling up the zipper on the back of her dress, her black evening bag dangling from one hand.

"I've looked! I've looked a million times!" She flung the small sequined bag at Marcus's face. "I don't have it! It's not here!"

Marcus recoiled in surprise but caught the purse, opened it, and fingered through its meager contents to be sure.

"I don't have the verification for my winnings either," Trina added. "That piece of paper. That's gone, too."

Marcus's face lit up with a sudden memory.

"Mac has it!" he reassured her. "I saw him slip it into his pants pocket last night."

Trina snatched her purse back out of Marcus's hands and headed for the door. "And you can fucking bet he has my ID in his pocket, too."

It was early evening as Marcus followed Trina out of the hotel and onto the Strip. He struggled to keep pace with her as she surged ahead. Even in high heels, she walked faster than he did. Hungover and confused, he suspected she was thinking faster than he was, too.

"Slow down a minute, will you?" he said. "What difference does it make if Mac has your ID? What's the big deal? If he has it, he can give it to you."

Trina stopped abruptly and faced Marcus with fierce eyes. "I can't get my money without that ID. I haven't figured out exactly what's going on, but I know something's wrong. I *know* it. Nothing that happened last night was an accident. Nothing about it was just for fun. Mac doesn't do shit just for fun. And neither does Slim."

She started walking again. Marcus tried to remain silent, certain anything he might say would only upset her. But after a few moments, his desire to ease her mind won out over his reticence. "Everything will be okay."

"Nothing is ever okay," she snapped.

He allowed himself the liberty of taking her hand, pleased when she didn't resist. "The money will be there when you go to claim it. Brent said so. Even if you have to get a new ID, the money will still be there. It'll just take a little longer, that's all."

They walked in silence before Marcus had another hopeful thought. "Have you tried calling him?"

"I've called and I've texted like a million times. He's not responding."

Marcus pulled Trina to a halt while he fished his own phone out of his pocket and attempted to call his brother while Trina glared at him. "It went to voicemail."

"Yeah, it did," Trina snapped again. She resumed her march toward the Sandbar Suites.

The walk in the evening sun exhausted them. Hungover and dehydrated, hungry but nauseous, angry and scared, they neared the place they called home, weary and bedraggled.

"Do you see their cars anywhere?" Trina asked as they approached the parking lot.

Marcus scanned the area to no avail. Neither Mac's truck nor Slim's Shit Mobile was anywhere to be found.

Trina led the way up the three flights of stairs and was the first to enter Room 310. Her everyday handbag, a cheap Michael Kors knock-off in fake red leather, sat in the middle of the dinette table. Marcus stood by as she upended the handbag and spilled its contents onto the table. Tampons, lipstick tubes, and loose change clattered across the Formica top as she searched through every nook and cranny of every pocket of the handbag.

She threw herself into one of the dinette chairs and buried her face in her hands. "It's not here!" she sobbed. "It's gone! They've got it!"

Marcus put his hand on her shoulder. "Don't cry," he pleaded. "Everything will be all right. You don't even know for sure that anything is wrong yet."

"Where the hell are they?" she yelled through her tears.

Marcus stood by helplessly as Trina put her head on the table and cried uncontrollably into the crook of her arm. Then she lifted her head from the table and turned to Marcus.

"What the fuck are they up to?"

Hours passed with no sign or contact from either Mac or Slim. Trina showered and fell asleep on the big bed. Marcus crashed on his little cot on the other side of the partition. He awoke from a deep, dreamless slumber when an overhead light was suddenly turned on and he looked up to find Mac standing in the doorway. He held a bouquet of plastic-wrapped flowers, like the kind you buy at gas stations.

Mac scanned the room like a man testing a frozen pond for thin ice. "Is she here?" he asked in a low voice.

"Sleeping," Marcus answered. "Where've you been?"

"There were things I had to do. Why don't you get out, huh? Give us some space."

With the least motion possible, Marcus shook his head. He backed himself into a corner of his cot with his knees drawn up to his chest, asserting himself in a small but defiant voice. "I'm staying. I'm not leaving her alone with you."

"You're not leaving me alone with my wife?" Mac snorted. "Brother, you're in way over your head here. Go down and sit with Slim by the pool. We'll talk later."

Marcus stared his brother down.

"Mac? Are you here?" Trina's voice rose in alarm from the other side of the partition.

"I'm here, baby," Mac said.

He jerked his head toward the door, trying to get Marcus out of the room. But Marcus held his ground as Trina appeared from around the partition. Dressed in one of Mac's oversized black T-shirts, she stood barefoot and shielded her eyes against the light.

"Where the fuck have you been?" she demanded. "I've been trying to reach you for hours."

"Yeah, I'm sorry. I can explain." Mac bowed his head like a naughty schoolboy and took one step toward Trina. He offered her the flowers.

"Are you fucking kidding me?" Trina slapped the flowers of out Mac's hands. "You think I want flowers? Think again! I want my ID, and my verification slip, and my money! Where the hell is it? Where's my money, Mac?"

"It's in a safe place—"

"It's in a safe place?!" Trina stepped forward and shoved Mac in the chest with both hands. "What the fuck does that mean, 'It's in a safe place'? What the hell is going on?"

Marcus wanted answers, too, but he said nothing from his place on the cot.

"If you'll let me explain," Mac tried to calm Trina down again, but she approached even closer. Her eyes aflame, she held up her left hand with its gold band in front of Mac's face.

"And I suppose you can explain this, too! What the fuck did you do to me last night?"

"*Do* to you?" Mac grabbed her hand and pulled it around behind her back. She squirmed to release herself from his grip, but he held her there while he whispered fiercely in her ear.

"I didn't do shit to you last night. You were on board with everything we did, from start to finish. You wanted everything you got last night. You begged me for it. So don't play the victim with me, you little bitch, or I'll show you what a real victim looks like."

"Stop it! You're hurting me!" Trina cried.

Mac pulled harder on her arm.

"Stop hurting her!" Marcus yelled.

"I haven't even started hurting her," Mac sneered, then shot back to Trina, "Now do you want to let me explain how things are going to be, or do you want—"

"All right! All right!" she shouted. "Let me go! You can explain."

Mac pulled her arm higher still. "You gonna behave yourself? You gonna be a good girl?"

"Yes!" Trina cried.

"Yes, what?" Mac demanded.

"Yes, I'll be a good girl!"

Mac threw Trina to the floor.

"Put those flowers in some water," he ordered. "Then we'll talk. And put some fucking pants on. I could smell your cunt all the way from the parking lot."

Trina picked herself up from the floor. She fetched an empty coffee can from the trash, filled it with water, shoved the flowers into it, and slammed the bouquet still wrapped in its plastic sheath onto the dinette table.

When she went around the partition to dress. Mac grabbed a beer from the fridge and took a seat at the table. He closed his eyes as if he were meditating. Marcus crept into the chair across from him, and Mac started when opened them again.

"Christ, what're you still hanging around here for?" Mac asked.

"I'm not leaving until I know the truth," Marcus said. "You can't treat Trina like that. She deserves better."

Mac snorted and sipped his beer. "That bitch is getting better than she deserves."

Trina reappeared, dressed in faded jeans and a white cotton blouse. She took two beers from the fridge and set one on the table in front of Marcus. She let her hand rest for a moment on his shoulder as she reached over him, all the while staring challengingly at Mac.

Mac snorted again. "You two are cute. Really. You're quite the pair."

Trina held up her left hand again. "I thought you and me were a pair. Is this for real? Are we really married?"

"Married as we'll ever be," Mac said. "Legal as shit. Crossed all the t's and dotted all the i's. We're Mr. and Mrs. Brown till death do us part."

"*Why* are we married?" Trina asked.

"Love, I guess."

Trina rubbed her face with her hands. "Just tell me, will you? Just tell me what the fuck is going on so I can get on with my life and figure out what to do next."

Marcus tried to hold her hand, but she slapped him away.

"Look, everything is going to be all right." Mac leaned across the table and Trina allowed him to rest his hand on her arm. "You're over-reacting. You can trust me."

"Yeah, right," Trina rolled her eyes. "Where's my money, Mac?"

"Our money," Mac corrected her. "Our money. We're married now. That money belongs to both of us."

"No way!" Marcus's fist hit the Formica tabletop, as if he were reenacting a performance of his father from his childhood. "Trina won the jackpot, not you! That money belongs to her! Every last penny!"

Mac leaned back in his chair and looked at both Trina, then

Marcus, dead in the eye, and almost smiled. "Not according to the law, it doesn't," he announced.

Trina sat up straight in her chair, alarmed. "What do you mean?"

"According to Nevada law, you and me are married. So, your assets are my assets."

"But I haven't claimed my winnings yet," Trina countered. "I haven't been able to find my ID. So nobody's got anything yet."

"Is that so?" Mac drank his beer and tipped back in his seat like a man without a care in the world.

"What do you mean?" Trina asked, her voice barely a whisper.

Mac slammed his chair to the floor and leaned into her from across the table. "I had your ID. I had the verification form. I had the marriage certificate. By law, what's yours is mine. They gave me the money. In cash. Best wedding present ever."

Trina fell back into her chair as if her body suddenly lacked the strength to hold itself upright.

"No fucking way," she whispered. "I don't believe you."

"Believe what you want," Mac said. "I'm telling you the truth."

"That's not fair!" Marcus protested.

Mac laughed in his face. "So, sue me," he taunted.

"You bastard," Trina said. Remaining calm, she sized Mac up, nodding her head as she seemed to piece the scheme together in her mind.

"So that's why you got me shitfaced drunk last night and married me. So you could steal that money. So you and Slim can waste it all on a fake fucking silver mine of yours."

"It's an investment. You can thank me later," Mac said.

"Fuck you!" Trina spat at him.

"Fuck yourself," Mac shot back.

He stood up and pointed toward the door. "Slim is down by the pool making the final arrangements now. That silver mine is going to make us a shitload of money. And I promise you—*I promise you*—we'll make that money back. And more."

Trina put her face in her hands. "Fuck me. Fuck me," she moaned.

Then she burst into a fit of wild laughter as she tossed her empty beer bottle into the trash and grabbed another from the fridge. She strode up to Mac and put her face close to his. "Can I at least have my ID back? I might need it when I go to the liquor store to restock this fucking fridge. I'm drinking the last damn beer."

Mac pulled her ID out of his wallet and handed it to her. "You'll probably want to update that with a new last name, Mrs. Brown."

Then he turned on his heel and left the room.

29

After Mac was gone, Trina glared at the closed door for a long moment before she lit a cigarette and sat back down at the table. Marcus was still glued to his seat, right there next to her, but she seemed to have forgotten him. She jumped when he started to speak.

"What are we going to do? I mean, what *can* we do?" He tried to rest his hand on her arm just as Mac had done. She shook him off.

"I don't know. I need to think." Trina's eyes darted around the room, as if the answer to her problems might be found in the years of grime embedded on every surface of Room 310.

"Do you think he's telling the truth? Do you think he really has the money?" Marcus probed.

"Oh yeah, he has the money," Trina nodded and drank from her beer bottle. "Those assholes saw their chance and they took it. They couldn't steal the money out of my savings, but they sure could liquor me up and steal it right from under my nose at Caesars Palace. Bastards! The question is: Where is it now and how do I get it back?"

Marcus took a deep breath and fidgeted with his hands while he pondered his next question.

"Is it really that important? The money, I mean? You've got your savings. Why not use some of it to get away from Mac and Slim? Forget about the casino money! It's not like you actually lost anything."

Trina turned to him slowly. "Are you out of your fucking mind? I was this close—this close—to having a hundred thousand dollars! If I'd had my ID with me last night, they would've written out a check to me right then and there. That money would be mine. It would be in *my* bank account where it belongs. And I'm not leaving this godforsaken dump until it is."

"Just leave now, before things get even worse."

"Worse?" She threw her hands up in the air as she paced the floor. "I work at the fucking Waffle Hovel. I live in a dump. I'm married to a man who beats me and steals from me. I've got you stuck to me like a burr in my ass. How much worse can things get?"

Marcus knew it was all true but to hear Trina say it out loud somehow made it all worse, much worse. For a moment, Marcus was at a loss for words, not because he had nothing to say, but because the thoughts he wanted to give voice to had been lurking in the back of his mind for years. For years he'd resisted bringing them into the light. He'd felt safer keeping those thoughts in the dark recesses of his mind. But now it wasn't just himself he was protecting. Now he needed to protect Trina, so he strung together the words that yanked those thoughts out into the full light of day.

"You don't know what they're capable of," Marcus stammered. "Slim and Mac. The two of them. Together. They're capable of killing. They're capable of killing you. *Mac* is capable of killing you."

Trina stopped pacing. "Mac isn't killing anybody, and neither is Slim. Mac told me about what happened when they were kids. How Slim accidentally killed a man when they were stealing copper from his house. The guy surprised them. Slim went nuts and killed the guy. It's not like he *planned* on killing anybody. It just happened."

"And it might just happen again! I've never known for sure exactly who did what back then, but I know they were both there. Who really beat that man to death? I don't know. But I know Slim took the fall for the two of them. Slim went to prison and Mac didn't, and Slim's holding that over Mac's head. Whatever they're cooking up together now, he's backed Mac into a corner. He's got him desperate. I'm afraid of what he might do."

Trina came back to the table and jabbed her finger in Marcus's face. "You're afraid? Well, I'm afraid, too. I'm afraid of not getting what's rightfully mine. And I'm not turning tail and running. If you want to leave, leave. But I'm staying. If they took that money in cash, it has to be here somewhere. And I'm going to find it if it's the last goddamned thing I do."

Now Trina pointed her lit cigarette to the door. "Those fuckers are out there right now planning their next move. You gonna help me, or what?"

"Of course, I'll help you. You know I will, I just don't know what you expect me to do."

"For Christ's sake, help me find the fucking money!" Trina exploded. She lit another cigarette and pulled back the curtain on the picture window. "Look at those assholes, making their big plans. They think the game's over, but it's not. I'm not leaving without a fight."

Marcus got up from the table and stood beside Trina at the window. He saw a calm smile cross her lips as she watched Mac and Slim. She nudged Marcus with her elbow.

"They haven't sealed their deal yet," she said, pointing her cigarette at them. "You can tell by their body language, by the way they're talking. If it was a done deal, that money would be gone already. They'd have handed it over to whoever the fuck they need to hand it over to, and they'd be bragging about their big accomplishment. They'd be waving documents in our faces, rubbing it in. Their big deal! Their big fucking deal!"

Marcus studied Mac and Slim from the third floor. He thought Trina's assessment probably was correct. There did seem to be a tension, an urgency, between the two men. When Slim's phone rang, he answered it immediately, and waved Mac away from him as he strode into the parking lot to take the call alone. Mac dragged his hands across his buzz cut and kicked the chain link fence that enclosed the pool.

"I bet they're asking them for more money." Trina laughed.

Marcus smiled tentatively, not sure how to interpret her mood.

"This is our chance," she said. "Their deal's not done, and until it is, that money stays right where it is. We just have to find it before they finalize their plans."

"You think so?" Marcus asked.

"I know so!" Trina said, steel in her voice. "And here's what we're gonna do. I'm gonna be the whipped bitch. I'm gonna go back to work at the Waffle Hovel with my tail dragging between my legs. They'll think they've put me in my place. And you—" Trina grabbed Marcus's arms with both hands. "You're gonna start your new job at Circus Circus. You keep your nose to the grindstone. They'll think they've got you beat, too."

"Come on!" Trina took Marcus by the hand and pulled him out onto the walkway. "Let's go *make peace* with the asshole powers that be."

Marcus was amazed by Trina's nerve and followed her down the three flights of stairs and across the parking lot to the pool. Mac was still there, pacing, agitated, and alone. Slim was at the far end of the parking lot, still talking on his phone.

"Christ!" Mac muttered as Trina and Marcus took their seats at the concrete patio table.

"You forgot the bread," Trina said lightly to Marcus.

"What?" he stared at her.

"For your ducks." She pointed to the aquatic squad that had come to the edge of the pool expecting Marcus to feed them as he normally did.

"Oh, right," Marcus said, too mentally depleted to think of anything else to say.

"What do you two want?" Mac asked. "We're conducting business here."

"We don't want anything," Trina said. "We talked it over, and I decided you have as much right to that money as I do, maybe even more. It sucks you went behind my back to get it. It sucks you made a fool out of me." Trina waggled her ring finger. "But we can forget about that for now. The money's yours. Do what you want with it. Like Marcus said, it's not like I've really lost anything, since I never had it in the first place."

Mac eyed Trina and Marcus suspiciously.

"Well, that must be one big-ass bitter pill to swallow," he drawled.

"It is a big-ass bitter pill," Trina agreed, fixing Mac with a steady gaze. "But I've swallowed worse."

"Have you now?" Mac retorted.

"I have." Trina held her left hand out in front of her to admire her wedding band. "But it went down easier, knowing that we're married. Which, legally, still makes half of that money mine, as well as half of anything that comes to you—to us, I mean—from the silver mine."

Mac took a long drag on his cigarette. "You bitches are all the same."

"You pricks are all the same."

They grinned at one another.

"Come here, wife!" Mac ordered, gruff but tender.

Trina climbed out of her chair and ensconced herself in Mac's arms.

"I still want my diamond. And my house."

"You'll get it all. And then some."

30

Who was fooling who? Were they in love? Did they hate each other? Had Trina changed her mind, or made up her mind, that she actually loved Mac? Did she want that house just for herself, or did she now want to share it with Mac?

Those questions, and more, rattled around Marcus's brain all of Sunday as life at the Sandbar Suites returned to normal, and on Monday he dutifully reported for his first day of work at Circus Circus. The required corporate orientation meetings were as boring as Howard, the bar manager who hired him, had said they'd be, so it was easy for his thoughts to wander into other areas.

In particular, he thought about the money, trying to imagine it as a tangible reality. *What would a hundred thousand dollars actually look like in real life? How much space would it take up? What denominations would it be in—hundreds, five hundreds, thousands? How large of a container would it take to hold all that green paper? How heavy would it be? What kind of a container would Mac or Slim have chosen for it? Where would they hide it?*

He thought about that last point a lot. Given their current living arrangements, it didn't seem to Marcus that Slim or Mac had many good options when it came to stashing their cash. Where, exactly, at the Sandbar Suites of all places, would you think you could safely hide a hefty bundle of money? There was no privacy there. Everybody knew everybody's business—who was working the streets, who was selling dope, who was working a straight job, who was fucking, who was fighting . . .

It seemed impossible to Marcus that word of Trina's windfall, and of Mac and Slim's stealing of the cash, had not somehow seeped into the awareness of the Sandbar Suites community. He couldn't imagine there was a locked door or a locked trunk of a car where that money would be secure for long. He assumed Mac and Slim had entertained similar thoughts. So maybe the cash wasn't on the property at all. Maybe they'd buried it in a secret place in the desert. Stashed it in a locker at the bus station—Marcus had seen that in movies. He supposed Mac could even have deposited the money into the bank account that only Mac had access to, although it was hard for Marcus to imagine Slim putting up with that the way he had.

But there was something about the idea of Mac being separated from the money that didn't sit right. It seemed to Marcus that would be a hard thing for Mac to do, no matter how safe the hiding place might be. Leaving all that money somewhere far away . . . No, Mac would want to keep that money close, no matter what.

By mid-day, it occurred to Marcus perhaps he could stop thinking about the money altogether. He assumed Trina was searching for it while he was stuck in the new employee orientation, so he texted her during his lunch break.

Any luck with the $$$?

When ten minutes passed without a response, he tried calling. But the call went to voicemail.

Marcus returned to the Circus Circus corporate offices for more training videos with his musings about the cash transformed into dread. *Was Trina okay?* That was his only thought for the remaining four hours of videos and online training sessions.

The second his new hire group was dismissed, Marcus left Circus

Circus and jogged all the way across town back to the Sandbar Suites. Out of breath, panicked, he burst into the apartment to find Mac and Trina next to each other on the big bed watching the evening news. They both turned to him, startled.

"Everything okay?" Marcus gasped, trying to get his wind back, trying to act casual.

"Everything's fine. What the fuck is wrong with you?" Mac said.

"Nothing. Nothing," Marcus said. "I just need to use the bathroom. Sorry for the interruption."

Trina fixed her eyes on Marcus with a meaning he was unable to interpret as he passed by her on his way to the bathroom. She was trying to tell him something, but he didn't know what.

He shut the bathroom door behind him with his body trembling. He took deep breaths, relieved himself, washed his hands, and re-emerged into the bedroom more composed but still uncertain.

His head felt light as he glanced in Trina's direction, scanning her face and arms for signs of abuse. But she looked fine. At least he saw no new bruises. It didn't appear she'd been crying. Everything seemed normal except for the intensity behind her eyes.

"Get the fuck out of here." Mac said. "We're on our honeymoon."

"Some honeymoon," Trina snorted. "I'm off to the Waffle Hovel tonight."

Mac got up and made sure Marcus was heading back out of the apartment. "Now stay the fuck out and leave us alone," and Mac shut door in Marcus's face.

Marcus was standing outside of Room 310, staring at the closed door. He realized the predicament Trina was in. She was Mac's prisoner now. She hadn't texted or called because Mac had never let her out of his sight, and he wasn't going to let her out of his sight while she was at the apartment until he and Slim had disposed of her money.

Marcus pondered the situation as he made his way down the stairs and over to the pool. *The money's somewhere in that room*, he thought. That explained Mac's behavior. He could see it now. He realized Mac

hadn't given Trina two minutes to herself the day before either, and
he'd probably kept her on a tight leash all day today, too. Mac knew,
given the chance, Trina would look for that money. If the money wasn't
in the room, Mac wouldn't have had any reason to keep Trina bound to
his side for two straight days.

From the patio table at the pool, Marcus stared up at Room 310.
The money was in that room! They hadn't buried it in the desert or
stashed it in a locker somewhere! It was right there within reach!
Marcus wondered if Trina reached her hand under the bed, would she
pull out a briefcase filled with hundred-dollar bills? He wondered if
she'd scrambled off the bed and searched underneath it in the few minutes Mac had left her alone while he used the bathroom or showered?
Had she looked in the closet or the kitchen cupboards? Or was she
paralyzed with fear, rightfully terrified about what Mac might do to her
if he caught her snooping around?

Marcus lay down on a chaise lounge and lit a joint. It was too much
for him to take in. He wished he'd never given Trina that fifty-dollar
bill. He wished he hadn't insisted she gamble it on the slots. He wished
she'd never won the big jackpot. He wished he'd never come to Vegas.
He wished he were someone—anyone—other than Mac Brown's kid
brother. He didn't exactly wish he was dead, just that he'd never been
born to Fred and Myrna Brown. He was a lost cause. Had been since
the moment he drew his first breath. And so was Mac. And so was Slim.
Maybe even Trina, although he wasn't sure about her. He thought Trina
maybe still had a chance. If she got her money, maybe things would
turn out okay for her.

That was all that mattered now was finding the money, giving it
all to Trina.

With that thought foremost in his mind, Marcus closed his eyes
and fell asleep while the sun was setting in the west. When he woke up,
it was dark, and the Sandbar Suites seemed eerily quiet. It was a rare
moment of peace, he thought. He listened again. No one was arguing
in the parking lot, no one was smoking a cigarette and chatting with a

neighbor out on the walkway, no Coke cans *cathunked* out of the vending machines, no flip-flops flipping and flopping as someone carted a
load of clothes to the laundry room.

Marcus checked the time on his phone: 3:00 a.m., three hours
into Trina's midnight to 7:00 a.m. shift at the Waffle House. Where
were Mac and Slim? Marcus scanned the parking lot for their vehicles.
Neither car was there. He peered up at 308 and 310. The lights were
off, the doors shut to both rooms.

Go look! a voice inside Marcus's head ordered him, but he felt as if
some dread force held him in place on the chaise lounge. It was terror,
pure and simple. The idea of what terrible things Mac or Slim would
do to him if they were to catch him searching the apartment for Trina's
money. He felt like a character trapped inside a horror movie, one part
of his brain screaming for him to GET OUT, the other ordering him
to look for the money.

He knew the longer he waited the more likely it was Slim or Mac
would return, and the chance to investigate would be lost. He almost
hoped they would return. He kept his eyes glued to the parking lot for
a good ten minutes, certain Mac's truck or Slim's car would pull into a
parking space at any moment, and he'd be relieved of his obligation to
Trina to search for the money.

When neither vehicle materialized, Marcus rose on trembling legs
and made his way to Room 310. Play it cool, he told himself as he
unlocked the door and took one step inside. You live here. You have a
right to be here. Mac's first thought won't be that you're looking for the
money. He'll think you're using the bathroom or getting yourself something to eat or drink. Besides, the money probably isn't even here. Mac
wouldn't have just left it here, would he? It's probably already gone.

If Marcus could've been honest with himself, that would've been
his wish—that it was too late, the money was already gone, and Trina
would just have to just accept it. It sucked, but he thought that would
be best all around. If he could honestly tell Trina he searched for the

money, but it just wasn't there. They got away with it. Case closed. End of story.

As he rummaged through clothes in the closet and the dresser, finding nothing, Marcus convinced himself that he wasn't going to find anything. Mac and Slim had the money with them and were doing whatever it was they were going to do with it. Even if they caught him looking for it, the worst they would do is call him a pussy, same as they always did. He started to relax, feeling certain he was already out of harm's way. And then he looked under the bed.

He spotted a small black Samsonite suitcase he'd never seen before.

31

Marcus felt a sinkhole open in his gut that might suck him into hell. He grabbed hold of the handle and pulled the suitcase toward him. The whole thing felt so light he wondered if there was even anything in it. That calmed his fears a bit. A big load of money would be heavy, right?

He shook the suitcase before he tried to open it. Something definitely thudded softly around inside. But a hundred thousand dollars? He thought not. And the suitcase wasn't locked. Surely if Mac and Slim had concealed Trina's winnings in a suitcase under the bed, they'd have at least locked it. But Marcus didn't see any locking devices on the suitcase, so for all he knew, Mac had just got himself a suitcase. No need to jump to conclusions.

Marcus set the suitcase on the bed, unzipped it, hesitated a second, then opened it up. There it was! Benjamin Franklin's face looked up at him from a handful of neatly bundled one-hundred-dollar bills. But it didn't look to Marcus like one hundred thousand dollars, or even a hundred thousand dollars minus whatever the casino took out in taxes. He remembered they always take out the taxes. So, his first thought was maybe this was his inheritance money. Mac had stuck it under the bed and Marcus could've taken it all any time he wanted.

But as his eyes adjusted to the sight before him, and he picked up one of the bundles of bills, Marcus knew this wasn't the inheritance money. There were seven bundles in the suitcase, each held together with a yellow paper band with "$10,000" printed on it, and then another slightly smaller bundle with "$6,000" on the band. He was looking at almost eighty thousand dollars. He held one of the bundles in his hand.

Suddenly lightheaded and weak, he sank onto the floor and rested his back against the bed. He stared at the money and felt the cell phone in his front shirt pocket rising and falling with every breath he took. A voice inside his head was screaming at him to call Trina.

But he didn't. Not right away, anyhow. Instead, he looked at the ten thousand dollars in his hand. Now there was a new voice in his head, and it said loud and clear:

This is yours!

Take it!

Take half and leave!

Leave right now!

Why shouldn't I?

He sprang up from the floor, rolled up his half of what was supposed to be his inheritance—five thousand dollars—and shoved it into the waistband of his jeans. He dumped the rest of the money out of the suitcase and onto the bed. He grabbed his toothbrush and comb from the bathroom and a handful of shirts and pants, underwear, and T-shirts from the dresser and crammed them into the suitcase. He was scanning the room for his jacket when the phone rang in his pocket. The vibration of it ripped through his body with the force of an electric shock. Caller ID showed it was Trina.

"What's going on?" she demanded when Marcus answered. "Where are you? Where's Mac? This is the first minute I've had to take a break."

Marcus's hands shook. Tears welled in his eyes. His breathing came in low, short gasps. He pulled the phone away from his ear and stared at it long enough to picture himself stepping out onto the walkway and hurling the phone all the way from the third floor of the building into the pool.

Do it! the voice ordered him. But he didn't. He put the phone back to his ear and let Trina's voice come through.

"Marcus, what the fuck is going on?" she pleaded with him, sounding close to tears herself.

"I just found your money," Marcus whispered. "It's right here in the room. You need to come home. Now!"

"Why the fuck didn't you call me?" Trina nearly screamed.

"I just found it!" Marcus whispered, defensive but firm. "Just come home."

"Oh, I'm there!" Trina said. And then she was gone.

By car, the trip from the Waffle House to the Sandbar Suites was just a matter of minutes, and Marcus knew Trina would be speeding to get there. His suitcase was packed. He had his jacket slung over his arm. He had the five thousand stuffed into the waistband of his jeans. Mac and Slim were nowhere in sight. Trina was on her way.

Marcus stared at the suitcase in the middle of the bed. He could picture himself leaving as if he were seeing himself in a dream, but he couldn't make his feet move toward the door. Like a zombie out of a horror movie compelled to do things against his will, he dropped his jacket on the floor, dumped his clothes out of the suitcase, stuffed all the money back in, including the five thousand dollars from his pants. He sat down on the bed to await his doom.

When Trina failed to arrive as quickly as he'd anticipated, he scrambled to shove his clothes back into the dresser drawer and replaced his comb and toothbrush in the bathroom. When Trina burst through the front door, he was sitting on the side of the bed, his hands folded in his lap.

Trina locked the door behind her, something Marcus had not done. She turned off the outside light, something else he'd not done.

"Jesus Christ! Is that it?" she asked breathlessly, pointing to the suitcase as she crossed the room.

Marcus nodded, numbly. He lifted the suitcase open for her to see inside.

She peered in. "Where's the rest of it?" she demanded of Marcus. "Where's the rest of my money? That's not all of it, is it?"

"It's all there. Ten grand per bundle. See?" Marcus handed her an unopened bundle.

Trina fanned the ten-thousand-dollar bundle in her hands, then reached into the suitcase and counted the remaining bundles.

"That's only seven!"

"Eight. I opened one."

"There should be ten! Where are the other two?" Trina put the question to Marcus with fire in her eyes.

"This is what I found," Marcus said, throwing his hands into the air. "The casino has to take out the taxes. Remember? Isn't that what Brent said? It's seventy-six thousand dollars."

"Oh! Right." Trina sat down on the bed, on the other side of the suitcase. "You're right," she said, her voice calmer and more under control. "Brent did say something about taxes."

She picked up a couple bundles of cash and examined them with an almost disapproving look as she returned them to the suitcase.

"I just thought there would be *more*. Like the suitcase would be full."

"I thought the same thing," Marcus admitted. "That's why I opened one up and counted. Because it didn't seem like enough. But that's it! There's your money!"

Trina exhaled loudly and turned to Marcus with a broad smile, which lasted about two seconds before a cloud crossed her expression.

"Do you know where Mac and Slim are?" she asked.

"Not a clue."

Trina's eyes darted to the locked door.

"They could come back any minute!" she said excitedly.

"What are you gonna do?" Marcus asked.

"I don't know! I don't know!" Trina exclaimed with a laugh. "I hadn't thought that far ahead!"

She jumped onto the bed, balanced herself on her knees, and gazed lovingly at the bundles of money in the suitcase. Her blue eyes were alive with joy. She couldn't stop smiling, and tried to hide her grin behind one hand.

"This is my money! Oh my God!"

She glanced down at her Waffle House uniform. To Marcus's alarm, she started ripping off her shirt, pants, shoes . . .

"I'm never going to have to work at the Waffle Hovel again!" She stood up exultantly, threw the clothes on the floor, and jumped back up on the bed. She gazed adoringly into the suitcase again. "Oh my God! I love this money, Marcus. I love this money more than any man! I love this money more than anything!"

She picked up bundles of cash, brought them to her lips, and kissed them, long and hard. She inhaled the scent of the bills as if she were smelling a rare blooming flower. She closed her eyes and held bundles of cash to her chest.

"Oh my God! I can't stand it! It's too much!" she gushed.

She started splitting open the sealed bundles of one-hundred-dollar bills, spreading them out in the suitcase so they took up more room. She opened all the bundles, then grinned at Marcus devilishly as she slipped out of her bra and panties. She pushed the suitcase out of her way and threw herself down naked on the bed.

"What are you doing?" Marcus, alarmed and aroused, had one eye on the front door, another on the naked whiteness of Trina's body stretched out before him.

"Dump it on top of me!" she ordered gleefully, pointing to the suitcase full of loose cash. She closed her eyes and took a deep breath.

"Dump it all over me! I need to feel it all over my body! Like rain falling from the skies, only it's money!"

Marcus hesitated.

"Do it now!"

Marcus picked up the suitcase and dumped the bills onto Trina's naked body. He felt guilty, as if he were emptying the contents of a trash can over her, but she cried out in ecstasy. She caressed the money against her skin. She rolled around in it. She kissed it. She got it tangled in her hair. She gasped for breath, then collapsed into a spasm of tears, burying her face in a pillow covered in one-hundred-dollar bills.

Marcus stood by the bed, watching the performance in mute astonishment, the empty suitcase dangling from his hand. He didn't hear the key turn in the lock but he heard the door open, and saw Trina go still at the sound.

Mac was home.

32

Mac stood frozen for a second, as if it wasn't immediately clear what he was seeing, as if he needed to understand what was in front of him. But it was only a moment before he crossed the room and ripped the empty suitcase out of Marcus's hand. Only a moment before he grabbed Trina by both arms, hauled her out of the bed, and threw her to the floor. That moment was all it took for Marcus to feel as if every last drop of blood had suddenly drained from his body. He couldn't comprehend why he was still standing, why he was still breathing. Surely he was dead. Surely Mac had already killed him.

But no, he was alive. He was still standing by the edge of the bed, watching events unfold around him. Trina was screaming, "Stop it! You're hurting me!" as Mac dragged her across the carpet by her hair and pulled her naked body into the recliner.

"Fucking worthless whore!" Mac slapped her face. "Fucking cunt!"

Trina shielded her face with her arms.

"I'm sorry! I'm sorry! Don't hurt me!"

Mac pulled her arms away from her face, glared at her, then shoved her back into the recliner with disgust.

"And you!" Mac turned his anger on Marcus, still rooted to the floor next to the bed. "What the fuck do you think you're doing? Who the fuck do you think you are?"

Marcus's knees finally buckled and Mac landed several powerful kicks into his ribs. He collapsed in a heap at his brother's feet and took the punishment as if it were something he deserved. He didn't try to move out of the way, he didn't try to avoid the blows. He didn't beg Mac to stop, but Trina did.

"Please, Mac! Please! You don't understand! It's not what you think! Let me explain."

"Not what I think?" Mac exploded. "Are you fucking serious?"

But there was less rage in his voice now. He shook his head as he looked from Trina in the recliner, to Marcus on the floor, to all the bills strewn across the bed.

"This looks pretty fucking self-evident to me," he announced. "My brother and my wife are fucking with my money! What the fuck do you need to explain?"

"Everything!" Trina cried. "Let me get dressed, and we'll talk about it."

"There's nothing to talk about," Mac said. But he didn't stop Trina from crawling out of the recliner and slipping on one of Mac's T-shirts as she got to her feet. Marcus pulled himself up into a sitting position and watched from his spot on the floor.

"There's everything to talk about." Trina pointed to the cash-covered bed. "That money belongs to me, and you know it! It's mine, and I'm not leaving here without it."

Mac moved close to Trina, towering over her. He gripped her throat with one hand, lifting her up onto her toes. She struggled to breathe and tried to claw his hand free from her neck as he spoke.

"Over my fucking dead body. That money is everything I need. Everything is in place now, and some little bitch from the Waffle House is not going to fuck up everything I've been working for. You're not leaving here with a single cent. You got that?"

Mac threw Trina across the room. She fell to the floor, coughing and gasping for air.

"I'm *this* close, *this* close to bringing this deal to a close." Mac turned his back on Trina and started collecting bills off the bed, shoving them back into the suitcase.

Marcus remained too numb to move. All he wanted was for Mac to pack up the money and leave. And when Mac was gone, then he'd leave, too. He'd finally had enough. But for the moment, he knew he just needed to stay on the floor and wait for Mac to get all the money back into the suitcase and leave. Then everything would be okay.

He mentally willed Trina to stay on the floor, too, and wait for Mac to leave. He reached his hand out to her, trying in his feeble way to communicate his thoughts to her. But Trina wasn't looking at Marcus. He watched in disbelief as she staggered up from the floor, her anger almost palpable, walked up behind Mac and slammed both of her fists between his shoulder blades.

Mac fell onto the bed, and Trina landed two more blows before he was back on his feet. He, like Marcus, stared at her in disbelief as she held her ground.

"It's my money." Her voice was a hoarse whisper. "Marcus gave me fifty bucks. I put it into the slot machine. I won a hundred grand. It's mine, and I'm not leaving here without it."

Mac's fist hit the side of Trina's face with enough force to send her head into the corner of the dresser before she fell back and crumpled onto the floor. Marcus heard the thud when her head hit the dresser.

"You fucking little cunt! You'll leave here with the clothes on your back, if you're lucky!"

Then Mac turned away from her and resumed shoving the money back into the black suitcase.

Marcus pulled himself toward Trina and touched her bloodied face. "Trina? Trina, are you okay?"

Her eyes didn't open. She didn't respond.

"Trina!"

Panicked, he shook Trina's shoulders. He called her name. But nothing he did got a response. He pressed his ear to Trina's chest. He heard no heartbeat. No breath lifted her breasts.

Marcus opened his mouth but only a gasp came out. Then he wailed at his brother, "Mac, help me! Call nine-one-one! Call an ambulance! She's not breathing! Help me!"

Mac barely looked in his brother's direction as he continued filling the suitcase with money.

"What do you mean she's not breathing?" he asked dismissively.

"I mean she's not breathing!" The words came out of Marcus in a high-pitched scream.

He fumbled for the phone in his front shirt pocket, then dropped it. He was on his hands and knees trying to pick it up with trembling hands when Mac kicked the phone to the other side of the room.

"What are you doing?" Marcus screamed. "We need to help her!"

"Calm the fuck down! You're overreacting, like some hysterical bitch. I didn't hit her that hard. I'm sure she's fine. She's just passed out."

"Are you sure?"

Mac pushed cascades of hair away from her face, revealing the bloody wound where her head had collided with the dresser. He held her limp wrist, checking for a pulse. He leaned his face close to her nose and mouth, checking for a breath. He pressed his hand to her chest, checking for a heartbeat.

Marcus watched, barely breathing himself, hoping beyond hope Mac was right. Trina was just unconscious. She was alive.

"Is she okay?" he asked.

Mac took one step back from Trina's body and shook his head.

"No, she's not okay," he said, his voice low and calm. "She's gone. She's dead."

"You killed her! You killed Trina!" Marcus sobbed.

"I didn't kill her!" Mac snapped. "It was an accident! She just died! There's a difference!"

"We have to call someone! We have to call the police." Marcus scanned the floor for his phone.

"No!" Mac spat the word with a ferocity that chilled Marcus's blood. "We can't do that! Not yet!"

Marcus gaped at his older brother. He'd always known Mac could be mean, but this was something new, something beyond the simple meanness of a barroom brawl, or beatings meted out to settle a score. Marcus had been afraid of his brother countless times, but the fear he felt now was infused with an anger he'd never experienced before.

Marcus pulled himself to his feet. "What do you mean 'not yet?'" he demanded. "This is happening now. This has to be dealt with now."

"Look! You don't understand," Mac said. His eyes were a mix of fury and desperation. "Everything hinges on me getting that money to Slim *right now*. Do you understand? This isn't some game we're playing. If I don't get this money to Slim, and Slim doesn't get this money to his contacts for the mine, Trina might not be the only dead body you have to call the cops about. Do you understand me? Do you?"

Mac brushed past Marcus, turned his back to him, and finished packing the money into the suitcase. Marcus planted himself in the front of the door as he heard the zipper sliding closed. Mac turned around to find Marcus blocking his way.

"Get out of my way," Mac ordered.

Marcus shook his head and, before Mac had time to even register the defiance, Marcus charged him. He slammed his head into Mac's gut, wrapped his arms around his big brother's waist, and landed him on the floor. He pummeled Mac's head with his fists, all the while screaming, "I won't let you get away with it! I won't let you get away with it!"

Marcus held the upper hand for just a matter of seconds before Mac threw him off and pinned him to the floor. Marcus's eyes locked on Mac's in pure hatred for what felt to him like the entirety of his life. Then Mac landed a blow to Marcus's head that plunged him into darkness.

33

arcus was in heaven. He woke up in bed with Trina lying by his side. Her long hair was loose, spread out around her on the worn white bedding like a reddish cloud. Marcus rolled to his right side, pressed his face through Trina's hair into the curve of her neck, breathing in the tropical scent of her shampoo. It was all he'd ever wanted. God must have forgiven him all his sins and laid him to rest in paradise. *Well worth it,* he thought, *to be killed by my own brother if it means spending eternity next to Trina.*

Except he wasn't in heaven. He was in hell, and hell was a place on earth where a man opened his eyes knowing the lovely woman lying next to him was dead. Hell was knowing his brother had not killed him, but the woman he loved.

The sun was just coming up when Marcus lifted his head off the pillow and staggered to his feet. Had he been a sensible man, he'd have found his phone and called the police. That's what he'd wanted to do before Mac punched his lights out. He'd wanted to hand the whole mess over to the authorities, let the chips fall where they may, bring this miserable chapter of their lives to an end, even if it meant sitting in a Vegas jail cell.

Perhaps that was still what he wanted. Marcus couldn't say for sure. All he knew as he pulled a sheet over Trina's exposed body was that he was going to find his brother. He was going to track Mac down and confront him once and for all. Give Mac a chance to turn himself in, tell his side of the story to the cops, and then, one way or another, Marcus would be done. Maybe Mac would actually kill him this time. Or maybe they'd go together to the police. Marcus no longer really cared which way the story went. He just knew it wasn't ending without him seeing his brother one more time.

He searched the apartment for their father's gun, knowing in advance it wouldn't be there. Mac had the gun; Marcus didn't doubt that for a second. Still, he looked, and in looking, he found their father's handcuffs, sitting on the dresser right next to the mahogany box that held their father's ashes. Their mother's box of dust was there, too, but she hadn't left her sons anything but sad memories. So, Marcus stuffed the handcuffs into his back pants pocket, collected Trina's car keys from her purse, and kissed her on the cheek before he departed the Sandbar Suites.

Marcus presumed Mac had returned to the silver mine to meet up with Slim. As he headed west into the desert, he struggled to recall the route Mac had followed the one time he'd taken Marcus to the mine. It took him more than an hour and several wrong turns before he spotted the sun glinting off the tin roof of the abandoned silver mine that Mac had attached his dreams of wealth and success to.

Had anyone asked him, Marcus wouldn't have been able to provide a coherent answer as to why he was even bothering to track down his brother in this desolate landscape. It was May, a time back home when the thick scent of lilac blossoms perfumed the air, and the sun just kissed your skin with its warmth. The leaves on the trees were exploding in a hundred different shades of green. Rivers and streams were overflowing with ice melt from the mountains, icy cold water running so fast and so loud, you had to shout to be heard over it. That was home, Marcus thought. This was hell, a place where the sun burned everything to ashes, where nothing pleasant wafted through the air, where nothing flowed wild and free, even if only for a season.

What was he doing *here*, in this graveyard of abandoned hopes, bleakness stretching out around him for miles in every direction? He couldn't explain it, not even to himself.

Marcus spotted Mac's red truck parked in the shade of one of the ramshackle wooden structures that dotted the abandoned mine. Mac was in the driver's seat, with the window rolled down, smoking a cigarette. Marcus brought Trina's car to a stop at what he hoped was a safe distance about twenty feet away. He stepped out of the car, shut the door behind him, and shouted to his brother.

"It doesn't have to end this way, Mac! It doesn't have to go from bad to worse. You still have a chance to do the right thing. You can turn yourself in. You can go in a different direction. We both can!"

He watched Mac shake his head, toss the lit cigarette out the window, and turn on the engine of the Ford F-150. He leaned his head out the window.

"Get back in your car and get the hell out of here while you still can, baby brother!" he hollered. "Just leave! This isn't your business."

"You're my business! You're my brother!" Marcus shouted as he took several steps closer to the truck. But his voice started to crack and lose its strength as he heard the words coming out of his mouth.

"We're brothers, Mac. We're all we've got left in the world. Let's leave together. Let's just go," he pleaded.

Mac revved the engine of his truck.

"Get back in the car, Marcus, or I swear to God, I will run you down like a dog in the road!"

Marcus kept moving forward, wondering with every step when his trembling legs would give out beneath him. He was less than six feet away when he heard the click of the revolver and felt a bullet whiz by just over the top of his head.

"I missed that time," Mac warned. "I won't miss again. Now get in the car and go home."

"I'm not leaving here alone!" Marcus shouted back. "You do what you want, but I'm taking you with me, one way or another."

Mac cocked the revolver a second time. He pointed it at his brother's head. But Marcus still didn't retreat. Mac lowered the revolver a couple inches, aimed it at his brother's shoulder, and fired.

The impact of the bullet sent Marcus to his knees. He grabbed the bleeding hole with his right hand and clambered back to his feet, screaming through his tears.

"I can't believe you're fucking doing this to me!"

Mac fired again. This shot kicked up some dirt near his brother's feet.

"Just get in the car and go," Mac said. "Please."

Holding his wounded arm, Marcus staggered back to Trina's car and settled in behind the steering wheel. He started the engine and turned the car around as if preparing to depart, but then he waited.

Mac gunned the F-150 and rammed it into the back end of Trina's Corolla. The rear bumper crumbled, and Marcus laughed at the sight of his brother's enraged face in his rearview mirror. He stepped on the gas and sped away from the silver mine. When Mac didn't follow, Marcus circled back around off the dirt roadway and barreled his car into the rear of Mac's truck.

Mac stepped on the gas and tore off down the road and Marcus gave chase. The F-150 far outpaced the mangled Corolla and was already leaving the mine when Mac circled back around. Marcus gunned the Corolla and raced straight toward the front end of Mac's truck.

"I'm coming for you, you bastard!"

Marcus couldn't have said what he hoped to accomplish with a game of chicken, but the look of bewilderment and hate on his brother's face was exhilarating. When Mac veered off at the last second to avoid a collision and drove off farther into the desert, Marcus turned the car around, and chased his brother. Mac dodged the Corolla a couple more times, but on the third go round, he floored the F-150 as fast as it would go, and T-boned the passenger side of his brother's car.

The Corolla was now crumpled in the front and the back and on one side. Somehow, it was still running.

"I'm not done yet!" Marcus shouted hoping Mac could hear him. "I'm going to destroy you!"

Mac looked at his brother with disbelief as Marcus backed up, pulled the Corolla around, gunned it, and drove into the side of his truck. The nose of the Corolla jammed under the body of the truck and punctured the gas tank. Marcus threw the car into reverse, and while the back wheels spun, throwing spires of red dirt into the air, gasoline flowed out onto the desert floor.

"Jesus Christ!" Mac yelled as he clambered out of his truck. At the same time, Marcus crawled out through the open window of the Corolla and fell to the ground.

"Are you satisfied now?" Mac demanded. "Have you caused enough damage?"

Marcus started giggling hysterically and crawled away from the mangled vehicles on his hands and knees. He reached into his pants pocket and retrieved a Bic lighter. He flicked the lighter on, and tossed it into the ever-expanding stream of gasoline.

Flames shot up into the sky and engulfed both vehicles.

"No! No! What have you done?" Mac screamed.

Still squatting on his knees, Marcus stared at the flames, not fully comprehending what, in fact, he *had* done. He watched in utter confusion as Mac swung open the driver's side door of the truck and crawled back into the heart of the inferno. It only started to make sense when he saw Mac kick what looked like a smoking black box out the door. It was the suitcase, with the money.

The flaming mass landed on the ground not far from the spot where Marcus was rooted in the dirt. He inched away from the flames while Mac ripped off his shirt and threw both the shirt and his body on top of the fire. Mac screamed as flames and melted plastic burned his arms, face, chest, and hair. He crawled around in the dirt with the intensity of a madman, scooping up armfuls of sand and dumping them over the noxious fire.

When the flames were extinguished, Mac collapsed face down in the dirt and wept.

"Fucking Christ! Fuck me!" Mac moaned.

Mac rolled over onto his back, and Marcus gasped to see strips of charred flesh up and down his brother's arms, chest, and face. Patches of his skin were reddened, others were black, all were encrusted with sand and oozing blood. Mac remained on his back, sobbing uncontrollably. Marcus had never seen his brother hurt this badly, had never seen him cry without restraint. He thought he should do something to help, but the novelty and horror of the situation paralyzed him.

Marcus said nothing. He did nothing but watch in stunned silence as Mac's tears gradually ceased to flow. Then, as if by an act of sheer will, Mac pulled himself up onto his knees, and started to sweep away the mound of sand he'd just piled up on top of the suitcase. With every move he made, Mac grimaced and whimpered in pain like a tortured animal. But he refused to stop until he'd uncovered the charred remnants of the small black Samsonite case.

The Corolla and the pickup truck were still burning like a bonfire. When Marcus shifted his position in the dirt to get away from the heat, Mac noticed him as if for the first time, as if he had forgotten Marcus was even there.

"Help me, for Christ's sake!" Mac sobbed. "Help me!"

Marcus scooted closer to Mac and the smoldering suitcase.

"What do you want me to do?"

"See if you can open it. See if the money is still okay," Mac whispered hoarsely.

Marcus hovered over the suitcase, testing the air around it with open palms, trying to determine if it was too hot to touch. It didn't seem to be radiating a lot of heat. When he touched the surface of the suitcase with his fingertips, he discovered the charred material was warm, but not hot. The plastic had cooled and hardened. Marcus was able to pull the suitcase out of the dirt, turn it around, and locate the zipper. Made of plastic, long strips of the zipper had melted. Marcus ripped the suitcase open with ease.

"Thank fucking God!" Mac exclaimed as he peered inside the opened suitcase. Some of the money was singed from the flames, but the bulk of it was untouched by the fire.

The two brothers were kneeling in the dirt as the bonfire of the two vehicles started to die down behind them. They both gazed at what remained of Trina's money.

Mac grabbed Marcus's wrist.

"You have to help me," he gasped. "You have to help me get this money to Slim. I swear to God, my life depends on it. You have to help me."

"I'll help you. I'll help you. I will," Marcus mumbled. "Just give me a second."

Mac covered his face with both hands, sobbing again. "I'll make it up to you. "We get this money to Slim, I'll make everything right, I promise."

With his eyes covered, Mac didn't see Marcus reach into his back pocket and take out their father's handcuffs.

"Everything's going to be okay," Marcus assured his older brother. "I am going to help you."

Mac sobbed even louder, promising again he'd make everything right when Marcus snapped one handcuff onto his brother's right wrist and the other onto his own left wrist.

Mac stared in disbelief at the handcuffs that now bound him to his brother.

Sounding sincerely perplexed, Mac asked, "What are you doing?"

"I'm helping you," Marcus answered. "I'm taking you to the police. We'll go there together."

"Are you out of your fucking mind?" Mac shot to his feet, yanking Marcus up with him. "We can't go to the police! I killed a woman, for fuck's sake! And Slim is going to kill both of us if he doesn't get this money."

"Fuck the money! Fuck this whole business!" Marcus shot back. "We're going to the police, and we're going there together. It's the only option you have."

Mac grabbed Marcus by the throat with his free hand.

"Where's the key?" he hissed. "Where is it?"

"At home," Marcus responded defiantly, almost laughing. "You're stuck with me. You can't escape."

"The hell I can't," Mac whispered.

He tightened his grip around Marcus's neck, squeezing harder and harder until Marcus's eyes bulged from his head and his body went limp.

34

Mac let Marcus's body fall to the ground, then leaned over him and pressed his ear to his brother's chest. Marcus was still breathing. His heart was still beating.

Mac scanned the horizon, trying to gain his bearings, trying to orient himself back toward the direction of the silver mine. He figured they'd been heading east when they drove away from the mine, but with the sun almost directly overhead now, he wasn't sure which direction was east or west, north or south. The only helpful sign he detected was the crazy tire tracks their careening vehicles had left in the desert dirt. That would have to do.

He leaned over Marcus's prone figure again, this time shaking his shoulders and slapping his face.

"Come on, baby brother. Wake up!"

Marcus opened his eyes.

"There you go," Mac said.

He grabbed Marcus under one arm and dragged him up to a standing position. Marcus leaned unsteadily against him, looking about with bleary bewilderment. It took several minutes before Marcus could stand on his own without Mac's support. But as soon as Marcus was steady on his feet, Mac snagged hold of one corner of the burned-out suitcase and took a first blind step in a direction he hoped would lead him back to the silver mine.

"Come on," he said. "Let's get this done."

Marcus fell to his knees, pulling Mac back into the dirt.

"I can't. I won't," Marcus whispered fiercely. "I'm done."

"Goddamnit, help me!" Mac shouted.

He tried to yank Marcus back up on his feet, but Marcus resisted. He lay down on his back and closed his eyes against the blinding brilliance of the sun.

"Fine! Fuck you!" Mac staggered to his feet, kicked the suitcase forward about six inches with his left foot, then grabbed hold of Marcus's cuffed wrist with both hands and dragged him across the desert. A hundred-dollar bill floated out of the burned and battered suitcase. Mac managed to snatch it out of the air. He crumpled it into a ball and shoved it back into the Samsonite.

Now he sat on his ass in the desert, lined up both his feet against the suitcase, and gave it a powerful kick. It skidded away from him about three feet.

"Yeah, by God!" Mac exclaimed.

He grabbed Marcus and dragged him again. Marcus laughed hysterically as his jeans were pulled down around his ass. The flesh on his arms was shredding, blood seeping into the dirt.

Mac repeated what already felt like a mantra. *Sit on ass. Kick suitcase forward. Drag brother.* He repeated the motions again and again, doing his best to follow the direction of their tire tracks in the desert. With every excruciating inch of progress, cash continued to escape from the melted zipper of the Samsonite. The suitcase, like Marcus, was in increasingly bad shape. Mac pursued every crisp bill that flew away from him, which elicited shrieks of laughter from Marcus.

Mac ignored the maniacal cackling and his own pain. Dehydration was causing the muscles in his arms and legs to cramp. The handcuff had sliced into his wrist, which was swollen and bleeding. He paused for a moment to catch his breath. A gentle breeze caught hold of two hundred-dollar bills. They wafted into the air like butterflies and drifted away.

"Oops! There they go!" Marcus giggled. Mac looked down at his brother who lay on his back in the dirt, his face scratched and bleeding, his arms shredded, his jeans now down around his knees.

"Give it up," Marcus implored weakly. "Just let it go."

"Shut up or I'll shut you up," Mac warned him.

"You're going to die chasing that money." Marcus's deranged laughter pierced the quiet of Death Valley.

With his free left hand, Mac landed a blow to Marcus's face that shattered his nose and splattered more blood onto the desert landscape. Marcus went silent, his eyes still open, a bloody grin plastered across his face.

"Fuck!" Mac moaned.

His strength nearly depleted, Mac resumed trekking across the desert floor on his hands and knees. He pushed the suitcase forward and crawled after it, dragging Marcus along with him, one torturous, painstaking move at a time. He stopped frequently to try against all reason to free himself from the handcuffs that chained him to his brother. But the bond held, and his only way forward was to haul Marcus along behind him.

Mac willed himself to keep going. Even when he was reduced to crawling across the desert floor on his belly, he kept nudging the suitcase forward and slithering toward it, his brother attached to him like a ball and chain. Even after he lost his sense of direction and was proceeding with all the accuracy of a blind man, Mac kept going. He lost track of time and lost track of where he was going, but kept moving. It was all he had left. He refused to give it up.

When he found himself inching up a slight incline, Mac choked out an exultant "Yes, by God!" and some of his strength returned. The silver mine was located in a hollow in the desert. Against all odds, Mac believed he was close to his destination. If he could just crawl up to the ridgeline before him, he'd be home free. He'd *roll* down the other side! He'd practically tumble into the silver mine. Slim would be waiting for him. The deal would go through. All would be well.

"Hang on, baby brother! We're almost there!" Mac whispered to Marcus as he dragged him up the small hill. Marcus's battered face grinned a silent response.

When Mac reached the top of the incline, he threw his arm around the frayed suitcase as if it were his dearest companion, as if the two of them had reached this summit together, as if the two of them could be proud of their accomplishment.

"We made it!" he croaked. "We made it!"

But as he peered over the edge of the ridgeline, there was only emptiness below. The silver mine was nowhere in sight.

Mac pressed his face into the dirt and watered the parched earth with his tears. The crying siphoned the last of his strength from his body. The suitcase slipped out from under his arm and tumbled down the slight ravine, opening wide to the endless blue desert sky. Money spilled out of it like seeds being released from a dried flower. Some bills remained where they landed. Others hitched a ride on the wind and flew off to destinations unknown.

Mac watched the fortune flutter away until he lacked the strength to do even that. He lay next to his brother and closed his eyes.

As he felt the sun baking into his brain, Mac conjured up Slim barreling around the desert in the purple Shit Mobile. He could hear him cursing the world and everyone in it and could imagine Slim narrowing his eyes, scanning his surroundings for all that money, all those green pieces of paper now drifting around Death Valley like some freed force of nature. The image cracked a grin across Mac's face as he felt consciousness slipping away.

He opened his eyes and tried to focus his gaze on Marcus. He wondered who would discover the two of them, handcuffed together, lying side by side in the desert. He wondered if they would be recognized as brothers, even though his eyes were brown, and Marcus's were blue.

Other books by
EDEN FRANCIS COMPTON

Emily
A world-famous playwright becomes obsessed with Emily Dickinson,
believing she has left clues in her writing of her trauma. He is forced
to come to terms with his own difficult past as he begins losing his
grip on reality.

Pre-Order Eden's latest book:

Catch and Kill

He thought he was untouchable . . .

Angie has long suffered from severe depression and anxiety, and her older sister, Scarlett, has always been her guiding light. Scarlett is not just an incredible, award-winning actress, but also a role model and the very definition of inner strength. So when Scarlett suddenly commits suicide, the shock and grief are nearly too much for Angie to handle.

Unexpectedly, Angie discovers that her sister's death was a direct result of being raped by one of Hollywood's most powerful and celebrated men . . . as well as the shocking cowardice of people closest to her.

Angie vows, in spite of her sometimes crippling anxiety, to bring this famous film mogul down herself. She snags a job with his company that allows her access deep inside his gilded world. But she soon realizes that an entire system has been put in place to enable him. She begins to amass a trove of evidence until a sudden betrayal sends her running for her life.

A heart-stopping thrill ride from beginning to end, Catch and Kill is about abuse by the powerful, those who conspire to protect them, and the dangerous path required to reclaim the truth.

https://mybook.to/catchandkill

Stay up to date:
Follow Eden on Amazon & Goodreads

https://www.amazon.com/author/edenfranciscompton